CONFESSIONS

CONFESSIONS

A Novel

SEAN EADS

HEX PUBLISHERS

This is a work of fiction. All characters, organizations, and events portrayed in this book are products of the authors' imaginations and/or are used fictitiously.

CONFESSIONS

Copyright © 2022 by Sean Eads.
All rights reserved.

Copyedits by Bret Smith and Jeanni Smith
Cover by Damonza.com
Typesets and formatting by Alec Ferrell

A Hex Publishers Book

Published & Distributed by Hex Publishers, LLC
PO BOX 298
Erie, CO 80516

www.HexPublishers.com

No portion of this book may be reproduced without first obtaining the permission of the copyright holder.

Joshua Viola, Publisher

Paperback ISBN: 978-1-7365964-9-4
e-Book ISBN: 978-1-7365964-8-7

First Edition: November 2022

10 9 8 7 6 5 4 3 2 1

Printed in the U.S.A.

For Brian, Lena, Asher, Ava, and Ansley.

My love to all of you.

NATHAN

I FOUND DAD SLEEPING ON THE COUCH. The front door was open, and I stood there rubbing the early morning ache from my eyes. Dad wasn't wearing shoes and his white socks were filthy. A vague childhood echo of my mom scolding me for running through the house with dirty feet entered my thoughts, followed by Dad saying, *"Oh hell, Peggy, let a boy be a boy."* If this happened on a workday, Dad was likely in the bathroom when he said it, maybe taking a pause from brushing his teeth to defend me. Then he'd go back to scrubbing or digging out grime from under his nails. He liked to be squeaky clean before heading off to another shift in the mines.

"Dad," I said, but he didn't move. His mouth was slack with one or two teeth showing. I wasn't sure how many he had left. Tim might know. All I knew was I had the dentures ready for when he died. I'd ordered them more than a year ago.

I went to the door, which was kept unlocked at night so Dad could always get back inside. Johnny and I didn't speak much or agree on anything when we did, but we both knew it was impossible to stop Dad from wandering. My younger brother Johnny still lived with Dad, so he knew better than I did and said Dad seldom left the backyard anyway. Even my cousin Rebecca, who stopped in often and was a lot more responsible than Johnny, seemed to think he was OK for now.

The assessment relaxed me a bit, but I still couldn't believe I'd fallen into a deep enough sleep not to hear him get up and walk out. I used to be sleepless when I took my turn here and committed to following Dad around for hours on end. But last evening's news had been too much for me, had overwhelmed me with a desire to sleep. *To sleep—perchance to dream.* I confess I did have a dream. A good one.

The kind that makes waking up to reality so hateful.

I turned to study my dad, oval-mouthed and old, rounded in the shoulders, everything about him edgeless and shadowed like the Appalachians at dusk. "I'm going now, Dad. It has to be an early start. Rebecca will be here before you wake up, I bet. Johnny, too, unless he's working. I never know. Don't—don't use the stove or anything, OK?"

I closed the door behind me, grateful Dad seldom cared for anything more than cold bologna, chocolate pudding and Jell-O these days.

The hearse was parked behind Dad's truck of twenty-five years, a black F-150 weathered to splotchy gray. It still ran, though. Johnny made sure of that and sometimes used it instead of his own. Dad's license hadn't been good in years, and he showed no interest in driving, but I still thought it wasn't right for Johnny to use the truck. When I suggested so, he simply gestured at the hearse and said, "Not all of us get a company car. I don't see why you have a stick up your ass about it. Did you take the dildo out to make space?"

I never remarked about it again.

I got into the hearse, started the engine and took another moment to rub my eyes. The sun had risen around an hour ago, but it still felt like dawn to me, and a glimpse of the electric red and orange sky brought a brief throb of pain to my forehead. Why did I suddenly feel like a college student who'd spent the night drinking? My actual age and sobriety belied both scenarios, but just then I didn't really feel OK to drive. Too tired, too drained. But Meghan said Steve wanted to figure out what to do about the baby and planned on being at the funeral home first thing. *Before* first thing, she said. Not that I cared what she wanted, no matter how bad the situation was. But Steve . . .

It was about a twenty-minute drive from Dad's place to work, but the drive ahead felt like a hundred miles. I reached what Wentz Hollow called Main Street and stopped off at the little corner store for coffee. The older woman at the cash register, Jan, according to her name badge, had seen the hearse pull up through the glass entry doors, as I'd parked right in front. She had a pale, alarmed look as she rang up my coffee. I figured she thought I must have a corpse in the back. Maybe she thought I was a ghoul. *How could he possibly be wanting coffee at a time like this? Doesn't he care?*

Coffee, coffin, to-may-to, to-mah-to, let's call the whole thing off. Christ, if only I could.

After Jan handed me my change, which I slipped into the acrylic donation case advertising the Ronald McDonald House, I turned to go. Then she said, "You poor man."

"I'm sorry?"

"It must be very hard. The work you do."

I thanked her and said that it sometimes was hard. She smiled as if I'd made her day, and I left.

I'd never solicit sympathy or consider myself desirous of it. I didn't become a mortician by accident, after all. You don't enter my line of work naive to the fact you'll be working with the dead. You're going to encounter the aftermath of terrible fates, you're going to face questions from the loved ones of the deceased, angry and even accusatory questions, as if they hold you responsible for what happened.

Sometimes grief reduces their speech to just those two words.

What happened?

I'd spent the night wrestling with that question and thinking about Steve. At some point, around 1:00 a.m., I realized I wasn't concerning myself with his dead baby at all. It was a different kind of *What happened?* and not mysterious in the slightest.

As I turned the hearse into the long driveway leading up to the funeral home, I forced my concentration to the task at hand. There was a car parked out front, its running lights on. Meghan and Steve Malone, here *first thing* like she promised. I took a sip of that coffee, scalding my tongue just a bit. I thought of my father and wondered if he'd woken up yet. Maybe he'd gone into the backyard, searching for whatever it was he sought. Then I thought of the Malone's baby, experiencing its first and last day on Earth in the space of a single breath.

That was the reality we had to deal with right now. Somehow I had to help them toward closure.

The hearse was kept in a garage at the back, but it felt awkward to drive past the Malones as if this were business as usual. Of course, for me it *was* business as usual, jaded or blasé as that may sound. The only other option was to park out front, leaving the hearse in plain sight of them. That couldn't be good for the Malones, having to look at it. Better to just get the hearse out of view, so I opted for the garage and walked around to the front, making sure I could be seen. Meghan Malone sat in the passenger side. She seemed to be having an animated talk with Steve. Were they fighting? I couldn't quite tell. Then Meghan's voice became audible. She was yelling at him. Sunlight off the window kept me from seeing Steve's face.

CONFESSIONS

Soon enough, I thought. After all these years, soon enough.

I made a point of passing in front of them and offered a curt nod, just to let them know I was here and ready for them. I still couldn't get a decent look at Steve's face, but his hands were on the steering wheel at 9 and 3. You could almost imagine him as a 16-year-old student being scolded by a driving instructor. Christ, Meghan was really laying into him. The one thing I could tell in my parting glance was her hands seemed to be in her lap, completely at odds with her evident anger.

Or maybe not. Grief makes us too conscious of our hands. You don't know what to do with them because you want to do everything all at once: punch, clutch, shove, pull. Standing in the back watching over several hundred funerals, I've come to pay more attention to hands than facial expressions. Some stand before a coffin with their arms at their sides, fingers balled into fists. Some place their palms on the coffin lid and close their eyes. Friends and loved ones stand side-by-side in mourning and sometimes a hand comes up and squeezes another person's shoulder. Sometimes a man raises his hand as if he means to touch his brother but freezes before contact. The hand hovers a fraction away from the other man's body and then makes an embarrassed retreat. What thoughts, what considerations occupy those moments of hesitancy? These people will never know that I alone have seen the gesture made and retracted, just as they will never understand how often my thoughts have urged those hands not to retreat. Our lives are impoverished by the unmade touch.

I began climbing the steps that led up to the funeral home's impressive porch, capable of hosting two dozen people at a time. Distance did little to make Meghan's voice any fainter. At the top step, I thought about turning and holding up my hands, like Moses commanding the Red Sea to part. Poor couple, shopping for a stroller last month, a coffin today. Somewhere in the world's shared day you could find weather appropriate for their gloom. But as I did look back to survey the land before me, it was impossible to deny Wentz Hollow was having a beautiful morning.

I went inside and left the door propped open, just to demonstrate to the Malones I was ready for them. A minute passed without them getting out of the car, so I decided to begin my morning routine. Routines are wonderful anchors in times of crisis. There was neither a funeral nor even a showing planned today, but I arranged a table of brown ceramic mugs in the foyer and then went to the kitchen to brew coffee. You must be prepared to offer things even if there's no one to receive them.

I brought the coffee out to the foyer table, along with a bit of cream and sweeteners. The Malones were still in their car. I left the front window and turned to survey my little kingdom. The viewing room was right ahead, in an area that once served as a ballroom, though the notion of anyone ever hosting a ball in Wentz Hollow amused me. The Wentz House was built around 1870 and became the town funeral home around 1950. Pretty much everyone within a hundred miles wanted to have their final star turn here, a last stab at glamor or status before returning to the common ground.

A bridal staircase took up the left corner and led up to my living quarters. Built of black walnut, its landing seemed a pooling shadow. There was a velvet rope across the entrance, a joke from the previous director, Robert Allen, who'd retired two years ago. I'd known Robbie in a professional capacity for years, encountering him at seminars and meetings of the National Funeral Directors Association. He'd just about choked to death when he learned I'd actually grown up in Wentz Hollow, and though we were not really friends, I was the first person he called upon announcing his retirement.

"Just wanted to let you know, Nathan. There's a business opportunity for you here. No real competition to speak of and the people are

nice. But of course you know that."

Did I?

At the time, I was 45 and working as a director in a chain funeral home in Texas, one of SCI's cookie cutter outfits. Not that people ever realize or even care how many funeral homes and cemeteries are owned and managed by corporations. Death is as commercialized as fast-food restaurants and big-box shops. That was part of the reason I decided to take Robbie up on his offer and buy out his business. Coming from my last job to Wentz Hollow made me feel like a Walmart clerk who'd just come into possession of a Mom & Pop Dollar General—except my quaint storefront was a mansion. I could be more personal here, more helpful to people in situations just like this.

Like I said, it was part of the reason I came back.

Wentz Hollow's population had grown by all of 300 people in the almost thirty-year-interim between my return and when I hitchhiked out of here after a senior year spent homeschooled. The town's population wasn't large enough to sustain a funeral home business on its own, but like Robbie mentioned, there wasn't much competition until you got closer to Lexington or Louisville. Lexington was nearest and it was still a three-hour drive. And as already noted, it seemed everyone in the surrounding area wanted their turn in the mansion.

I turned, certain I heard the door open. It had not. I exhaled a held breath. My hands shook a bit. Steve's *going* to come in sooner or later, I told myself. I wondered how I'd see him. I mean, would my imagination reconstruct the middle-aged man into the 17-year-old boy I'd known? Or would reality overcome romanticism?

The world was full of too much reality today.

A door to the right of the foyer led to my small office. On the far left was another opening, doorless, that led to the showcase room where customers could inspect sample coffins and urns, tombstone options, memorial plaques. I headed to my office in part because the single window there looked out onto the parking lot. I opened the blinds and glanced down on the Malone's SUV. The passenger side door was now open. Meghan Malone looked frozen in place; her right foot planted on the pavement. Were they still arguing? What in the hell was going on?

Well, I thought, *it won't be much longer.* There were two chairs on the guest side of my desk, and I made sure to pull them out. They were already spaced to give adequate leg room for a smaller person like Meghan, but Steve was a sturdy, tall guy. 6'3", as I remembered. I didn't want him to even have to adjust the seat before sitting down. It should feel like his favorite chair at home.

I sat down and took another sip of coffee. Aside from a couple of large houseplants, the office decor hadn't been updated since I took over, which meant it pretty much felt like a 1970's time capsule. The walls still had paneling, and the room itself was on the dim side. Usually, I was too busy here to notice such details, but just then I had nothing to do but stare at a couple of hairline cracks in the ceiling as the toes of my shoes delved into a carpet far too plush to be modern. None of this would fly in an urban setting, but in Wentz Hollow it felt right. The process of change in small towns happens at a pace Darwin could appreciate. You might even forgive the locals if they wondered why they even needed a funeral home or a cemetery. After all, when was the last time anyone around here ever died?

Steve and Meghan had the answer to that question. So did the Henshaw family. I had Mr. Henshaw in my mortuary room, waiting to be prepared for tomorrow's visitation. His care would only take a few hours, but I wanted to get his case finished and his body moved into the viewing room before noon today.

CONFESSIONS

"Hello? Mr. Ashcraft?"

For as large and as old as the front doors were, they moved with a whisper quietness appropriate to solemnity. I hadn't a hint the Malones had come in until Meghan called out from the foyer, and I hurried out to greet them. But only Meghan stood there waiting, looking around with her brow furrowed until I came to meet her with my hand outstretched. I kept eye contact with her, but my concentration was on the empty doorway.

"So what do I got to do?" she said.

"I'm sorry?"

"What do I got to do to get this over and done with?" Her voice carried that strong Appalachian twang that never left you, no matter how hard you tried to shake it or how many diplomas you earned.

"First let me say how sorry I am for your loss. I realize how difficult it must be for you and Steve."

"Is there paperwork? Something to sign?"

"There'll be a Certificate of Stillbirth, but that's a matter for you to take up with the hospital."

"Oh, I've been over that already," Meghan said, waving her right hand. She took a step forward and looked toward the viewing room. "This place hasn't changed a bit. We had my Aunt Pauline's funeral here when I was 13. Everyone said it was the most beautiful wake they ever went to."

I offered a curt smile. "I hope you were put at ease."

"I didn't really know her."

"I see," I said, taking a glance at the front door. Meghan must have noticed.

"He ain't coming in. I said he had to, but he just can't bring himself."

"Are you sure? Maybe if we give him a little longer—"

"He's not coming in. So let's just get this over with, OK?"

There was nothing I could do except curse my horrible

fantasizing about reconnecting with Steve. *Let's just get this over with.* It could be the motto of my life and my work. I could put it on my own tombstone, rendered in Latin to give it that buff of classiness.

"I think we should start in the—" I started to say *showroom*, which is what it was, but that seemed too crass a word to use just then. "Let's start in here."

We walked past the viewing room and the staircase and entered what had once been intended as a private dining room. It was in fact the room in which William Wentz died, according to Robbie, though I don't know how he came upon that knowledge. Merchandising being just as important in the funeral business as in the automotive industry, this was the room I'd bothered to upgrade, to modernize and make *glossy*. Robbie had only kept two wooden caskets in the room, but I had several, both wood and metal, in addition to shelves of gorgeous urns, burial clothing options, all manner of customization and personalization. As an industry friend of mine once said, an entrepreneurial mortician's slogan should be, "One stop shopping for the day you'll be dropping."

I stepped to the side and let Meghan look around. She started hugging herself like the temperature had dropped 20 degrees. Her glance didn't rest on anything for very long. She made the briefest touch of a coffin made of poplar with a deep cherry finish and brought her fingertips to her chin, an almost thoughtful pose. "Gosh," she said.

How I wish I were looking at a day like last Wednesday. I had a couple in their early 30s come in, forward-thinking Dave Ramsey-types who wanted all of their financial affairs in order, including burial arrangements. An unusual attitude at their age for a decision most people delay until their 60s, if they make it at all. So many people feel such an understandable squeamishness toward death they can't even bring themselves to make a will, much less step into a funeral home and go coffin shopping. But the couple from last Wednesday were clear-eyed enough about it and decided to turn the process into a good time. Their spirit rubbed off on me and I started showing off my wares like a car salesman. Full gallows humor mode engaged. It seemed improbable they hadn't discussed it before, but midway through the process they each learned the other would rather be cremated. This realization made, they stared at each other with even greater understanding and devotion, and I stood between them with my hands clasped together like a marriage counselor who's just led his clients to an important breakthrough.

After they left, loneliness announced itself the way it so often did when you've spent time with people who are all couples, when the night is winding down and only you are driving home alone. That Wednesday, of course, it was the couple driving away from me. I stood at my office window watching their car depart, shocked by the sensation that I wanted our business transaction to lead to something more. Couldn't it? I had their telephone number. I had the husband's email address. His name was Richard, her name was Sarah. *Sarah*, I thought, *you're a damn lucky woman finding a guy like Richard.*

And vice versa, I'm sure.

With no arrangements to occupy the rest of that Wednesday, I sank into the lingering loneliness of their departure. I touched the paperwork they'd left behind, running my fingertips over the cursive of Richard's signature, thinking again how fun he was—*they* were—and wondering what plans they might have tonight. A movie—out or in? Dinner— also out or in? They wouldn't know how the funeral director they met hours earlier (fun himself, right—what a character!) would be thinking about them, wanting to spend time with them, maybe forging a friendship. I did not return to Wentz Hollow to die, yet each day I felt I needed to add a tablespoon of embalming fluid to my coffee just to keep myself from disintegrating.

My profession attracts introverts. Some imagine it attracts the morbid, weird, or depraved, but that's trafficking in stereotypes. I can be socially awkward, though, with difficulty starting conversations. One of the unforeseen benefits of being a funeral director is that it attracts the curiosity of others. I therefore enjoy letting people pepper me with questions, sometimes even apologizing along the way, as if they've committed a taboo. Waving away someone's apology and dismissing it as unnecessary is a great way to show ease and demonstrate likability.

—But what exactly do you do with a dead body? I mean, are you involved in dressing it?

—Oh, of course, Richard. I mean, it's not going to dress itself.

—How, though? I thought dead bodies got stiff. How do you do that?

—It's interesting you ask that, Richard. Rigor mortis is not a permanent situation at all. Still, you may have noticed that all the clothing I had on display is slit up the back, sort of like a woman's dress. This helps a lot.

—That's really cool. I had no idea about all this.

—I'm sure there's a lot I don't know about your line of work too. Why don't we grab coffee sometime and . . .

"Mr. Ashcraft, don't you have something smaller?"

I shook myself out of my fantasizing. "Sorry?"

She gestured at the coffin. "It just feels like I'm putting one marble in a great large box. I don't see why a baby would need something this big."

"They do come in different sizes," I said, stepping closer. "There's a size just for infants."

She shook her head. "I really need to get Steve in here. He's the one who wants all this. Hang on, will you?"

"By all means."

CONFESSIONS

She walked out of the house, leaving the front door open. I stood in the showcase room, looking down at the buffed, perfect wood floor as my pulse quickened at the renewed possibility of seeing Steve. Then my throat constricted at the thought of trying to talk to him, and I knew I needed water. I was halfway across the foyer, heading to my office, when Meghan Malone returned. She slammed the door behind her and paused, rubbing her temples a moment.

"OK," she said. "We're not doing burial. We're doing cremation. Why the hell he didn't say that before I don't know."

"Is he coming in?"

"Hell no. There were some urns in that room, right?"

"Yes."

"Then let's look at them."

She went into the room ahead of me and went to the wall shelves where I had ten different funeral urns on display. Meghan just stood there, pulling at her hair a bit.

"I can't believe this bullshit," she said.

"Don't be mad at him," I said.

"I'll be pissed off if I want to be pissed off. I swear to God he never mentioned cremation. That's not what I want."

"In my experience, it's common for fathers to . . . to feel it more, especially at this stage. In a way, none of this has been real for either of you. It's one disbelief after another, and that disbelief is sort of a light. Then you arrive at a place like this, and the light gets snuffed. By not getting out of the car, Steve's hanging on to that flicker for as long as he can."

Meghan began to cry. Nothing unexpected in a funeral home, of course, and I had many boxes of Kleenex stashed throughout the building. I produced one from behind an urn and handed it to her.

"Maybe I should go out to the car and tell him he's needed," I said. "That might—"

"No. I'll be done in a second."

She went on dabbing her eyes. I withdrew and snuck fast across the foyer to my office. I looked out the window. Steve had gotten out of the SUV. He was standing beside the open driver's side door, almost clutching it. He looked off to his left. Maybe the impossibility of eye contact made for the best circumstance. His shoulders remained broad like they'd been in high school when he was slugging his way to a baseball scholarship.

A baseball cap kept me from seeing if he still had all his hair, and the door blocked any glimpse of his torso. But I wasn't looking at him with present eyes anyway. I knew it because as I watched him, I experienced a second, throbbing pulse—the heartbeat of time. We have our carotid artery, but there is temporal blood coursing through us as well, sometimes deadening, but more often awakening. Call it a kairotic artery, perhaps, that brings us to a sudden and crisp rapport with the past. Just then I saw him as he looked in the hallways, as he looked rounding third base, as he looked in the school parking lot with friends, as he looked when he passed me that first note in math class. All that measure of hopeful, beautiful youth contrasted against a middle-aged man whose child didn't last even half an hour in this world.

I heard Meghan Malone crying even louder from the showroom. I hurried back to her with a fresh box of tissues.

"I looked out on Steve," I said.

She nodded.

"He seems OK," I added.

The reassurance seemed to make her cry harder. She let a few wads of used tissue fall to the floor and took up the nearest urn. It was pewter with a laurel leaf pattern etched just below the neckline. Meghan seemed transfixed by it as she sniffled. I wondered if the maternal instincts and fantasies she must have been nurturing had seized control of her, because she held the urn along the length of her forearm, the cap near her right breast.

"It's heavier than I figured. Like when you pick up a clay garden planter thinking it's plastic."

"Urns come in different sizes, just like coffins. What you're holding is an adult urn. Extra large, in fact."

Meghan laughed at that and put both hands to her mouth as if in shock. In doing so, she dropped the vase. It banged hard on the floor and she began to hyperventilate and apologize, begging me not to make her pay for it.

"It's OK," I said, picking it up. "See? It's metal. In fact, I'm glad you could see a demonstration of how tough an urn like this is. It won't shatter, and with the screw-top lid, you don't have to worry about any ash escaping."

She began to settle down. Panic had dried up her tears, and all at once she seemed relaxed.

"It's just I never would have thought there'd be sizes like clothing. But there's some really fat people, aren't there? They must leave a lot of ash."

"Yes," I said, not wanting to explain how ash quantity was related only to the density of a person's bones. "We cater to the obese and the slender alike."

"It's weird that everything's so . . . practical."

I smiled. "That's a really great observation you've just made. Grief unmoors us. Mundane details we can relate to help us keep a toehold on our sanity."

I thought she'd be pleased by my praise, but a colder look came over her expression. "I think it's awful. I think it's gross there are urn sizes and coffin sizes. I don't give a shit if it's practical. I think you're awful but I'm even worse. The only person not awful is Steve. None of this is his fault. He wouldn't be in this situation if it weren't for me. Do you know what I'm saying?"

There was a hard clarity in her eyes as she waited for my

answer.

"You can't blame yourself. It's not your fault about the baby—"

"Do you *know* what I'm saying, Mr. Ashcraft?"

The repetition was icier, spoken neither as a question nor as a plea for understanding. As I considered the possibilities of what she was trying to say, a wave of nausea struck me, upsetting a stomach filled only with coffee. Swallowing back on a stab of acid reflux, I came to the conclusion I felt she wanted me to reach.

"Your personal life is not my business."

"How many funerals have you done, Mr. Ashcraft?"

"Well over a thousand cases."

"Cases?"

"Sorry," I said. "That's industry terminology."

"You make it sound like you run a detective agency."

Strange as it may sound, I'd never thought of it like that. Or if I had, it'd been so long ago the novelty had worn off.

"I guess death is the big mystery," I said.

My remark lingered between us like an unpleasant odor. She turned back to the urn display and said, "I want one that's cheap, and I want it ceramic. *Got that?*"

I nodded. "Are you sure Steve wouldn't want to come in and see them for himself? I mean—"

"He's getting his way on the cremation. That's enough. Besides, if he really was going to come in, he'd have done so by now. In the back of his mind he probably knows there's no reason to be involved here. None of it concerns him."

We said very little to each other over the next twenty minutes as we went to my office and I processed the order online. I read out some prices and descriptions while she tapped away on her iPhone. She just said, "That sounds good" and "As long as it's ceramic" to each option. I didn't have a crematorium, so I told Meghan I'd work with the hospital and a third party on those arrangements. She didn't ask about the cost.

I'd seen this sort of reaction in people before—relief instead of grief, the sense of death as freedom from an unwanted burden. In most cases, you mustn't judge people. Some have been caring for an ill parent for years, sacrificing all their happiness in the process. Having not returned to Wentz Hollow for my mother's funeral a decade earlier, I understood not everyone mourns the way other people think you should. But this was the first time a client's attitude made me feel ill.

"So it's all done, right? Ceramic urn?"

"Just like you requested."

Meghan paid with a credit card, and I walked her to the front door. Steve was back in the SUV, clutching the steering wheel, staring straight ahead. He wasn't as dazed as he appeared to be, though. His head turned, following Meghan as she came around the front to the passenger side. *God*, I thought, *please look my way. Do you even recognize me? Do you even know who I am?* The engine was already running. Steve was ready to go. He'd been ready all this time. The idea we could be within thirty yards of each other after all this time and not acknowledge it broke me. I had Meghan's credit card receipt in my right hand and I seized upon the chance to get closer. I called out to her. She had the passenger side open and she stood frozen, almost gaping at me. Steve was just staring at her. It was as if his neck couldn't turn left.

As for the horror in Meghan's expression, what did she think I intended to do? Repeat her insinuations to her husband? Make a scene. I approached her without looking at Steve.

"Better not forget your receipt," I said, handing her the paper. She snatched it from me and got into the SUV. I stayed in place as they backed away from me. The SUV turned left and then Steve looked at me. How many world tragedies had taken place since the two of us made eye contact?

I raised my hand and gave a little wave. The Malones

drove away.

I lingered in the empty lot a few moments longer before giving up the ghost and going inside. With the door shut behind me, I took a deep breath, unhooked the velvet rope across the staircase and started up to my living quarters on the second floor.

I climbed the stairs contemplating what Meghan said. Whatever she'd done, whatever she felt, whatever the state of her marriage might be were not my business. And what was I to her except the face of the last hoop she had to go through to put a mistake behind her?

He's getting his way on the cremation.

I stopped a few steps shy of the upper landing. Was she lying about that? If the baby wasn't Steve's in the first place, then wouldn't she prefer the quickness of fire over the frozen eternity of embalming?

I pivoted and looked down the staircase, the fingernails of my right hand digging into the railing's old wood. She *is* lying, I told myself. She wants cremation and she wants to make sure the ashes are put in an urn she can shatter. Then it's just a matter of time before some house-cleaning accident occurs and a broom sweeps the ashes and shards forever out of sight and mind.

Au revoir, erreur.

The scene unfolded in my imagination with great clarity. I saw the urn sitting on a mantle above the fireplace. Meghan goes about dusting, moving her arm in ever exaggerated swipes. Finally her wrist knocks the urn to the floor, leaving two large shards to the north and south and gray ash spread from east to west. A nasty little compass scene, a horrified shriek and sob from Meghan even if she's alone in the house when it happens, and then a resolute march to get the dustpan. Sweep, sweep, sweep. Trashcan. Then a once-over with the vacuum to get any lingering baby out of the floor joints.

CONFESSIONS

As I headed down the stairs, my imagination leapt to Steve's response. I felt his palpable hurt, my throat hard with his true sobs. I felt his longing in my own chest, the raw emotion of losing the baby a second time and not being able to have closure since Meghan had already disposed of it all. He'd be too stunned to ask why she hadn't at least tried to save the ashes in a jar. The idea of his baby vacuumed up and discarded would break him. I felt the tremble that would send his broad shoulders shaking.

No, Meghan, I'm not going to let your little plan work, I thought. I entered my office and pulled up her order to make the necessary change. It didn't take long at all to find an identical urn made of bronze rather than clay. It was much pricier, but I paid the difference out of pocket, as well as the extra $50 cost for immediate overnight shipping. *Good luck trying to break this one, Meghan. You're going to be polishing that damn urn for the rest of your life. I owe it to Steve. You're going to pay.*

I dried my palms against my pant legs and began to pace. The best thing for me just then was getting to work on the Henshaw case and channel all this energy into something productive.

I went to the front of the viewing room. Mr. Henshaw's coffin was already in place. There was a raised dais with a lectern a few feet behind the coffin, and at the back of this little stage, hidden by black curtains, was a double door that led to my embalming and preparation room. In the glory days of William Wentz, this had been the manor's kitchen, but only a stainless-steel industrial sink in the right corner gave any suggestion of the room's past life. A mobile mortuary refrigerator capable of holding four bodies took up the left wall. It was stainless steel as well and at first glance looked like the world's most impressive filing cabinet. The top drawers were chest high, and I opened the one containing Mr. Henshaw. I'd performed his embalming yesterday.

Robbie's assistant had also been an older man who decided to quit when Robbie retired, and I had yet to find a replacement. Doing all the work myself could be difficult, but the relaxed pace of life and death in Wentz Hollow allowed me to be leisurely. I used a cadaver lift to move Mr. Henshaw out of the refrigerator, positioning the sturdy straps around his legs, torso and neck. The hydraulic machine took his naked corpse out of the refrigerator, and I steered it over to the preparation table in the middle of the room. Centering Mr. Henshaw along the table's length, I then gentled him down onto the surface and unhooked the straps.

"Sorry it's just me for company right now, Mr. Henshaw," I said, placing a hand on his chest. "Mind if I bend your ear?"

I pressed my lips together as a little shiver jolted my shoulders. In all my years as a mortician, I'd never lowered myself to conversing with the dead. Doing so may be common in my profession, but the idea always struck me as an act of profound disrespect or a touch of madness. There should be something sacramental about working with the deceased, and I'd always performed my duties in silence, without even background music. You should do your duty as if the family of the dead might somehow see you doing it at any moment. What would their feelings be if they saw you jamming out to "Hungry Like the Wolf" as you pumped their father full of embalming fluid? No, the dignity of death and the honor of the profession demanded silence. Silence even in thought, really. Somewhere along the line I'd learned to make my mind go blank during the time spent preparing a corpse. The processes and procedures were so ingrained that I did not need to think, but the concentration remained in the quietude of the moment, perhaps in the same manner it persists for any craftsman dedicated to his trade.

Yet here I was, chatting away to the body of Mr. Henshaw. My cheeks burned from shock and embarrassment. I backed away from the table until I hit my shoulder blades against the double doors. I walked off the dais and past the coffins and up the pew rows until I reached the foyer.

You hear people talk about doing things without realizing it, acting without any conscious direction. That's what happened to me when I left the funeral home and started walking. There was an old walking trail across the street that winded its way along a creek and took you right into the center of town. The drive was no more than ten minutes, but the trail meandered and took closer to half an hour. I figured I was twenty minutes on the trail before realizing I'd left Mr. Henshaw sitting on the prep table, unfinished. Had I locked the front door? Had I even bothered to close it? Feeling my pockets, I realized I didn't even have my cell phone if someone needed to reach me.

"Damnit," I said, looking back, hoping I might somehow only be a few yards from the main road. But I'd gotten far enough along the trail that the funeral home's high, distinct roof was obscured by trees.

I started back, furious with myself. But anger only drove me a few steps before I stopped again. I *couldn't* return to work, not yet. I thought of Steve sitting in the SUV, but I remembered a different look in his eyes, years earlier. I couldn't see well enough to know if he'd been crying this morning, but I knew what his eyes looked like red and tear stained.

I needed the company of the living, even if only to enter the corner store and eavesdrop on the sale of a carton of cigarettes. A quick stop in town to center myself, then I could walk the road and get back to Mr. Henshaw fast enough.

Quickening my pace, I got off the trail in just under ten minutes. Sweat had dampened my clothes and a blister seemed to be developing on my left big toe. I went two blocks east, still intending to visit the corner store. Then I saw Johnny's truck parked at the curb. He must be doing some electrical work for one of the businesses. Who knew what he might be up to though. Had he even gone home to check on Dad first, or had he rolled out of some woman's bed and driven straight here?

I didn't want to risk encountering him. I turned north, crossed Main Street, and found myself in front of Tim's dental office. We had something in common. Like so many businesses in small towns, his practice was located in a refurbished house. Mine just happened to be a lot larger. His examination chair was in a remodeled bedroom and his waiting room had once been someone's parlor.

In fact, when I first met him, that's just what he said to me. *Step into my parlor.*

It'd been one of those rare days when I could take off and spend the afternoon with Dad, and all he kept talking about was Tim. I didn't know who this was, as Johnny never told me anything. At first I thought Tim was a figment of his imagination, but then Dad told me where to find him, and we pulled up at the building I stood in front of right now.

A dentist?

Dad had already bounded up the steps to the porch, leaving me speechless and smiling. Anything that made Dad happy was wonderful, and I came up to the open door and looked inside. Tim stood there grinning as Dad slapped him on the shoulder and fawned over him, more puppy dog than senior citizen. Then Tim and I made eye contact.

There's a fantasy movie from my childhood called *Highlander*, about a group of immortal people fighting each other. These immortals experience a tingling awareness when they're in each other's presence. Years later, after I got out of Wentz Hollow and started college, I thought of that movie the first time I encountered another gay man. I'd not heard the term *gaydar* yet, but everything about him sent a shock of recognition through me—as well as possibility and hope.

So when I met Tim that first time, we stared at each other like two immortals getting the measure of each other. This was about a year ago, and we'd managed a handful of encounters since then, always occasioned by my dad, who'd greet Tim like his long-lost best friend and then roam about his office like a childlike alien as the two of us made small talk. I kept meaning to ask him for a drink, nothing major. A toehold on the mountain climb of a relationship. But I hadn't. God knows I've misread cues before.

I entered, hoping I didn't stink of sweat. His front door had a jangling bell that doubled as his receptionist. I closed the door behind me, hearing the floorboards creak from down a little hallway that led to his examination room. Tim appeared in his crisp blue oxford shirt and black trousers. The bottom half of his white lab coat was buttoned and bunched up around his waist because his hands were stuffed into his pants pockets. The top of his lab coat draped around his narrow shoulders. He was maybe 30 or 31 but looked even younger, like a kid playing dress up. I loved how he was skinny-fat and a little cherubic in the cheeks. I'm sure every old lady in Wentz Hollow just wanted to pinch him and offer him a piece of Wurthers.

"Nathan," he said, looking past me. "Where's Bart?"

"Dad's at home. He's fine."

He nodded. "Are *you* OK?"

"I just need to talk. You busy?"

I expected him to say no and wave me toward a chair, so it surprised me when he flashed a pained look back down the hallway.

"I can come back if you are. It's really nothing—"

"No, no. I don't have any patients. It's just—well, it's already been a day."

"That makes two of us," I said.

"What do you mean?"

Tim surprised me again by grabbing my wrist after he asked

the question. He let go after a single squeeze and apologized.

"Is something wrong?"

"No," he said. "I just had a phone call from home, that's all. Family drama."

"I can relate."

"With a brother like Johnny, I have no doubt. Seriously, Nathan, take a seat. I don't have anything on the books until 10:00."

"What time is it now?"

"Nearing 9:00. You look like you've been up a while."

We started down the hallway to his examination room. Along the way, he closed a door that led to his office.

"Funeral home directors keep strange hours," I said.

"I can imagine."

We entered his examination room and he pointed at the chair as he perched on a nearby stool.

"Seriously?"

"It's the most comfortable seat in the house," he said. "I've even taken naps on it."

I sat down. He was right, I did seem to melt into the chair's contours. This just reminded me of how little I'd slept, and I squirmed out of it and got to my feet.

"No time for naps," I said, walking over to the east wall. His dental diploma from the University of Washington was there, as well as last year's poster advertising the Kentucky Wildcats Men's Basketball team. To the left of both hung a framed quote attributed to Kahlil Gibran. I read it out loud.

"*Your pain is the breaking of the shell that encloses your understanding.* Deep," I said, turning back to him.

"I try recommending meditation to anyone facing a root canal. They opt for the anesthesia every time. Would you like some now?"

That got me laughing. I rubbed my eyes. "Don't tempt me."

"If I inject you, will you tell me what's going on?"

"I wish I could, but it's work-related. There's a code of ethics for funeral directors. I imagine dentists have one too."

"*Of course.*"

Tim's answer was so terse I thought I must have insulted him by accident.

"Sorry."

My apology seemed to annoy him. "Just get back in the chair. I'll give you a free examination. Might as well make all this awkwardness worth our time, right?"

"I don't have time for a cleaning."

"Then I won't give you one. Sit. Now. Comprende?"

I thought about my cellphone which could be ringing away. I thought of the line of people who might be at the funeral home wanting to make arrangements. Neither were likely to be the case just now, but imagination makes everything a certainty.

Tim patted the seat. "I promise I won't pry out any teeth or information. It's fitting you'd take your secrets to the grave."

He put on latex gloves which made his hands seem smaller and adorable. Some of his blond hair was darkened by sweat.

"Are you sure about this?" I said. "I did a rush job brushing and flossing this morning before getting on the road. I'd be ashamed to have you see."

He patted the chair again, with more emphasis. "Most people brush so poorly that I can tell what they had for dinner the night before."

I laughed again and surrendered to the chair. Was this flirting? Were *we* flirting?

"I thought you lived in the funeral home."

"I do."

"Then why were you racing to get there in the morning?"

"I spent the night at Dad's."

"How is Bart?"

"About the same," I said.

Tim's lips pressed into a tight line as he told me to open up. The rim of his mirror scraped against my teeth. I stared at his face. His eyes looked up from my mouth and we met each other's gaze a moment. I became hyper aware of my hands gripping the edge of the armrests. I thought of Tim touching my face. How obscene to talk about codes of ethics and then want him to violate them. Of course he wouldn't. He was too good a person, too professional.

"How's Bart's xerostomia?"

"Heth whuth?"

Tim removed the mirror and sat back. "His dry mouth. I told him it's speeding up his tooth decay, but he didn't seem to care."

"The way Dad is now, it probably didn't even register."

"I told Johnny to start offering him sugarless hard candy. Nothing stimulates saliva like having something to suck on."

He grinned. Before I could think of a response, he got up and put the mirror in a plastic basin on the counter.

"It wouldn't hurt if you and Johnny could team up on this," he said, his back to me. "Bart's quality of life would be a lot better if he'd just let me pull those last few teeth and make him a good set of dentures."

"I know. But it's not going to happen, Tim."

"The dentures, or you and Johnny joining forces?"

"Both. But Dad wouldn't let those teeth be pulled no matter what. I wouldn't have called him a vain man before he got sick, but when I was growing up the thing I remembered most was his smile. You'd see those teeth and think he must be a salesman. I think he liked working in the mines and getting his face dirty because it made his teeth seem whiter. I can even remember him at the dinner table, rubbing his front teeth with the napkin. Like a butler cleaning the family silver, you know?"

He returned to his stool, his hands in his lap. "A dentist's dream."

"For all the good it did him. Wentz Hollow looks like a metropolis compared to the holler where he grew up. There was lots of stuff in the well water but none of it was fluoride. Yet somehow he never got a cavity. My grandparents wore false teeth by the time they were in their 40s."

"Interesting," Tim said. "Some people have the right DNA and never get cavities at all. Their teeth tend to be smoother, and their saliva remineralizes the enamel against bacterial erosion. Which just proves my point about the severity of his dry mouth. Without having enough spit, the bacteria's taken over with a vengeance. It makes us pay if . . ."

His words voice trailed off in the same way a breeze dies down suddenly, leaving you regretting its absence. As the silence lengthened, I thought about many recent things involving my father. Before I returned to Wentz Hollow, Rebecca had appointed herself as the family crier, emailing me all the news. When Mom died ten years ago, I wouldn't have known without her. Johnny wouldn't have told me. Would Dad? He'd mirrored Mom's hardness to me, but I wanted to believe the softness I saw overtaking him was just the emergence of his true personality. Rebecca was the one to tell me Dad was becoming forgetful, just niggling things at first, like where the car keys were, or the last two digits of Uncle Brad's phone number. But then you had to wonder why he was thinking of the number in the first place since his older brother died before Mom. Then, the first time I came back to the house, Rebecca and I stood on the porch listening to him yelling, *"You put Brad on! I know it's the right number!"* My cousin and I looked at each other, but Rebecca couldn't hold my gaze, and I knew she'd understated Dad's condition. Then we went inside, and he saw us and hung up and came over to me like the sweetest old man who ever lived. His hug stunned me, and Jesus Christ how I hugged back.

"Tim, can I tell you something?"

"Anything. I'm glad we're talking."

"This morning, before it was even sunrise, I took a shower, and I opened the medicine cabinet. Dad's toothbrush was there in the same green plastic cup that's been there for decades. I bet two hundred toothbrushes have occupied that cup, because Dad was conscientious about wear. I don't know what made me do it, but I picked up the toothbrush and looked at it. The bristles were matted as if it'd been used to scrub the floor for a year straight. And bone dry. I don't know the last time they got wet. Then I looked at the tube of toothpaste next to the cup. It may have been squeezed twice. The expiration date was two years ago."

He reached out and squeezed my right wrist. "It's OK, Nathan. You can't brush Bart's teeth for him."

"I couldn't stand that it was dry. I ran the head of the toothbrush under the tap until it was soaked and then I put it back in the cup and closed the cabinet. Why does every medicine cabinet door also have to be a goddamn mirror?"

I was on the verge of crying. I might have cried, except Tim said, "You want a tissue?" and I thought about how I offered a box of Kleenex to Meghan Malone just a little while ago. I didn't want to replay that scene with me in her shoes and I forced back the tears.

"I don't know what to say, Nathan. Where the fuck is Patch Adams when you need him?"

I got out of the chair. "You're a lot better than Patch Adams."

"Well, I've got nitrous oxide. Who needs to be funny when I can just gas you?"

We laughed and headed through the hallway to the lobby. I was ahead of him, and he put a hand on my shoulder.

"You don't ever stop, do you?"

"Stop what?" he said.

"Being cheerful."

Tim pulled his hand away. His expression changed, becoming serious. "Man, I'm betting I'll really need a drink tonight. How about joining me?"

We stood there, two Immortals realizing each other at last.

"I'd like that."

"Then that's a yes?"

"It's a yes. In fact, why don't you come over tonight after 8:00?"

His eyebrows raised. "To the funeral home?"

"I can't help where I live."

"Nathan," he said, "I can't wait. Don't mind if I bring my toothbrush, do you? I like to brush first thing in the morning."

Tim gave a sly smile. I can't imagine what my expression looked like, but I felt an incredible exhilaration, equaled only by an awkward sheepishness.

"I'll make sure my toothpaste isn't expired," I said, trying to joke but sounding too earnest to my own ears. Tim just laughed and said he'd see me tonight. I walked out and turned down the sidewalk to take the short route back to the funeral home. Most people don't leave a dentist's office feeling giddy unless they've been dosed with laughing gas, but I felt a certain glide to my steps, like I was ice skating all the way home. Fortunes and outlooks turn fast all the time: sunlight bursts through a cloudy day or sudden rain clouds roll in over your picnic. The heart skips a beat from terror or excitement all the same. Morticians, more than most, get reminded that the revolving door of luck is just an illusion. We think all things circle back, but you're walking a line to a terminal point.

But no one should philosophize before noon.

TIM

THERE'S A MOVIE I had to watch in 10th grade history class called *Spartacus*, and someone in the film says, *"As the teeth go, so go the bones."* I wasn't thinking about being a dentist in 10th grade. Hell, I was barely watching the movie. How could I when Connor Monroe was wearing shorts? The classroom lights were off and the blinds were pulled, but Connor even looked hot in the dark. He sat one row over and two chairs up on the right. His legs were bouncing like he had the jitters and his calf muscles flexed and relaxed, flexed and relaxed. Goddamn. It's funny what excites you when you've never had sex. I was a perverted little horndog anyway, but no gay boy could resist Connor Monroe. He was captain of the basketball team and those legs of his were long and perfect.

Despite the distraction, I must have been paying a little attention to the movie, because that line about teeth and bones wormed its way into my memory six years later when I finished my bachelor's degree in biology. My mom asked me what I was going to do now. Teach high school? The idea sucked. Then I remembered, *As the teeth go, so go the bones.* "Mom," I said, "I'm going to become a dentist." The decision made both my parents smile, and that was good enough for me.

Looking back, you could say I always had a thing for dentistry, even in early childhood. I remember being 6 or 7, and we were packing for some road trip. My parents presented me with a travel kit that included a miniature folding toothbrush and 3-ounce tube of Colgate. I have a distinct memory of obsessing over the toothbrush, getting up at night to open and close it like a pocketknife. I was very impressionable and easily impressed. It's highly possible that if my parents had given me a tampon instead, I'd now be a gynecologist.

I've always been a leap-without-looking kind of guy, so I didn't do a bit of research on my new career choice. I therefore didn't realize I was committing to four more years of school, a learning pace of eight teeth per year. I sure as hell didn't know I was going to rack up $100,000 in student loans, which I'd start paying off at the ripe age of 30, as soon as I walked away from the University of Washington with a diploma in hand that read *Timothy Sawyer, DDS.*

Ever hear of the National Health Service Corps Loan Repayment program? I hadn't either until graduation came around and the crippling reality of my debt set in. The way it works is, if you're willing to put in two years at a designated *Health Professional Shortage Area,* you get $50,000 of your student loan wiped out. My parents went on smiling, but their smiles became frozen whenever the subject of my student loans came up. They really couldn't help me.

So I signed on with the government's loan repayment program and announced I was going far away.

"To where?" Dad asked. "Africa? Latin America?"

"Some place called Toothless, Kentucky. Population: zero teeth."

CONFESSIONS

One of the best things about my parents was how bitchy I could be with them. Mom and Dad were both leftists, the kind of people who hoped their baby would be gay and therefore interesting. Other parents might reprimand their son for mocking his future patients, but even my mom snickered and said, "Hell, that's the entire South, Tim. Can't you at least go to a Third World country where there are some standards?"

We had a lot of laughs in the weeks ahead as I prepared to move, and the Service Corps trained me on my obligations. Then came the day of departure. My dad hugged me and then very seriously said, "Your mom and I want you to be careful, you know? About being gay. We're proud of you for the man you are, but it's a different place you're going to. Just stay safe."

"I'll be fine. It's not like I'm flamboyant or anything."

The skeptical expression on my father's face threw me. Did he really see me as some sort of screaming queen who needed the Hoover Dam to hold back an occasional lisp?

Then Dad teared up a little, muttered something about Matthew Shepard, and clapped me on the shoulder. "You're going to do great out there, Tim."

"Damn right I will!"

That was thirteen months ago. In less than a year, I'll have completed my obligations with the government and have half of my student loans eliminated. Best of all, the Service Corp helped me establish a little practice in the only nearby town, Wentz Hollow. I was making OK money, living expenses were cheap, and the work wasn't terrible. I confess I had some stereotypes about Kentuckians before I arrived. I figured I'd be dealing with people whose cheeks were stuffed with chewing tobacco, people who were down to their last three yellow, rotten teeth, people who'd been gumming their food for years. Imagine my surprise to learn Kentucky ranks first in the nation in fluoridation of drinking water! Part of my obligations with the Service Corps included taking my services on the road and visiting all the nooks and crannies of existence further east, where Wentz Hollow was referred to as *town*. The people there had their share of health problems, but it wasn't quite the dental apocalypse of my assumptions.

So I was getting along, and if I stuck around for a couple more years past my obligated time, I'd have enough money saved to be debt free. Then I could get the hell out of here and go back to Seattle.

But two more years in Wentz Hollow?

Jesus.

I tried to do any number of calculations in my head. Dentists aren't necessarily the best mathematicians. We only have to count to thirty-two, after all. I imagined being 35 years old, debt free but without any savings. How many thousands of dollars would I need to start a private practice in Seattle? Or should I just go work for Comfort Dental? The possibilities became a swirl. What was the point of thinking ahead at this point anyway? I'd jump when the time felt right.

In the meantime, Wentz Hollow had itself a dashing, affable dentist who took cash, card, check, and almost every insurance including Medicare, Medicaid and CHIP. From baby's first tooth to grandma's last, the folks of Wentz Hollow and the surrounding countryside had an anti-cavity cavalier at their beck and call.

Adopting an outrageously cheerful demeanor was my primary coping strategy when it came to the reality of being forced to work and live in Eastern Kentucky. Call it the Tao of the Homosexual, that ability to create a character. To play a role. It's easy enough to do if you've watched any TV from the last sixty years. *Northern Exposure, Evening Shade, Twin Peaks,* etc. I began streaming any show that featured a doctor or a barber or just a next-door neighbor full of folksy wisdom and humor. I soaked that stuff up through my pores and created *Tim Sawyer, Rural Dentist Who Totally Wants to Be Here*. Honestly,

CONFESSIONS

75% of the character rests in the stance: hands in the pockets up to the wrists, palms flat but placed more along the sides of the thighs than the front. This creates a relaxed, unassuming *aw shucks* affect. Then all you have to do is be nice.

I told my parents about *Tim Sawyer, Rural Dentist* and they totally misunderstood, thinking I was going around talking in an Appalachian drawl and memorizing a bunch of homespun wisdom I could vomit out at a moment's notice. But that crap would never fly. How could I explain that when you're creating a character, it's all about body language? How you stand and what you do with your hands creates a non-verbal autobiography. I said, "Mom, imagine if you went to a dentist and he appeared in the doorway, arms crossed at his chest like a bar bouncer. Wouldn't you fear for your teeth?"

"I guess I'd be a little concerned," she said, laughing.

"Exactly," I said. "I'm creating a whole new kind of dentist. I don't even want them to think I have hands. I want them to think I'm capable of sweet talking a bad tooth into falling out."

"Well, I'm biased," Mom said, "but I don't see how anyone could resist your charms. I know it's none of my business, but . . . have you *met* anyone?"

Despite our relative openness with each other, my parents seldom made direct inquiries about my love life, so her question startled me. Back in Washington, during college, I was having a lot of sex. *(Thank you, Grindr.)* One might even call me a whore. In four years, I don't think I ever saw the same guy more than twice. None of my sex partners measured up to those heated memories of Connor Monroe, but you wouldn't find me complaining. I had evolved beyond the simple kid who could be satisfied stealing glances at a jock's legs. My social life became this sweaty free for all that didn't subside much even when I entered graduate school. A dentist-in-training has needs and an understandable oral fixation. But I learned fast that I'd fallen into a very different culture. You sometimes hear the notion that certain professions attract specific demographics—the whole "Is every male flight attendant gay?" thing. I never figured dentists to be card-carrying Republicans until I found myself enrolled with a roomful of fellow hopefuls. Here I was at the same damn university where I'd done my bachelor's, but it felt like a mirror universe populated by Mitt Romney clones.

Never being too political, I rolled with the situation. Plus, I am, as they say, *straight acting,* which isn't the same as acting straight. If someone accused me of doing that to get by in Wentz Hollow, I'd be pissed off. The only *acting* I'm doing is that of a geographically displaced young dentist pretending to feel at home in a little town located in the part of a state where all four Grindr accounts have a tumbleweed for their profile picture.

"No," I said. "No one yet."

"Well, hopefully that changes. Your Dad and I are thinking about you."

Imagining my parents sitting around wondering if I'd had a hookup in Kentucky gave me a bit of a shiver, but I knew Mom meant to sound caring rather than creepy.

The simple truth is I'd lived like a monk during the entirety of my time in Wentz Hollow. The nearest gay scene was in Lexington, almost a three-hour drive. I ventured out that way a few times and found for the most part it wasn't worth the cost of gas. 23-year-old me, ready to move heaven and earth for a piece, would laugh at such sentiments. Have I become old before my time? Is there something in the water besides fluoride? Did my DDS degree now mean *Don't Drive for Sex*?

These details might seem meandering, but there's a point to them as sharp as the tip of your canine teeth. After a few months in Wentz Hollow, once I'd gotten set up in my office but still didn't have too many patients, sometimes I'd sit in my examination chair with the intention of taking a nap. But instead of sleeping, I found myself staring at the room's white walls. I had my diploma hung there, next to a framed quote that felt so appropriate—*As the teeth go, so go the bones.* The rest of the wall was bare, and I let my memory try painting portraits of past hookups there. It shocked me how little I even remembered most of their faces, and those I did recall had no names. Maybe this shouldn't have been such a surprise. With a lot of those guys an exchange of names never even happened. We're not talking hours upon hours of quality time spent in each other's company. Still, how could I have been with all those dudes and never once think about dating any of them?

Wanting a relationship should have been the first sign I was starting to be changed by life in Wentz Hollow. Some might escalate it from mere sign to *warning signal.* Was I transitioning to a romantic? Call it a coping mechanism, call it the primary product in an excuse factory, but as a kid, whenever my emotions became too much, I reminded myself that feelings are just an illusion cooked up by brain chemistry. Thank serotonin for your happiness, blame your anger on acetylcholine, praise dopamine for your horniness. And as for acute loneliness, well, that was—

Real.

You can't be lonely, I told myself. Not when you have a bunch of friends just a text message away.

That was true to an extent. My first month in Wentz Hollow, I was group texting more than ever before, almost live blogging my day at times. *Just finished up inside another mouth. Jealous, bitches?* But those jokes got stale and by the third month I wasn't texting at all. Or receiving texts, for that matter. The true depths of my isolation hit me about six months into my stay. I'd just finished with a new client named Meghan Malone, who'd flirted through the entire session and seemed almost reluctant to leave until her cell phone rang and she said,

"Guess I better go."

"Was that your boyfriend?"

"Oh, gosh no," she said, adding a wink. "I'm single."

"How tragic," I said, laughing.

"Maybe you could help me change that."

I offered my politest grin. "See you in six months, Ms. Malone."

She laughed as if I'd said the most idiotic thing. "Bye, Hermey," she said, and left before I could ask her what she meant. I went back to my office, put my tools in a sterilization bin, and settled back into the examination chair, which was still warm from Meghan's body. The last forty-five minutes had been so strange. It wasn't the first time a woman ever flirted with me. Like I said, I'm pretty masculine. But as I replayed the session in my thoughts, I realized I'd flirted back just a little.

Well, why not? I thought, staring at the wall, which by now hosted my diploma, the latest poster for the University of Kentucky Wildcats men's basketball team, and a replacement quote I'd found online from Kahlil Gibran. *Your pain is the breaking of the shell that encloses your understanding.* I was still perfecting my character and decided my original quote was a bit too plain. I could be folksy *and* profound, and Gibran did the trick. He was all the rage back in Seattle. Every bookstore carried his stuff, and you'd find his quotes on T-shirts and coffee mugs.

In this part of Kentucky, not so much.

I left the chair and went over to stand in front of the quote. *Your pain is the breaking of the shell that encloses your understanding.* I shivered. I *was* lonely, and loneliness was my pain. That's why I'd flirted with a *woman* of all things. I was *lonely* and not just *horny*.

The difference struck me like an epiphany, and I backed away and went to the hallway bathroom. I splashed myself with cold water and studied my dripping face in the mirror.

I'd changed. I'd become—mature. Once again, all the memories of past hookups shot through my mind like a series of flash cards for a test I'd already passed. There was no regret about not really knowing any of them. I was a different person then. They now served to remind me I wanted something else. Something better.

I was a young gay dentist stuck in Kentucky, and *somehow* I was going to meet a boyfriend to fulfill my new, more sophisticated emotional needs.

Enter the local funeral home director.

Or rather, enter the local funeral home director's *father.*

I was wiping the water from my new, mature face when I heard the bells ring on the lobby door. I stuffed my hands into my pockets, got the palms just right, and strolled down the hallway to greet whoever it was.

The old man standing there matched every stereotype I ever had about a Kentuckian, right down to his denim overalls worn over a checkered red shirt. His rolled shirtsleeves revealed skinny, liver-spotted forearms, the hairless skin waxy like a banana peel. A few determined hairs arced from left to right across the crown of his head, as if he'd sat down with his barber, pointed to a photo of the Gateway Arch and said, "Give me that look." I said hello but he didn't seem to hear me. He stood there looking around with the door wide open behind him. The old guy looked like a stray dog that had accidentally walked into a veterinarian's office and was just starting to recognize its mistake.

"Sir? Are you OK?"

Then another man appeared in the doorway, and a burst of excitement made me question whether I was just horny after all. Goddamn, this guy was beautiful, hot and fit in a way only blue-collar workers can achieve. Gym bodies are great, but they don't match up to those who spend all day laying concrete or tearing out walls. These guys may not have six pack abs and

5% body fat, but they're solid in a real-world way. It shows most in their forearms, I think. Really toned, broad forearms. He stood about 6'3", with dirty blonde hair and a bit of stubble that looked like a splash of gold dust on his sunburned skin. I figured him to be about my age, give or take a couple of years. His arms were tanned, thick at the biceps and triceps and smooth all the way down to the wrists. His blue t-shirt stretched tight across the chest and clung along the slim tapering of his torso. His blue jeans were a bit dirty, and his sneakers must have been white once upon a time, but damn.

Damn.

The younger guy said, "You the new dentist?"

"Not sure about new," I said, grinning. "Been in town about half a year now. You fellas here for an exam?"

The old man opened his mouth, an almost perfect oval. At first I thought he was showing me he was indeed here for a cleaning, but then he began rocking a little from side to side. He looked to be about 5'7", though I guessed he'd been a few inches taller before age shriveled him. He walked over to the nearest wall. The waiting room was decorated in thrift shop chic, full of paintings of ships weathering stormy weather, boys running through the countryside, all that sweet Country Time Lemonade stuff. The old guy leaned in close to one, pointed at it and laughed.

"That sure is a funny picture," he said.

I looked at him and then at the stud, who rolled his eyes. "He'll call a tombstone a funny picture. I'm Johnny Ashcraft. This is my dad. He needs his teeth looked at pretty bad."

"Welcome in, sir. It's sure nice to meet you. What's your name?"

"It's Bart," Johnny said.

"Now I know your dad can speak, because I've heard him," I said. You know some jokes will fall flat the moment you make them.

"Got time to give him a look over?" Johnny said.

"I can do that. I've got my chair right down the hallway."

"Good luck getting him to it. Best just to wait and eventually he ends up where you want him to be."

"Are we going there?" Bart said, pointing at the picture but turning to talk to me. His voice had a higher pitch than I expected, wispy and strained, like he suffered from a mild speech impediment. It was obvious most of his teeth were gone, including the maxillary central incisors, aka his two front teeth. I wondered how long he'd been without them.

"No, you're not going into the damn painting," Johnny said. He took hold of his father, his long fingers completely engulfing his dad's wrist. "We're here to see the Doc about your teeth. Remember all the pain you're having?"

"I'm not having any pain."

"The hell you're not. So let Doc take a look at you."

"You're the doc?" Bart said, leaning toward me. He had terrible breath but I fought off showing a reaction.

"I sure am, Mr. Ashcroft," I said, holding out my right hand.

"Ashcraft," Johnny said. "Not that it makes much difference."

I mustered all the aw-shucks folksiness I'd developed so far. "Well, it does to me. If a man can't get another man's name right, he ought to apologize. Am I right, Mr. Ashcraft?"

Bart moved past me. Johnny followed him. His right arm brushed up against me as he did. It felt meaningful. God, I'd take back every bad thought I ever had about Wentz Hollow if this guy ended up being gay.

"Dad, you be good and let Doc take a look." He looked back at me and said, "He's only got about eight teeth left anyway. Should be an easy job."

"I see," I said, trying a conspiratorial smile.

Bart made his way down the hall, stopping to look at any

possible thing of interest along the way. He started into the bathroom, but Johnny pulled him away and said, "The chair's in *that* room. Doc's not going to see you sitting on the can."

Both their backs were to me, but I could see how Bart froze up at the sight of the chair. If his mouth was as bad as it seemed, I had to wonder if he'd ever been to a dentist in his life. Maybe there'd been a bad experience as a child that scared him off, or maybe he'd grown up in a place where there wasn't a dentist. That's why the Service Corps had sent me to this neck of the woods, after all.

Bart began to wander about my exam room. Johnny sighed and said, "Hang on, Doc. I'll hold him down in the chair if I have to."

"I've got another idea."

"You do?"

"How about you take a seat first. I'll take a look in your mouth and we'll show Bart there's nothing to worry about, right?"

"Think I'll pass on that idea, Doc."

"Johnny never liked the dentist," Bart said. "Peggy always had a time of it when he was little. Nathan was always good with the dentist, but not John."

"No reason to be afraid, John," I said, grinning.

"I'm not afraid."

"We'll keep your secret, won't we, Bart?"

The old man turned with his mouth as ovaled as could be and his eyes sort of squinty. Then he slapped his thigh and rocked from side to side again.

"You know I ain't scared of a damn dentist," Johnny said. "But Dad, if it'll make you happy, I'll sit in the chair and let Doc take a look. But only after he's done with you."

"Sounds fair to me," I said. "What do you say, Bart?"

He looked like he wanted to turtle, shrugging up his shoulders until they were almost level with his ear lobes. He held the position for several seconds. I thought of a child who's been shook by a sudden, scary noise and can't unwind. By now I'd worked with the elderly enough to discover how childlike they can be, particularly in stubbornness.

Just when I thought Bart would never agree, a change came over him. He touched his mouth like it was a new discovery, looked between Johnny and me, and said, "Maybe I better. Since I'm here."

"I promise to be gentle."

"But I don't want him in the room," he said, pointing at Johnny.

"Now Dad—"

"You heard what I said, John. You go wait and let the men talk."

I stepped out of the way of a father-son staredown, let it go on for several seconds, and then clapped Johnny on his very solid shoulder. "Don't worry. Your old man doesn't bite, does he?"

Without looking at me, he said, "Dad's all bark. Yap, yap, yap, right, Dad?"

He turned and walked back to the waiting room. I watched, taking in every step until he took a seat out of sight.

"OK," I said in my quietest tone, debating whether or not to shut the door. I decided against it and sat down on the stool next to the chair. "Come on over, Bart. Let's get to know each other."

He shuffled over but didn't sit. He bent to look at the white ceramic cuspidor mounted to the right. His manners seemed so childlike I decided to indulge a hunch and I turned the water on. A steady murmur of running water filled the silence, soft and gentle like the sound of a flushed toilet refilling, only more muted. To me it was a pleasant, tranquil white noise.

"I always like that sound," I said. "Like a creek bed, right?"

He gave me that oval-mouthed smile and started to turn

around.

"What are you thinking, Bart? Want to sit down?"

He went to the wall and peered at my diploma a moment, then moved over to the basketball poster. He pointed and turned to me, his mouth once again a wide oval. "You a Cats fan?"

"Since birth," I said.

"When I was little, my daddy and me always listened to Cawood call the games. My daddy would say Cawood is just like us. Daddy mined coal."

"That's really interesting, Bart. Why don't you come sit and tell me—"

"I'll just stand here a bit," he said.

"Well, that's not really how a dental exam works."

"I don't need one."

"How about letting me take a little peek inside anyway? It's my job."

Bart shifted over to the framed quotation from Kahlil Gibran. His body shifted, almost teetering as he followed the words from left to right. He reached to adjust the right strap of his overalls. Then he turned back with that open-mouthed smile of his and said, "That must be a good one, because I sure don't understand it."

I laughed at that, but before I could reply, he shuffled left to reinspect my diploma. "You a real dentist? You look like a kid."

"I'm as real as my teeth," I said, grinning and tapping on my first premolar. "Better use me while you can. Before too long all the dentists will be robots."

My joke worked. People around these parts hate automation more than most. They listen to Rush Limbaugh and shake their heads at stories about truckers getting laid off in favor of self-driving rigs. Bart didn't laugh at all, but I'd already gotten used to his mannerisms. He slapped his thigh and kept his mouth nice and open. This told me he was cracking up.

After a moment, he said, "I'm glad I won't live to see it."

"Amen to that."

He straightened. "You pray?"

I'd already been asked several variations on this question in my first few months in Wentz Hollow, and I knew how to answer it. Be God-fearing, be a Wildcats fan, and hate the Louisville Cardinals, and you'll go far in these parts. Be anti-abortion as well, and you can run for Congress.

"Sure do," I said.

"What church?"

Now I didn't know how many churches were in Wentz Hollow, and the only denominations I knew even a little bit about before moving here were Catholics, Mormons, and Methodists. But there was a Southern Baptist place up the street from my office, and that's the name I gave. I knew it because I drove past it every day.

"That's a good place."

Bart launched into a story about how his small church had merged with another one to form Calvary Hill Baptist. "I can't remember just when it happened. Must have been when Nathan was about 2 or 3. There were thirty of us in one place, and seventy in the other. Together we might have been the largest church in the county."

"Would have? What happened?"

Now Bart did something I'd come to notice whenever his mood threaded the needle between reflection and agitation. He turned his head to the right and looked like he was about to spit. It was such a weird tic, and I didn't know what to make of it the first time. Later I learned he'd chewed tobacco for years and it was sort of a shadow motion, a muscle memory. Whenever he made that spitting motion, I knew he had to get something out.

He went and took a seat in the chair. He did this with

all the visible unease of a man lowering himself into his own grave, and I noticed he never quite let the back of his skull connect with the headrest.

"Same thing that always happens when folks get together to worship God. One man ends up hating another man, or their wives take a dislike to each other. Then the first group only wants to listen to their preacher, and the other group won't abide any preacher but their own. Lots of shouting, not enough praying. Nathan must have been about five when it all ended. I'd have quit going after that, but Peggy wouldn't have it. Church meant so much to her."

One thing I really liked about the people around here was how they dropped names in their stories without any context, as if they assumed the listener had grown up with them or something. As Bart kept talking and the names began piling up, I tried to imagine anyone else telling the story in the same way, and I couldn't do it. My mom would say, "Then my younger brother Patrick came over" or "Then Patrick—that's my younger brother—showed up." But for people around these parts, details like that were like butter spread over a hot biscuit, something already melted into the bread of understanding.

Bart went on with his stories, his fragile hands clasped together at the base of his rib cage, and I began to feel more like an intrigued psychiatrist. It was the first time my sense of role-playing became something authentic. I lost track of time, falling under the spell of his soft voice, losing myself in the melancholy of memories that weren't always given in coherent threads. Nevertheless, I found the tapestry charming.

My listening seemed to gain Bart's trust. I remembered what I was supposed to be doing and said, "I better take a look at your mouth." He opened up without any hesitation and I pulled the stool closer and moved in with my inspection mirror. As soon as the mirror passed between his lips, however, the tension returned. I heard a slight cracking sound and realized it was his fingers gripping at the vinyl armrests. His eyes moved side-to-side the way a trapped animal's might, making me feel like I was now playing a high stakes version of the old game Operation. If the mirror bumped against anything, Bart would explode.

I closed my nostrils against the reek of his breath and steadied my hand and angled the mirror to see the back of his mouth.

Any medical professional gets used to seeing bad things, horrible and sickening conditions, illnesses that cause a natural revulsion. You don't go far in your program without a lecture on the importance of compassion and controlling your expressions. I'd seen my fair share of poor oral health. All that said, I confess I didn't look in Bart's mouth a second longer than I had to. He had nine teeth left, yellowed and not firm at the roots. The gums were inflamed by gingivitis, and when the edge of my mirror made the barest graze, Bart gasped and flinched like a man being tortured. I could not imagine how much pain he must experience throughout the day.

"OK, that's good, Bart," I said, hoping I didn't sound defeatist. "I think we have something we can work with here."

His small Adam's apple bobbed. There wasn't much spit to swallow. His dry mouth was evident. He turned his head and just stared at the basin.

"The first thing we want to do is get that pain under control."

He nodded.

"I imagine it must be pretty bad."

Bart nodded again.

"How would you rate it on a scale of 1 to 10?"

The poor old guy looked at me. His eyes narrowed like we might be playing a guessing game. "5," he said.

There was no way it could be under a 7 even on a good day.

"Are you taking anything like Ibuprofen?"

"Oh, I like that stuff. I take tons of it."

I put my hand on his forearm. "That's a figure of speech, right? We don't want you taking *tons*."

He looked toward the basin and for the second time I saw that odd motion of his where he acted like he wanted to spit. "I forget what all I take. John may know, or Rebecca."

"Do they live with you?"

He blinked. "John has done good for himself. He's an electrician. Never going to go broke doing that."

I smiled and sat back on my stool. "Did you teach him?"

"Gosh, no. I was a miner like my daddy. Shame to see coal die. Some of the best times in my life were in the mines. But it's not what I wanted for my boys. I knew that the first time I saw Nathan. Those little arms and legs, that beautiful face. I tried to imagine it black with coal. *No, sir*. Mines for me, but never for him. I took both my boys down there to show them they could have something different. Johnny I worried about. But as Nathan grew up I knew I could relax. He won that blue ribbon at the science fair and I knew he was special. For a month he had it on a string and wore it around his neck, just as proud as can be until Peggy got mad about it."

"Why did she get mad?"

"Oh, she said he was prancing. We argued about it a few times. A boy shouldn't prance. I didn't notice, but she saw him more than me. I guess in the end she was right, but . . ."

I leaned closer. "But what?"

Bart's eyes squeezed shut. "He's gone on and done just fine for himself as well. Both of my boys have. I guess he's not squeamish being what he is. I don't see how he can stand it."

"Now I'm really curious," I said, laughing. "Is he a doctor?"

Before Bart answered, Johnny stepped in.

"Thought I'd hear a drill going by now. Dad, you talking

CONFESSIONS

Doc's ear off?"

"It's fine," I said. "I like hearing stories."

This was the truest thing I'd said all day, and another bit of self-discovery made since coming to Kentucky. When I think back on all those college hookups, there was never a lot of talk before, after, or during. I can't say I was interested in hearing their life stories, and some definitely had been talkers, going on about their hopes and fears even as I raced to get dressed. I wasn't interested in their mouths when it came to speech. I might have walked out on some of them mid-sentence; it was hard to recall. Thinking about it made me feel like an asshole. Part of me thought I was being ridiculous. After all, the app was called Grindr, not Listenr. But all those hookups wanting to talk afterward, wanting a psychiatrist or a priest or a friend . . . wasn't I poorer for not bothering?

And now I found myself genuinely interested in the half-remembered anecdotes of a very old man. I guess in coming to Kentucky I'd traded oral sex for oral history.

Johnny walked over and stood next to us. I was still perched on the stool, which made it a real catbird seat since my eyeline was just a little above his crotch. "With all that talking, I guess you got a good look into Dad's big mouth."

"He sure did, John. He said it's all OK."

Johnny looked at me. "My ass. What's the truth, Doc?"

"First we'll want to do something about his gum pain," I said, and then stopped myself, realizing I was responding to Johnny's natural dominance. I pivoted to speak to Bart. "You mentioned Ibuprofen, but that can only do so much, and it's not a good idea to be taking it all of the time. Right now I want to get you on Orajel. It's over the counter, but I've got a supply here that you can have. I'll show you how to apply it."

"Well, that sounds like just the thing," Bart said.

"It'll help a lot with the pain and inflammation. We're going to need to have some X-rays done on your mouth too."

Both men flashed the same skeptical look I'd noticed on everyone around these parts when I mentioned X-rays. It was the paranoia of the poor and uninsured, the certainty I was trying to run up their bill. Hell, who could blame them? Medicaid fraud is everywhere in these parts, and dentistry has its share of bullshit. You have dental chains funded by private equity investors who make demands about profit margins and revenue targets. Dentists get pressured to push unnecessary surgeries and overtreat minor problems. But that wasn't going to be me. Not now, not ever.

So, I understood their reaction when Johnny said, "Get out of the chair, Dad. We won't be back." I stood up as Bart wiggled himself up, grumbling. The idea *he* thought I was scamming him really hurt. It was like I'd earned his trust only to betray him on a dime.

"There won't be a charge," I said.

"Nothing's free, Doc."

"I swear. Bart, listen to me. The X-ray has to be done. You've got significant tooth decay. I need to see how deep it extends into your jaw. There's an old saying I like. 'As the teeth go, so go the bones.' Your jawbone could be in big trouble. An X-ray is the only way to know."

"We're not going bankrupt over five teeth! Come on, Dad."

I looked at Bart. He stood in his place, looking back and forth between us. He looked like a lost boy facing a fork in the road. Johnny's face was bright red with beads of sweat blistering his forehead. The muscles flexed in his forearms as his hands clinched. Medical debt was the most sinister of potions. Just a whiff of it could turn Jekyll into Hyde real fast.

I held out my hands to show them I understood their worry. "It's all covered under the government, and I tell you what. If it isn't, I'll eat the bill myself. You can have that in writing. The only thing I want is for Bart to be pain free. But

CONFESSIONS

I have to know what I'm dealing with first."

Johnny took a step closer.

"You'll really put that in writing?"

"I can type it or write it out in longhand. Typing would be better," I added, smiling. "No one can read my handwriting."

Bart walked right up to me and held out his hand. I shook it.

"You're just like my boy Nathan."

Before I could answer, Johnny said, "You know, I'm getting that feeling too, Dad."

How a simple wink could be so mocking, I don't know. But Johnny managed it, and I found myself blushing.

"And you go to church!"

Looking at the ground, I muttered something about missing a service from time to time.

I forced myself to raise my head just as Bart flashed another of his oval smiles. He pointed to the empty space where his front teeth once were and said, "The Lord doesn't mind some gaps."

I got Bart the Orajel and showed him how to apply it. I couldn't get either of them to commit to the X-rays or even a follow-up appointment, but I did get a dinner invitation before they left. One thing about the south—or at least rural Kentucky—is how fast relative strangers ask you over to their house for supper. And they say *supper*, not dinner. But Bart said breakfast, which threw me. He kept saying how I had to come over for breakfast as I escorted them into the lobby. By that point I'd gotten used to being invited into my patients' homes, but I'd always been vague about accepting. Bart, however, wasn't vague at all. I had to come to breakfast *tonight*. Then, Johnny piped in and said, "Yeah, join us tonight for breakfast, Doc."

"But breakfast is in the morning."

"Dad calls everything breakfast now. That's fine with me,

I like a good breakfast beer. You and I can have KFC and some drinks, and Dad will slurp down mashed potatoes since it's all he can stand half the time." I looked at Johnny and tried to figure out his game. Did he really want me to come over? What had that little condescending wink been about? He was still hot enough to make the idea of throwing back beers with him tempting. I was also intrigued by this brother of his, Nathan. Would he be over for breakfast too?

I had to find out.

The moment I said yes, Bart slapped his thigh like I'd given him the greatest gift ever. He wrote his address down on a piece of paper and then bounded out the door, looking for fresh adventures. Johnny watched him go and shook his head. Then he motioned for the paper and looked at it. "Son of a bitch," he said. "Dad actually remembered where he lives. Half the time he gives people the address for the post office. You must have the magic touch."

"That's what they say."

"Oh, I *bet* they do, Doc."

He threw another wink at me, laughed and walked out, shutting the door behind him. I went to the side window and watched them leave in an old blue pickup with a ladder strapped across the rooftop, its bed filled with power tools. Johnny drove the truck just the way I figured he would, racing toward stop signs and then slamming his brakes. I wondered if he drove like that the whole way home, and if he did it just for amusement or to make his dad sick. *Dumb redneck trash*, I thought.

But redneck trash I wanted to fuck.

I went home a few hours later, showered, and shaved. I was sifting through the shirts in my closet, fretting over the decision, when realization struck. Why was I acting like a man getting ready for a date? I looked down at my chinos, shook my head and got out of them. KFC and beer in rural Kentucky:

CONFESSIONS

this was a blue jeans and T-shirt affair at best. Old habits die hard, and I selected my tightest tee. If his brother was there, I wanted to show him what I had to offer. Hell, I might as well show Johnny too. *Because you never know.* That was the quote that should have been hanging in my office. Wiser words had never been spoken.

But I discovered a different kind of tightness as I pulled on the shirt's hem and turned to look at my reflection on profile. There's a thing called the Freshman 15 that refers to how college freshmen usually gain 15 pounds over their first two semesters. There should be a condition called the Southern 20 for people who move south of the Mason-Dixon line. The success of any form-fitting shirt depends a lot on the form, and I saw first trimester padding where the straight plank of my stomach used to be.

"Oh my God," I said, squaring myself back to the mirror. I pinched the flab. It didn't seem like all that much when captured between my thumb and index finger. Holding it, I made a slow pivot right again, staring at my belly's reflection. It was like watching an optical illusion as I became more and more parallel with the glass: Not bad . . . not bad . . . a little chubby—*FAT.*

How the hell had this happened? Did the dentist need to go to the eye doctor? How could I have been so blind?

I backed away from the mirror as if my reflection were a doctor confronting me with a terrible prognosis.

"OK," I said, trying not to hyperventilate. "You've let your diet go. You've got a job that keeps you sitting around a lot, and you're not exercising like you used to. You're in a land where all things are fried. Here's how we're going to handle this. You're going to start walking. You're going to download home exercise videos. You're going to do pushups in-between appointments. You're so over carbs. You'll drive to Lexington or Louisville or Cincinnati to find the nearest cool sculpting place, and you're going to get this nasty beast frozen off you."

I didn't have a scale in the house, but I weighed 150 pounds when I graduated dental school. At 5'10", that put my BMI right in the middle of normal weight. Where the hell did I stand now? What did this flab between my fingertips translate into? Five pounds? Ten? Twenty?

I cast the shirt off me and began to run in place, raising my knees as high as I could, wearing nothing but underwear and socks? I did it for twenty minutes and then I pinched the fat again. Maybe a little lesser?

Hydroxycut, I thought. Cardio, Keto, pushups, and Hydroxycut. With my metabolism, I'll be back into shape in two weeks.

My heart rate slowed as I thought myself back from the edge. The tunnel wasn't too long, and the light at the end blazed bright. I was just grateful to discover my mistake in time, thanks to my best tight shirt. Right now it was my enemy, but we'd be friends again in no time. I opened the top left dresser drawer and took out a pair of blue jeans, which were five years old. With great concern and dread, I tiptoed into them and eased them up my legs with all the steady care of a bomb disposal technician. Unlike my preference for tighter t-shirts, I'd never gone for skinny jeans. I liked a regular fit. As the waistband passed my knees, I noticed the constriction. Jesus Christ, even my thighs had become fatter. The fabric began a joyless Koala bear hug up my leg but I kept going, sucking in my gut, holding my breath as I faced the awful reality of being unable to button my pants.

But they did button. Relieved, I exhaled. My stomach muscles relaxed and the flab spilled over the top of the jeans. I thought it looked like the head of a joey poking out to take a look at the world, and I dashed to find my one really oversized T-shirt, the one that used to make me look like a skater boy because it reached down to my thighs. Its slimming effect wasn't everything I could dream of, but it'd work for tonight.

As you can imagine, though, my mindset wasn't the greatest for KFC and beer. If I had Bart's number, I would have called to cancel. Instead, I bit the bullet and set off to the Ashcraft homestead, which ended up being on a lonely country road about twenty minutes south of my practice. I'd never have found it without my phone GPS, and when I pulled into the gravel driveway the house felt unreal and a little sad. It wasn't in bad shape, but it appeared to sit on a lot of vacant land. A field stretched toward the horizon on the opposite side of the road, and a very tall tree stood off in the distance, silhouetted against the sunset. I couldn't make out many details, but its black form seemed leafless and lightning-struck.

I parked behind two trucks. One belonged to Johnny. Was the other one Nathan's? Was he here? I imagined a shyer, smarter version of Johnny waiting for me, waiting for *anyone* to save him from Kentucky and his brother. We could be made for each other, and here I was making a poor first impression. God, why did I have to be so fat? Why had I let myself go? I stepped toward the porch and the inevitable rendezvous. I smelled honeysuckle and heard crickets. I wondered if I'd be able to hear them around the kitchen table, filling the uncomfortable silence of the awkward meal to come.

The front door opened and Johnny stepped out. He was wearing a muscle shirt, the kind where the sides have been cut away. His torso was smooth and tanned, with the right amount of hair showing on his stomach. I remembered on the spot the couple of times when Connor Monroe wore something similar, and how dangerous those moments had been because they kidnapped my eyes.

"Hey there, Doc," he said. He had a Bud Light in his left hand. His right hand casually lifted the hem of his shirt up and dabbed the cloth along his forehead. A rich, dark treasure trail climbed the ladder of his abdominal muscles, which probably could have been a six pack if he didn't drink as many beers. I was surprised he didn't have any tattoos. Then he dropped his shirt down and flashed a grin that said, *caught you looking.* His arrogance would have been hot if I knew more about him. Was he a straight guy who likes attention no matter where it comes from? Did he just enjoy teasing any queer who came his way? If only there wasn't an edge of meanness about him. For all I knew, gay bashing was his favorite past-time and he belonged on a Southern Poverty Law Center watchlist.

"Hi, Johnny. Did you have a good day?"

"Fair, Doc."

I took a step onto the porch. "I don't know if you should call me that."

"Dentists aren't docs?"

"Well, they are, but—"

"Then quit being a bitch about it."

I nodded, at a loss for words. I smelled the beer on his breath and guessed he wasn't on his first bottle.

"Do anything interesting?"

"Just been putting up with Dad. We got the chicken. You ready?"

"Sure. I'm not too hungry, but I'll have a little."

He turned and flung the bottle. I lost sight of it and didn't hear it land in the grass. "Hate it when beer gets warm. We got plenty more. Dad don't drink so it's all for me."

"Does your brother drink? What's his name again? Nathan?"

"The queer."

"What?"

"Liquor," Johnny said, grinning. "Did you think I said something else?"

"I know what you said."

"You sure? Because a lot of times we hear what we want to hear, right?"

CONFESSIONS

Johnny opened the screen door for me. The main door was already opened. I just stood in place feeling cold. Then Johnny said, "Well come on, Doc. Dad can't wait to talk your ear off some more. After you get tired of it, you and I can sit out here and drink."

"That'd be cool."

He lifted the bottom of his shirt again, not quite as far as last time, and laughed.

I entered the house and found Bart at the kitchen table, a green and white Formica table with four chairs that lorded over squares of cracked linoleum. The tiles were white with generic grimy blue crests. There was almost an identical pattern on the wallpaper.

"Hey, Dad, your new best friend is here."

Bart opened his mouth big at me. I thought he might get up, but when he didn't, I opted to take the seat to his left.

Johnny went to the refrigerator and took out a fresh beer. "Dad's in a real happy mood, Doc. That stuff you gave him for his gums might as well be cocaine. Hell, he was feeling so good I had to try a little bit of it myself."

I stiffened. "You didn't really do that, did you? There's the possibility of side effects."

He unscrewed the bottle cap and tossed it on the counter. "Oh, it was just a little dab. Put it right down here like a pinch of dip. Besides, I read the box first. Since I'm not breastfeeding or looking to become pregnant, I think I'm good."

"That's still my medicine, John. You shouldn't take it."

"You're right," he said. "Especially when I've got better stuff here."

He brought the bottle back to his lips.

The briefest look of disapproval crossed Bart's expression. Between that, the décor and some of the things I'd heard Johnny say, my imagination started weaving a backstory for these two. I saw Johnny bullying Bart non-stop, year after year, knowing he could get away with it because Bart was old and didn't want to be alone. He needed someone to stand up for him. Then and there, for this night at least, I decided that someone would be me.

But our meal together for the most part lacked tension. We made enough conversation to drown out the crickets. Johnny became chill, placing the chicken bucket in the middle of the table. He then laid out the side dishes and put down three paper plates. I looked in disappointment at the fourth spot, assuming its emptiness meant I'd not be meeting Nathan tonight. Once again I found myself wondering how much he looked like his younger brother. The amber kitchen light really favored Johnny's skin and hair, and I had a great, up-close look at his body's firmness. It occurred to me I wasn't even trying to hide my lust. Maybe this is how I'd have acted in high school if Connor had been a cocktease. As he served us our food, Johnny seemed to make ever-more elaborate stretches and reaches across the table, guaranteeing his shirt rode up or the open sides revealed his nipples and his armpits. Goddamn, I was taking him in, storing material for masturbation fodder. That he said nothing dumb or offensive was the cherry on top.

Then he belched.

"*John*," Bart said, a sudden parental edge in his otherwise soft voice. "Be nice at the table."

"A man's got to get the gas out one way or the other."

"You can still excuse yourself."

"Well, excuse me," he said, and then turned his head and belched again. "Excuse me twice."

By the time Johnny finished, he and I each had half the bucket on our plates, as well as two biscuits, a big dollop of mac and cheese, and potato wedges. Bart's plate had a volcano of mashed potatoes in the middle with gravy running down the sides like lava. I looked at my meal and felt undeniably hungry. I also felt the tightness of my jeans. It's one night,

CONFESSIONS

I told myself. One indulgence. Tomorrow you start off fresh. Tonight's a loss but the real war begins tomorrow.

"You don't mind paper plates, do you, Doc? Dad sold the china after Mom died."

I looked at Bart to see if father and son were having some sort of feud, but the old man looked oblivious. Still, I didn't put it past him to be waiting on my answer like a hawk.

"I'm really good with paper," I said. "Use it myself most of the time. I hate washing dishes. Wish they could make paper pots and pans too. Maybe I'd cook a little more."

Bart opened his mouth and tilted his head back a bit as he clapped his right hand against his thigh. His smile was a black hole.

"Less talking, more eating," Johnny said. "Doc, I gave you the legs and thighs just because you don't strike me as a breast man."

I glanced at Bart, who just blinked at his mashed potatoes.

"Well, thanks for looking out for me, Johnny. I'd hate to give in to temptation. Mind if I get one of those beers?"

Johnny went to the refrigerator. As he did, Bart picked up his fork and began working on the mashed potatoes, and his eating made an exaggerated slurping noise. *Poor old guy*, I thought. The state of his teeth hadn't happened all at once. Like a man stuck in quicksand, he'd been sinking into his misery bit by bit over the years, making accommodations with the pain instead of facing the problem.

Johnny brought me the beer and said, "Christ, Dad, you're going to make Tim sick."

"I'm fine," I said, taking a quick swallow. "So, Bart, the Orajel is really helping?"

"Oh, it's just the trick, Tim," he said.

"I'm glad to hear that. Can't wait to help you even more."

Bart said nothing to this, and I looked across the table as Johnny took his seat. He ate with his head bent down, eyes

67

focused on the food. *He* was a breast man. Two of them overcrowded his paper plate, and he'd heaped mac and cheese over them like cake frosting. I picked up my fork. As I did, Bart raised his head, his eyes wide. I thought he was scared, thinking he'd escaped any further talk of his teeth. But instead he said, "Grace."

"I'm sorry?"

"How could I forget to say grace?"

"You forget all the time," Johnny said.

"I've *never* forgot grace, John. Why did you let me? Your mother would never let me . . . well, never mind. We'll say it now."

He held out both his hands to us. Johnny sighed and reached across the table to take his dad's right hand. Not having any friends or family religious enough to say grace at the table, I sat there a moment feeling like a cultural anthropologist among an Amazon tribe. Then I felt a little kick against my leg and looked over at Johnny. He gave the slightest nod, serious in his eyes. I looked at Bart's left hand, still stretched out toward me. Bart's eyes were closed. I'd assumed he was praying in silence and only now realized he was waiting for my touch.

I took his hand and closed my eyes. Bart began speaking at once, his voice even softer than usual.

"Lord, we thank you for bringing Tim into our life and for allowing us to share this meal with him. We ask for Your blessing and that You'll touch him and guide his hands and make him an instrument of Your mercy. Watch over us in everything we do. Watch over those that can't be with us and bring healing to those we've . . . to those who aren't here . . ."

I opened my eyes. Johnny's were open too but he kept his head bowed. Bart's closed eyes were aimed straight at me, moving left to right under the lids as he read the words off some internal screen that had begun to flicker. As Bart's struggles became greater, Johnny moved his hand out of Bart's grip and slid it further up his father's arm to the shoulder. I saw him squeeze it twice before saying, "That's good, Dad." Bart stopped talking and opened his eyes. We looked at each other.

"Amen," he said.

He started in on his mashed potatoes again. Johnny picked the skin off his chicken and ate it. I took up a biscuit and for a minute or two neither of us said a word.

"Bart, did you say your other son lives in Wentz Hollow?"

"Nathan does all right for himself."

"That's not what Doc asked, Dad. Yeah, he lives in town. You know the old mansion, Wentz Manor, or whatever it's called? It's a funeral home now. That's where Nathan is, hanging out with the dead."

"He lives in the funeral home?"

Johnny laughed. "Gives him cover."

"We should have called him," Bart said. "Did you try to call him?"

"I left a message," Johnny said, but the way he muttered it gave me doubts.

"Well, I hope I get a chance to meet him sometime."

"Stick around Wentz Hollow long enough to die, and you definitely will," Johnny said.

I laughed. "Maybe before I'm only capable of giving him the silent treatment."

"It'll still be a good time, Doc. Especially for you."

"What's *that* supposed to mean?"

"Nothing. Just having fun."

"Nathan's done good for himself. Both of my boys have done all right. They're good people."

"One of us is," Johnny said.

I grinned. "Don't worry, man. There's still time to change your ways. Maybe a self-improvement book?"

Johnny waited until Bart was looking at the mashed potatoes, and then smirked and flipped me off. A few minutes later, he scooted his chair back, stood up and took his plate over to the trash can. Then he took another beer from the refrigerator. "You two keep jawing. I'll be out on the porch. Come out and join me when you want, Doc."

After Johnny left, Bart showed his toothless, oval smile.

"John's sure taken a shine to you, Tim."

"He has?"

"You'd be a good friend for him. The boys he used to run around with weren't nice like you. Don't think any of them amounted to much, but Johnny did OK for himself taking a trade. Wiring a house is better than being in the mines, but I reckon it's lonely work. I never felt alone in the mines."

Bart raised his face and gazed at the kitchen light. Silent now, with his soft voice still echoing in my mind, it felt like a stone oracle had come alive, spoken, and became inanimate again.

"I'd like to hear more about the mines. Some of my other patients were miners too."

"I never got past 10th grade, but I did OK for myself. There was a time when you could get by. I took my boys into the mine when they were children."

I smiled. "I remember you telling me."

"I did?"

"Yes, sir."

"I took them down there to show them how hard it was. I did good but I wanted the boys to have more. So did Peggy, God bless her. She wasn't always right, but she always had her way."

He turned his head like he was going to spit, and then looked up at the kitchen light again. His eyes were watery, and the light entered between his parted lips and revealed his small, pink tongue.

I assumed his wife must be dead. I sat there wanting to become a dentist of memory, drilling down into fading recollections, discovering and filling the abscesses.

I listened to him for another half an hour as the food went cold and the beer became warm. Then Johnny called into the house.

"Hey, Doc! You still letting Dad talk your ear off?"

Bart touched my forearm. "You better get going, Tim. John's better company."

"I don't know about that. I'm really enjoying talking to you. Why don't you join us?"

"I never drank much. Having alcohol with my boys doesn't seem right. I'll probably go to bed now."

We got up together. I was faster and helped get him to his feet. Bart almost leaned into me for a second and patted the top of my hand before weaning himself away. He went through a side door into a dark room, navigating without turning on any lights. Then he was gone. I looked at the cracked linoleum a moment, then walked into the living room, which I'd breezed through the first time. Now I had a chance to really see it. The furniture was old and simple, worn, and the air had the slightest scent of mildew. There was no coffee table, but a cherry wood credenza stood against the wall to my far left. It hosted a number of framed photographs. It'd honestly been a while since I'd seen one. Even my grandparents preferred digitization and held up their smart phones when they wanted to show off their grandkids. The photos I saw now belonged to many different generations. Some must have been taken between 1930 and 1950. I bent to one yellowed picture and saw Bart's smiling face. The mouthful of teeth I'd imagined were captured well here, and I grinned. It looked like a high school picture, though Bart said he only had a 10th grade education. If the kid in the photo had been in high school with me, Connor Monroe would have had competition.

I didn't spend as much time looking as I wanted. I saw photos of what must have been Bart and his wife. There was a picture of Johnny, a high school graduation snapshot. Johnny stood there accepting his diploma, looking at it as if he doubted its reality.

But no photos of anyone I'd presume to be Nathan. No whiff of his existence.

"Hey, Doc! C'mon out!"

I turned and tried to wedge my hands into my pockets. This just reminded me of how tight the jeans were through the thighs.

One more beer only, I thought. *Then, tomorrow, circuit training.*

I came out to the porch, lit by a single bulb. Johnny was in one of two old lawn chairs, situated side by side, separated by an open cooler filled with ice and beer. He'd changed clothes since I'd last seen him, replacing the jeans with cotton jogging shorts. His muscled legs had dark hair on them, and he'd taken off his shoes and socks. His feet were propped up on the porch railing and his hands were locked behind his head. There was no pose that could have excited me more.

"Nice night, huh?"

"Yeah," I said, taking my seat. I grabbed a beer from the cooler. Calories be damned. If Johnny was going to give me a view like this, I'd spend the next few hours nursing a six pack.

For the sake of not being a total letch, however, I did bother to take a look out at the surrounding darkness and the night sky. Seattle had too much light pollution to make backyard astronomy practical, but the stars above Wentz Hollow belonged to bright constellations. Children around here wanting to wish upon a star had about a million to choose from.

"Heard you laugh during grace," he said.

"What? I'm sure I didn't."

"It's a dumb thing to do anyway. Thanking God for fried chicken."

I laughed at that and nodded.

"KFC," Johnny continued. "More like JFC."

"Huh?"

"Jesus Fucking Christ."

"Oh," I said.

"He's imitating the way Pastor Dan prayed. Same words. Except Pastor Dan used to throw in all this perverted sounding stuff. 'Lord, please look after Johnny as he gets over chicken pox. Touch his body, Lord, and heal him.' It took everything I had not to crack up every time I heard him asking Jesus to go around feeling people up."

"That *is* pretty weird."

He threw his bottle and it disappeared into the dark. "Jerk me off, Jesus. I need a handjob so bad."

"You do, huh?"

As a dedicated queer, I suppose it's impossible for me to keep an edge of innuendo out of my voice when talking to a hot guy. I heard it in my tone. Johnny smirked again and reached over for another bottle.

"You like what you see, Doc?"

"I won't lie."

"It amuses me when guys like you stare. But don't let it go past looking, Doc, or you'll lose a few teeth. Not much of a threat when it comes to a dentist, though. Guess you'd just put them all right back in your mouth."

"Do you hit gay guys a lot?"

"Hit on me, you get hit. Leave me alone, you get left alone."

"But you like being . . . appreciated?"

He laughed and drank. "Appreciate away, Doc."

We didn't talk for a couple of minutes. The noise of the crickets became deafening.

"What about your brother? From the way you talk, I take it he's also—"

"Yeah, he's a faggot."

"*Dude.*"

"OK, he's a faggot dude."

"He's your brother."

Johnny laughed. "It's not like you know him. Why do you care?"

"Do you use the N-word? I'm not black, but that's not right either."

"I look racist?"

"Looks have nothing to do—"

"But you think I am, right?"

"I don't know you."

He sat his bottle down on the space to his left. I couldn't read his expression at all. His eyelids were half shut, like he might be passing out. A few minutes passed, the longest stretch of silence we'd endured. What if I'd pissed him off? What if he was deciding whether or not to beat the shit out of me? It was getting late anyway, and I'd stayed a lot longer than I intended.

"I better get going," I said, standing up.

"Got your phone on you, Doc?"

"Yeah. Always."

"Take it out."

"Why?"

"I'm gonna give you Nathan's number."

"Huh?"

"He'll like knowing there's another queer around. Maybe he'll even stop fucking the dead."

"Look, Johnny, that's enough." My voice had a quaver I couldn't make go away. "I don't know what's going on with you and your brother, but you don't have the right to talk to me like that. Don't call me a queer."

"I better watch myself. Don't want to piss off the only dentist in town. I bet you have all kinds of ways of getting revenge if I ever had to take a seat in your chair."

"I assure you I'd never do that."

He said the words back to me in a mocking falsetto, and

then hit my shoulder. It was going to leave a bruise, but I could tell he'd held back most of his force. This was him being *playful*.

"Jesus, Doc, *relax*. It's cool. Just trying to be friendly."

"By calling me a queer?"

"A duck's a duck," he said. "But if you're a duck that doesn't want to be called a duck, I'll call you a moose. I'll call you whatever you like, Doc. But give my brother a call. Birds of a feather and all that."

I should have taken Nathan's number, but anger got the best of me. "No thanks," I said, and left the porch. Johnny didn't call out. I figured I'd have to endure hearing his laughter all the way to my car, but he didn't laugh either. I just had to put up with his silence. I kept hearing it even inside the car, even after I started the engine and drove off.

Even when I got home and started crying.

MRS. LAWRENCE

ABOUT FIVE YEARS AGO, at the start of my retirement, I considered writing down everything that happened. A memoir of sorts. But to what end? I couldn't answer that question so I forsook the project until eight months ago, on the day Meghan Malone came begging for help. That night, after I finished researching and could remember how to prepare the ingredients for the drink she wanted me to make, I started thinking of all the students I'd helped or tried to help. Of course, I reminisced about Nathan Ashcraft, though I question whether I've ever gone a month without my thoughts steering toward him. Given enough decades, any teacher will forget the names and faces of the pupils who cycle through their classrooms, even those they especially enjoyed or hated. But no teacher forgets a student she destroyed.

He may be the last in a succession of about twenty presidents of the Sarah Lawrence Hate Society, local chapter established in Wentz Hollow in 1982, though it often feels like a state-wide organization. Principal Thompson was the first president with Coach Skinner as vice president, treasurer, and secretary. Only in a place like Wentz Hollow could such fat, ridiculous men be considered *powerful enemies.*

I had others, just as I had other students besides Nathan and Meghan. Many went on to acquit themselves well. They graduated and moved away from Kentucky—obvious proof of common sense. Even those who never left Wentz Hollow took honest jobs, married, and no doubt tried to be good husbands and wives, and then good parents once nature took its course. After thirty years, I saw many such examples of nature, children and even one grandchild of former students—fresh rings in the cambium of the family tree, that place where dendrochronology and genealogy fuse.

Not all of my students came to good ends, of course. No one who teaches for any length of time can avoid this reality, even in rural Kentucky. One need not be in Chicago's worst high school to have students kill or die, rape or be raped, go to jail—or escape from one. No point in naming names. I did my best to educate them, to stand up for them when they needed it, and to urge them to think for themselves.

Sometimes, maybe, my urging became a push.

I must have met Nathan Ashcraft in 1987. I believe that was the year I was asked to judge the science fair projects of the Wentz Hollow junior high students. (I suppose all of the University of Kentucky's professors were preoccupied). The twenty entries I reviewed included many of the usual suspects: the potato battery, the baking soda and vinegar volcano, the conductivity of pennies, Paw-Paw's last tooth dissolving in a glass of Coke. Then I came across a bright but nervous-looking boy standing behind a table that had a dead frog hooked to a battery. The poster next to his project bore the rather impressive title, *An Inquiry into Electrical Current and a Frog's Nervous System.* The pretentiousness alone almost earned him the first-

CONFESSIONS

place ribbon, coupled with my natural affinity for dead frogs. When he applied wires to the battery, the amphibian's legs twitched, sparking either interest or disgust from everyone passing by. I made sure to visit him last, and I spoke to him about his frog galvanoscope. He nodded like he knew what I meant, and then frowned and confessed his ignorance.

He never knew it, but I awarded him first place for that act of honesty, for that moment of bravery. His accomplishment stayed in my memory a few years later, when he was a student in my 10th grade biology class. He was not a star student in any sense. Decent with anatomy, but his eyes glazed over when the subject turned to proteins and nucleic acids. These deficiencies were not important to me. After all, I didn't expect Wentz Hollow High to be producing any Nobel Prize winners. But the courage and honesty he'd shown--*those* mattered. Those were not teachable traits.

Call my enthusiasm for Nathan a personal bias then; an appreciation of commonality. I was about as different as they came in Wentz Hollow: a fiercely liberal biology teacher, a free-thinker, an activist. A rabble rouser, some said. Complaints to the school board about the egregious size of the athletics budget do not earn you many allies in towns like Wentz Hollow. Nor do signed letters to the editor arguing for the election of Walter Mondale and Michael Dukakis, though Kentucky did finally come around and vote for Bill Clinton. Expressing my opinion even made coworkers uncomfortable, resulting in remarks like, "I don't see how this is a biology teacher's business" or "Why don't you teach political science if it means that much to you?"

My husband Frank used to joke that my favorite form of conversation is an argument, and my favorite conversations centered around religion and politics. Science too, of course, but science ends up intersecting with religion and politics in a hundred ways. Local affairs and social issues should be everyone's concern regardless of career. In biology, changes and transformations occur regardless of desire. A caterpillar cannot refuse the butterfly. As a biology teacher in Wentz Hollow, however, I saw nothing but cocoons kept in check by powerful political and cultural forces. It could be a world of butterflies with just a little courage, a little honesty.

That's all I wanted for Nathan Ashcraft.

I had no suspicions about him at all, nor would I have expected him to seek me out as a confidant on such matters. Perhaps if I gave the school's official "health talk" things might be different, but in Kentucky there seems to be a long-standing tradition that only the football coach can teach boys and girls about sex. So, Skinner had the students huddling up and taking a knee to watch him yank a condom over a cucumber, which must have been traumatizing for the boys since at their age none of them sported more than dill pickles at best. Those poor humiliated boys and those poor disappointed girls, both genders facing unrealistic size expectations because of a piece of fruit. I suppose just getting to mention contraception in a public school in this part of the country counted as a minor miracle. Nevertheless, over the years I often presented my case for a more thorough curriculum, taught by me *sans* cucumbers and *sans* sports metaphors. Sometimes you knew when Coach Skinner had given his annual talk because you heard the newest crop of boys snickering in the hallway and asking each other if they'd gotten into some girl's *end zone*. Nor was it unusual, on any random morning following Skinner's presentation, to see a boy come in, make eye contact with a friend, smirk, and raise his arms in imitation of the touchdown signal.

Nathan Ashcraft was never so odious.

I remember the Friday he sought me out. Sixth period was my free hour, and I stood at the industrial sink rinsing out lab glassware from the previous class's inept experiments.

Fifth period happened right after lunch, and in my experience student IQs always dropped about ten points to assist digestion. So I was at the sink, feeling tired, staring at the water going down the drain when I heard—

"Mrs. Lawrence?"

His voice, so soft and tentative, almost didn't register over the sound of the faucet. I looked over my shoulder and saw Nathan standing there, hands in his pockets, shoulders shrugged. He wore an oversized T-shirt that might have reached below his thighs if the fabric wasn't bunched around his wrists. I smiled, turned off the hot water, and removed my face guard. He came toward me, a junior not too different from the sophomore I'd had in class. Other than seeing him a few times in the hallway and exchanging hellos, we'd not spoken in months.

"What's all this?" he said, looking into the basin.

"Failed alchemy," I answered, and he smiled. I held up a dripping glass. "Do you know what the difference is between this and the students in fifth period?"

He shook his head, his eyes wide and earnest.

"This is a graduated cylinder. I doubt the fifth period students will be graduating at all."

Nathan laughed. His laugh had a much higher pitch than his voice, and a quality similar to several rapid-fire hiccups.

I removed my latex gloves and discarded them.

"I don't mean to interrupt you."

"I was just finishing up," I said. Rather than traditional seating, my classroom consisted of ten long tables, each with four stools. I pulled up two stools and sat down. "Can I help you with anything?"

"I was just walking by. The library got so boring."

Some adolescents are good liars by the age of 13, while others never quite acquire the selling nuances of body language and tone. Nathan lied like someone begging not to be believed. I knew my role was to play along until he'd convinced himself whatever dark truth he wanted to share had in fact been dredged out of him.

I mentioned having no suspicions about him, and that's in part because he kept his head down most of the time. When you're surveying faces from the front of a classroom, standing above the fray as it were, you notice all the stolen glances students give each other. The subtle turn of the head, the fleeting gaze that follows the length of this girl's arm, that boy's leg. Longing bubbles out of kids at this age, especially when the desire can't be shown for one reason or another. These observations might seem amusing, but over time they become a teacher's secret heartbreak as you start putting two and two together. Why is it I always catch Jill looking askance at Alycia even though her head's aimed right at me? Does Rebecca realize James spends most of the hour staring at her hair? Then there's Mark, who must have a crick in his neck because every three minutes he keeps turning his head to the left and makes a half-circle sweeping motion. It's a casual thing, like a purposeful stretch. But it just so happens his eyes never quit staring at Scott's legs during the arc of his movement. Mark never sees how about thirty seconds later Scott makes a little sideward glance to his right, always finds Mark staring straight ahead at me, and the briefest flash of regret shows in his face. Such occurrences are like watching two gears running out of sync. You just want to stop the class and go make their cogs mesh.

When I was a much younger teacher, in my mid-20s and still a relative stranger to Wentz Hollow, I assumed my colleagues shared this wish. How naïve. Jackie Welch, part of the English faculty, acted like I was some sort of pervert when I brought up my observations during a staff luncheon. *Sarah, what in God's name are you saying? Why are you even noticing things like this? You're supposed to be teaching, not people watching! Kids figure it out on their own. They don't need us acting like some*

CONFESSIONS

sort of matchmaker. She then claimed no teacher could be effective if their minds were busy imagining the love lives of their students, and I was lucky she didn't report me to Principal Thompson. I said it was just an observation, not an obsession. It was as if I'd made some horrible confession without even realizing the sin.

In the six or seven years between that conversation and the day Nathan approached me, I'd had several intimations of the dissatisfactions to come. I was beginning to think transubstantiation existed after all. Priests turn water into wine, high school biology teachers turn their careers into nooses. You try to make a difference and end up feeling like you've spent every day dropping lit matches into a wet paper bag.

But in the fall of 1990, the start of Nathan's junior year, I was immersed in the passion for change. It had been a summer of despair for me as George H. W. Bush built up his army in the Middle East sandbox and called it *Desert Shield*. Everyone else acted so damn giddy. Wentz Hollow had no Muslim population, thankfully, or who knows what might have happened. Racism is always bred from ignorance and fear, but small-town racism has a peculiar repugnance, a special stupidity. I watched it ratchet up in 1990 and I saw it again after September 11, 2001. Then there was what I call the Illegal Immigrant Panic of 2006, when someone vandalized the nearest Mitsubishi dealership, blackening out or removing the T from every vehicle, turning the name into *Mi Subishi*. Rumor had it a marauding gang of Hispanics were marking their territory and declaring their intent to take over the state. Mi Subishi, Mi Kentucky, I guess.

But 1990 was a special sort of insidiousness, the country's building military orgasm after eight years of Reagan's jingoistic foreplay. When school began that fall, I expected a fresh seriousness among the faculty and students. What we got was an obnoxious pep rally to kick off the football season and that damn Coach Skinner standing in the middle of the gym floor, a megaphone in his right hand, his left fist pumping as he shouted, *"We're going to WAR! We're going to WAR!"* The students hollered and stomped their feet on the bleachers like some redneck Nuremberg Rally and I stood off to the side, trembling as I watched the cheerleaders wave their pom-poms and dance around Skinner like he was some kind of maypole.

I wrote a very long editorial that night and hand-delivered it to Geraldine Huntsman's front door. Geraldine was editor, publisher, and almost sole writer of the *Wentz Hollow Herald*. We never liked each other, even back then, but our town's little Charlotte Foster Kane knew the value of *shit-stirring* when she saw it. Not that my aspirations were so base. I only wanted to reiterate the seriousness of the world's geo-political situation and how inappropriate it was for our benighted—I used that word—Coach Skinner to compare football and armed conflict, especially since sex education already occupied that coveted role.

No bomb in the entirety of the Gulf War made an explosion like that editorial. Neighbors refused to talk to me. I received the cold shoulder and ate by myself in the staff room. My car was egged more than once, and the *Herald* received more retaliatory letters to the editor in one month than it had in the past decade. Coach Skinner at least wasn't passive-aggressive. He was just aggressive, storming into the staff room and calling me a cunt and a bitch. I stood my ground, and no matter how frightened I may have looked, no matter how much my heart pounded, I'd never felt more alive or righteous. At around 5'10", Skinner had a few inches on me, but it was easy to see how he thought himself to be much taller. He hovered in front of me puffed out like a king cobra, not realizing he was trying to intimidate a mongoose.

I filed a complaint with the school board since the confrontation happened in front of several witnesses. The bitterest blow came when those witnesses melted away during the investigation. I'd always accepted being unpopular among the staff, the subject of eyerolls. But realizing the other teachers—all women—would side with a Neanderthal who used words like *cunt, bitch,* and one or two instances of *dyke,* showed me I couldn't count on anyone but Frank.

But even he became grim. He worked for a small accounting firm, and once people realized he was my husband, clients called to say they'd take their business elsewhere. For a while there seemed a chance he'd be fired. I must admit our marriage grew tense for a couple of weeks, and though it went against every fiber of my being, I decided to write a retraction letter. I announced the decision that morning at the breakfast table. That evening, Frank presented me with a gift-wrapped present. Opening it, I found my editorial, clipped from the paper, mounted on a matboard and centered in an 8.5"x11" frame. He'd handwritten a message on a sticky note and attached it to the upper right corner.

Don't ever stop being you.

I've seldom cried in my life. Tears aren't easy for me, and I didn't cry in that moment either. But I came quite close. He held me and I thought, *No, I won't change.* Thank you for reminding me to stay true to myself. As terrible as the ostracization and the threats had been, I told myself I should be grateful for the experience. It reminded me of what some of my students must face every day, the peer pressure to conform, the constant message of *Don't ever* start *being you.*

To say the memory was fresh when Nathan came to me that day would be an understatement. I wrote the letter in late September; it was now early November and Frank had given me the picture frame just two weeks earlier. Observing Nathan as he stared at the floor, I thought of how I must have looked when I was on the verge of surrender.

"So, the library was getting boring?"

He nodded. "A little bit."

"Well, it's good to take a walk now and then. My husband and I go on one every night if the weather's good."

"Oh."

"Do you have anyone you like walking with?"

"I guess not," he said.

"How about someone you'd *like* to walk with?"

It was such an innocuous question I barely counted it as a probe. But Nathan frowned and shook his head. Then the grief lines etched across his face so fast it was like a cracking mask. He began crying, and I hurried off my stool and went to shut the door. There were still forty minutes left before the next class bell.

I took a fresh beaker, never used, and filled it with cold water. "Here, Nathan, drink this."

He looked at the beaker and said, "Tell me it's something to change me."

"It's just water."

He sipped at it and wiped his eyes.

I risked putting a hand on his shoulder. "I doubt there's anything about you that needs changing. What do you want to make different?"

"I don't know. I better go."

"Let's talk some more, Nathan."

"*Please* just let me go!"

"Of course, you can go if you want to. But I hope you'll stay. You came here for a reason, right? You need to talk and you felt you could trust me."

"I don't know. I was just walking."

"*Nathan*."

"Goodbye, Mrs. Lawrence."

He thrust the beaker of water at me and headed for the door. I couldn't just let him go. He'd already shown so much courage, but he needed help.

"Nathan, I'll have to let the school counselor know about this."

He whirled back to me, trembling. "No, no, no, you can't. She'll call Mom and Dad."

"I'll make you a deal. Sit down. Talk to me, and anything you say will be our secret. I promise."

He stood there on the verge of hyperventilating.

"Come on," I said, patting the first stool. "I bet whatever you have to say won't be as bad once it's out and not screaming around the inside of your skull."

Nathan sat down with his hands tucked under his thighs. His legs dangled and swayed, and he kept his attention on the floor. A few flakes of dandruff showed in his thick brown hair. His hunched posture accentuated the length of his T-shirt. He seemed swallowed by the fabric.

"Whatever it is, just say it. You have no idea how brave you're being."

He stared at his lap. "I don't feel brave."

"Maybe that's when we're strongest. You're a special student, Nathan. I knew it from the moment I first talked to you. Remember the science fair? Remember the blue ribbon?"

He smiled. "Yeah."

"You were pretty good then," I said. "But you're even better now. You're strong enough to say whatever it is that's bothering you."

He took a deep breath. His whole torso rose up like it was just tethered to his waist. Here was this teen boy, scrawny, speckled with dandruff and acne, and he seemed to be drawing himself up to his full height like some hero out of Greek mythology. Or so an English teacher like Jackie might say. Instead, I remember thinking I was witnessing a human version of deimatic behavior.

He let out his oxygen and mumbled the secret as he deflated.

"It's quite fine, Nathan," I said at once, not wanting even a few seconds to pass before giving my approbation. "It's estimated around ten percent of the population is homosexual. That would mean in any given classroom there are going to be at least two other students who feel the same as you."

He seemed to take no comfort in this statistic, assuming he even heard what I said.

"Please don't tell my parents. Please don't tell the counselor."

"No, of course not. It's *our* secret."

I told Frank while we were having dinner. I didn't give him Nathan's name, of course, but I had to share the other details. He listened, obviously riveted as I went over what happened. His younger brother Allen was a homosexual, but thankfully Frank hailed from an educated West Coast family, as refreshing as a sea breeze compared to the prejudice surrounding us.

"I wish I could figure out how to help him," I said.

"You listened to him. That's enough."

"It has to be better than that, Frank. It has to be *more*."

"What do you mean by more?"

I dabbed the corner of my mouth with a napkin. "Frank, this student is the first to come out to me, but he's not the first homosexual I've taught. He can't be."

"I'm sure."

"I'm not just guessing, either. I'm speaking in terms of statistics. Plus, sometimes, a teacher can just tell."

He grunted and ate.

"And every one of those students was suffering," I said. "Suffering, and I stood by and let it happen. Jesus Christ, the curriculum doesn't even let me mention the concept of homosexuality!"

"You don't teach health."

"I'm the school's *biology* teacher, Frank! Homosexuality is a biological fact, not a matter of health. It's been observed in animals going back a few thousand years, and I'm not supposed to utter a damn sentence about it?"

"What good would that do for a group of kids?"

I found myself glaring at him. He was seldom obtuse, and I had the sense he was trying my patience on purpose.

"When you feel like a total outcast, hearing something that reaffirms your normalcy is important."

"By hearing animals can be homosexual?"

"By hearing homosexuality is part of the natural order. I thought you'd be more supportive of this. What about Allen?"

Frank shook his head. "Sorry, I'm imagining Allen when he was 15, and I can't see getting any comfort from learning two male ducks might hatch an egg together. But knowing Allen, he was probably having sex with his biology teacher. I know he was seeing the football coach. He was pretty proud about it."

I had an unwelcome flash of imagination. Nathan and Skinner. I shuddered and got up, seizing my glass.

"What are you doing?"

"Turning water into wine the only way I know how," I said, and went to the kitchen. I poured the water down the drain and uncorked a half-empty bottle of shiraz. This conversation called for a full pour.

I saw Frank eyeing the glass when I sat down. His tone became more conciliatory.

"Maybe you could start sliding in a few references during your lectures. Kind of an in-passing sort of thing."

"Perhaps."

He smiled. "We can have fun guessing how long it'll be before the kids tell their parents and one of them makes a complaint to the board. I'm assuming you're doubling down on getting fired at this point?"

I said nothing to this, in part because my vision hadn't crystallized yet. But I had a rough idea of what needed to be done, and there was nothing *in-passing* about it. The situation required a boldness Frank couldn't accept, and if my greatest supporter wouldn't champion my agenda, I might falter before I even got started.

This town, this state, this country needed a slap in the face to wake it up, not shy prods and pokes. I woke early with this determination the next day and told Frank I'd be out and about until the late afternoon. Then I made the three-hour drive to Lexington and the Margaret I. King Library at the University of Kentucky. My intent was to spend the day scanning through periodic literature indexes and education journals, gathering any and all published statistics on homosexual students—rates of suicide, instances of bullying, drop-out figures. I spent $20 photocopying articles, and by the end of the day my right wrist felt like it needed a splint from all the note-taking. The stack of results padded three file folders, though I doubted either the quantity or quality would impress Principal Thompson or any school board member. But it would be there, heavy *proof* of the problem Nathan Ashcraft represented and bore on his narrow shoulders. As I sat down at the kitchen table Sunday morning to better organize the information, I couldn't tamp down my growing delight. When Frank shuffled in, heading for the coffee maker, he stopped and said, "Jesus Christ, Sarah. What are you grading?"

"They're not student papers," I said. "It's research. Solid, scientific research."

"Are you running your own experiments on the side? Do I need to be worried you've got a clone of me growing in the basement?"

"I'm perfecting the original model," I said, smiling. "The clone won't have a tongue."

He bent down to kiss my cheek and must have caught sight of the top article in my stack: *Lesbians and gay men on campus: visibility, empowerment, and educational leadership*. He jerked back, no longer looking like he needed any coffee.

"What the *hell* are you up to?"

"It's called marshaling evidence."

"Evidence for what?"

"There's a cancer in my school, Frank. It's called homophobia, and it's hurting everyone."

"But homophobia goes far beyond Wentz Hollow High."

"*Obviously.* When a body is covered in tumors, you have to start somewhere when you remove them. In this case, the body is our nation, and I think Wentz Hollow, Kentucky, is a fine place to begin. It just takes the right teacher and the right student to get the process going."

Frank paled. He turned around and began putting scoops of coffee into the filter.

"I've learned a valuable lesson from all the dustup over my newspaper editorial," I said to his back.

"Have you?"

I patted my stack of research. "The editorial was an emotional plea. It was based in *truth*. Now I'm working with numbers, and they're based in *fact*."

"Aren't truth and fact the same thing?"

"That's part of the lesson I've learned, Frank. Truth has an emotional quality to it. Facts don't."

"I think you'll find there's still plenty of emotion in the facts as well."

"I'm aware of that. The Board can call me crazy and, they can even fire me, but the numbers won't change. They're here in black and white.

The coffee maker began to percolate. Frank turned around to face me. "Just don't push too hard, OK? I don't want our neighbors throwing Molotov cocktails through the windows."

I laughed. "Better stock up on fire extinguishers."

"I mean it, Sarah."

"I mean it too, Frank."

With my big stack of articles gathered in the space of a day, Frank must have feared I'd be putting my plans into motion by the end of the week. But I really had learned something from the editorial blowback: look before you leap, think before you jump. This time I was going to go slow, be methodical, and consider all the possible angles and approaches.

When I returned to school on Monday, I experienced an almost conspiratorial feeling as I walked the halls, taught class, and ate alone in the staff room. No one understood or realized I was building a bomb, and its explosion was going to change the school, the town, the state, the country. It was time to blow up old prejudices, sweep away their rubble, and build something much better.

But only when the time was right.

I spent that day counting the minutes to the sixth period. When it came, I left the classroom door open and sat at my desk and clutched my hands like someone praying for deliverance. Five minutes passed, then ten. I'd not seen Nathan in the hallways. Maybe he was out sick. Fifteen minutes. Why did he have to approach me on a Friday? He had the whole weekend to backslide, to regret, to . . . take rash action? Twenty-two minutes. No, if he'd harmed himself, the whole school would already know. There's no privacy in a town like Wentz Hollow. Twenty-five minutes. Twenty-six. Maybe he's in the library. Maybe I should take a little trip to the library just to make sure he's all right. Thirty minutes. Half an hour of our precious time together ruined. Why, oh why didn't he—

"Mrs. Lawrence?"

I pivoted toward him and raised my eyebrows. "Nathan! Tired of the library again?"

He shrugged. "A little."

"Well, it's nice of you to stop by. I was just thinking about our talk on Friday."

He looked at the floor.

"Are you feeling well?"

"I don't know."

"I'm always here for you if you want to chat some more. Actually, you'd be doing me a big favor. I have so many questions."

This made Nathan raise his head. He seemed shocked.

"About me?"

"Sure, about you. About all the students just like you too."

"I don't think there are any," he said with a nervous laugh.

"Well, as I said, if the ten percent theory is correct, there must be around fifty. Assuming a 50-50 split, that means twenty-five boys, right?"

His eyes widened, which made me smile. I could see his horizons broadening, his hope expanding.

"They're all like you except in one way," I said. "You had the courage to come forward. You sought someone out."

"I cried."

"That's natural."

"I was in the library, by myself in a study carrel. And I—"

Nathan squeezed his eyes shut. His face had become bright red, and I forced myself to stay quiet and wait for him.

"I just felt so alone. I could see Steve sitting at the table, and he was holding Danielle's hand. They were leaning across the table and staring into each other's eyes and I—I wished I was her."

He wiped his eyes.

"I just feel so guilty," he continued. "I think about some of my friends all the time."

"Of course you do."

"I mean I think about them at . . . night."

I nodded. "Like I said, of course you do."

"You don't think it's wrong?"

"I think it's the most natural thing in the world. Everyone does it. The mind fantasizes. It dreams. Dreaming is the most important thing. It shows us things as they could be. It could be a dream as large as world peace or a dream of you and Steve leaning across the table toward each other in the library."

He must have caught himself smiling and put a hand over his mouth. The bright happiness in his eyes still showed forth. I wanted to ask him which Steve he meant, since there were several possibilities. But he must mean Steven Malone, who was a senior. Tall, athletic, broad of shoulders and smile. The typical confident and cocky jock possessed of natural charisma, destined to become a salesman or a politician who'll get married, get fat, and have a ton of extramarital affairs. But for the moment, he was the all-American boy.

Oh, Nathan, I thought. *You can do so much better.*

"Can I ask you something?" I said.

"Sure."

"You mentioned feeling guilty. If you were thinking about girls who were your friends, would you feel the same way?"

"Uh, no," he said, as if I'd asked the dumbest question imaginable.

"Why?"

"Because . . . because they'd expect it."

"Why would they expect it?"

His answer got lost in fluster. He made a few attempts to formulate a response, and then blurted out, "Because it's not lying."

"Yes, Nathan," I said. "Honesty above all. That's what you're about. That's what you value."

As, of course, did I. What a team we'd make.

"I want to tell the truth to my mom and dad, but I know how they'll be."

"Then don't. Not now. Not yet. Wait until the time is right. The important thing is to know you're not alone. There are other students in this school who feel the same way you do. The key is to get you all together somehow. You could meet in a room—this room, even—and feel safe to talk about your feelings."

Nathan's eyes shifted down and to the left as my idea soaked in.

He shrugged.

I didn't push any more that day, or the next several times he came to me over the rest of the semester. The seed had been planted; now it was time to water and see what germinated. In the last two weeks before winter break, Nathan stopped by my classroom every day. Sometimes he'd help me wash beakers and we'd stand at the sink talking about life. He told me about his much younger brother, who drove him crazy. He told me his father worked the night shift in a coal mine and how his mother watched *The 700 Club* on a little black-and-white mini-TV perched on the kitchen counter.

"It must be interesting having a little brother that much younger than you. I bet he idolizes you."

Nathan smiled. "He's a pest. As soon as I get home, he starts climbing all over me."

"He misses his big brother."

"Don't get me wrong, Mrs. Lawrence. I love him and all."

I laughed. "Of course you do. You want things to be great for him. You want to keep him safe. That's what big brothers do."

"Johnny's always laughing and—I like that. I want him to be happy. I want to stand up for him."

"You already are, in ways you probably can't even guess. Just be you."

He nodded.

We had other conversations that were far less serious and possibly pushed the boundaries of propriety. But it never became unethical. Nathan's guard dropped the more he trusted me. Under other circumstances, a thirty-something school teacher wouldn't be his confidant on any subject, and certainly not about romantic crushes. Were Nathan effeminate in a stereotypical way, he might have gravitated to some group of outcast girls who accepted him as one of their own. But he was not fey in voice or mannerism. Lacking any other option, I became his private outlet.

"Did you see Steve today?" he said during our sixth or seventh get-together.

"I don't believe so."

"He's got a new haircut. I really like it. He looks good with it buzzed. But it wouldn't matter even if he wore it shoulder-length, or if he was bald. I mean, I wouldn't care."

"*That's* true love."

Nathan spun in a full circle atop the stool. "He's perfect!"

"Perfect, eh?"

"It's the truth. I wish he would notice me."

"You've never talked?"

"We sit beside each other in Trig, but I'm not the sort of guy he talks to."

"Nathan, don't idolize anyone who acts like they're too good to even notice you. And never, ever believe you're inferior to anyone else. Because you're not."

I wished I hadn't ended the meeting sounding like I was criticizing him, but I feared that's how he took it. He didn't come the rest of the week. Then, the next Monday, he all but raced into the classroom right after the sixth-period bell sounded.

"Mrs. Lawrence," he said, red in the face and almost breathless. "You won't believe it."

At first, I thought something terrible had happened, but then I saw him grinning. I took a stool and pulled another one close. He had too much energy to sit down.

"It's Steve," he said. "In Trig this morning."

"What happened?"

"He wrote me a note. Look, I've got it right here."

CONFESSIONS

Nathan took a piece of paper from his pocket. It had been folded eight times, and he sat smoothing it out with all the care of a napkin-folder who has studied every sentence by Emily Post.

"He's really cool," Nathan said. "And funny. Look at what he wrote."

He handed the note to me. Before I could even read it, Nathan repeated the words. "'Are you as lost as I am?' Isn't that awesome?"

"So funny," he continued before I could respond. He began pacing back and forth, skipping a little. I studied the note some more, remembering how our last meeting ended. Could he have written the note himself? Was this a way of saving face? I had no knowledge of either boy's handwriting. But as I looked at Nathan, my doubts vanished. Happiness can be faked, but I saw elation here. He'd become as bubbly as a Lawrence Welk show. I remembered the first note a boy ever passed me in class, sometime around 4th grade, and how receiving it temporarily rearranged my world.

Are you as lost as I am?

Yes, I thought, *what if you are?*

"Did you write him back?"

"I was too scared, but I mouthed *Totally.*"

"What did he do?"

"He smiled and nodded. Isn't that great?"

"To quote my favorite student—*Totally*. Did you talk after class?"

"Huh? No. He just got up and left. But I mean he could have written this note to anyone. He chose me."

"Probably because you're funny and a good person."

"It'd be crazy if he thought of me as a friend," Nathan said, finally taking his seat on the stool. "Everyone he hangs out with is on the baseball team. I think he plays golf too."

"I didn't realize we had a golf team."

"What? Oh, I don't know. But he wrote me this note. He was making a joke and he included me."

He took the note and held it in his lap. I wondered if this was the hundredth or the thousandth time his eyes had traced each letter. As I stared at him, contemplating how glad I felt that he'd shared his happiness with me, I thought to myself, *This is it*. This is what I envision. This is the happiness of acceptance I want students like Nathan to feel, so they all can experience transformation through joy.

Now, if only Steven Malone could in fact be homosexual as well.

"So, what's the next step?"

"Next step?"

"I recommend getting a hamburger together."

"I can't do that!"

"Why not?"

"Because he wouldn't want to go."

"Why do you think that?"

"I just know," he said.

"You just know that he doesn't like hamburgers? Nathan, look at how happy you are right now. Don't you like how light it makes you feel? How hopeful?"

"Yeah."

"Well," I said, "there's more of that in store for you if you're willing to take risks and fight for what you believe."

Nathan got very silent. His happiness evaporated and I realized I'd pushed too hard.

"It's just a note," he said, not making eye contact.

"You're right. Hopefully there will be a lot more. The two of you could be great friends. Maybe best friends."

The bell for seventh period was about to sound and he got off the stool and began folding the note, taking the same exaggerated, adorable care he'd shown before.

"Thanks for listening, Mrs. Lawrence. Thanks for . . .

understanding."

"You're welcome, Nathan."

After he left, I let out a breath I seemed to have held for the last thirty minutes. Maybe there was such a thing as fate and Nathan's was beginning to sample the joy that had always been in store for him. But action is the surer thing. I'd rather sow seeds than trust in a garden to spring up of its own accord.

I left school that day thinking that when I saw Nathan tomorrow, I would begin the careful cultivation that this town, this state, this country, and this world needed so very much.

NATHAN

WHEN I GOT BACK to the funeral home, I decided to take a shower before returning to work on Mr. Crenshaw, since the dead should never smell cleaner than the living, at least until they get embalmed. Before I undressed, I caught my reflection in the bathroom mirror. Enough quick dismissals and cold rejections at gay bars after reaching my 40th birthday had broken most of my vanity, but enough remained to make me frown at the notion I'd looked this bad when I entered Tim's office. My face was red like I'd been on a beach for hours and my thinning, sweat-soaked hair resembled a dying, overwatered lawn. It was a good thing I didn't have access to a mirror when we were talking. It might have robbed me of the confidence to—

My God, I thought. *Do I actually have a date tonight?*

Coming to terms with the reality of a date when they're uncommon in your life isn't entirely unlike a happier version of the seven stages of grief. For me, anyway, it always begins with shock and denial and ends on acceptance and hope.

It's just a drink or two, I told myself. Expect nothing more, and you won't be disappointed.

But the eternal boy in me wanted to turn the clock hours ahead to preview a great night. I walked into the living room, where I had my sofa and television. There was a single dirty plate on the coffee table, and I scooped it up and hurried it to the dishwasher. Otherwise, the room seemed clean enough for hosting, though who knew what a dentist's standards might be. I moved to the bedroom. The bed was made. I didn't remember making it this morning and it took me a moment to remember I'd spent the night at Dad's. It's a strange thing when you quit calling the house where you grew up *home*, but I made that transition too long ago to feel complicated about it now.

How was Dad? Had Rebecca come over yet? Where was Johnny? I supposed if anything had been wrong, I would have received a call from someone by now.

I turned on the shower, undressed, and stepped in. As the water pelted my head, I pictured my hair liquifying, slipping out of their roots, sliding down my body to the drain. In many ways, that's the essence of hair loss, it just doesn't happen all at once and in such a grotesque manner. If you lose anything slowly enough you adjust to it as you go, sort of like a gradual anesthesia. Is it better to suffer an abrupt loss or the slow and steady decline? A question for the philosophers, I suppose. And like I said, no one should philosophize before noon.

It wasn't a philosophical turn that brought my thoughts and imagination back to Steve and Meghan's dead infant. I saw Meghan staging an accident to make the urn fall. Over and over it fell, and because I changed the order from ceramic to bronze, it would not shatter. Meghan would never be able to break it. She wouldn't be able to hurt Steve more than she already had.

The protective feeling surging through me just then

was stranger than imagining sudden and absolute baldness, stranger than not thinking of your childhood house as home, and stranger than the idea of a date. The idea of me protecting Steve or being able to offer protection seemed absurd. I thought of us in high school when he was invincible and towering. The notion of someone trying to bully him and the notion of me stepping in to guard him didn't square with any sense of reality. But a boy has the simplest understanding of bullying and torment, and an even simpler comprehension of how to fight back. God, the lessons we learn about all the ways to break and bruise!

I was putting on an old, comfortable pair of blue jeans and a faded red T-shirt, the clothes I usually wore when working with the dead. As I buttoned the jeans, however, my cellphone started ringing. It was the ringtone I'd programmed for the county hospital, alerting me I needed to answer it no matter what time it was or what I might be doing. Movie titles to the contrary, Death does not take a holiday.

When I heard that ringtone, I could assume my services were required because someone had died. This time, I answered it assuming I was getting a follow-up call regarding the cremation arrangements for the Malone's baby.

"This is Nathan Ashcraft."

The caller identified herself as a dispatcher from the county hospital and then said, "Mr. Ashcraft, I'm calling on behalf of the Lawrence family."

"The *who*?"

She repeated the name. I felt for a chair that wasn't there and managed to get to the sofa. The dispatcher seemed to be rushing through the details and I found myself making her repeat them as the confusion grew. One moment she was speaking too fast, in the next too slow.

"I'm sorry," I said, leaning forward, staring at the carpet. "What's the deceased's name again?"

"I show it as Sarah Lawrence."

"OK," I said. "That's what I thought."

"Her husband says funeral arrangements were pre-arranged with you."

Must have been back when Robbie was here, I thought. "I'm sure that's the case. I'll be there in half an hour."

I hung up and placed the phone on the coffee table and stared at it like a traitorous friend.

"Mrs. Lawrence," I said. "Goddamn."

Death may have gotten her, but I bet Death was now sitting at home pressing a bag of ice against a fresh black eye.

You don't know that it's *her*, I told myself. Even in Wentz Hollow there could be more than one Sarah Lawrence. I rose, pocketed the phone, and finished dressing as I forced myself to focus. I still needed to finish with Mr. Henshaw. His case had to be my priority until I had him ready for tomorrow's viewing. Even drinks with Tim must wait until that duty was fulfilled.

Mrs. Lawrence.

I changed into khaki pants and a dress shirt, slipped on brown penny loafers, and went downstairs. I locked the front door and grabbed the keys to the hearse from the top drawer of my office desk. I considered the old filing cabinet in the corner, detailing customers and cases going back decades. I had ambitions of digitizing all of those records one day. Mrs. Lawrence's file should be among them. Maybe a quick look could verify whether or not—

No.

First things first, I thought. *Get the client, return with the client, store the client, then attend to Mr. Henshaw. Don't even open the body bag.*

I went around back. The garage was a converted carriage house large enough to hold three hearses. I had only one, likewise purchased from Robbie, with almost 100,000 miles on it.

CONFESSIONS

I remembered the odometer every time I listened to the ignition turn over a few times before catching. There was also a persistent rattle, maybe something loose in the exhaust system. And the faintest squeal of brakes.

I backed out of the garage.

A hum kicked in after a few minutes on the road, probably indicative of a failing transmission. Or maybe portending nothing more than worn-out ball bearings.

I turned the car around in the parking lot and headed toward the main road.

An oil change, a tune-up. Check the spark plugs. Check the tires.

I turned onto the street. The tank was half-full. I drove and watched the odometer turn, number after number rolling over. The natural order of things, miles and hours counting up toward a reckoning. Addition that leads to ultimate subtraction: this is the math of life.

The fuel valve or whatever it's called. A bunch of gaskets. Like death, like life, all of it a mystery. Evil under the sun, evil under the hood. Why did I keep neglecting to make a maintenance appointment? Can't have the hearse stalling in the street as I'm leading a funeral procession. That would be bad. Quite unprofessional. Everything you cannot stand.

The hearse moved like a lead coffin on wheels, sluggish and hard to control. Easy to cause an accident, except there's never much traffic in Wentz Hollow. That would be the ultimate irony, a hearse killing someone in a road accident. If the hearse remained drivable, you could just load up the fresh dead in the back and continue on your way. So much time saved. So much—

I screamed.

I had enough presence of mind to check my blind spots before moving into the next lane. Then, I activated the hazard signal and pulled onto the shoulder and parked. With both hands on the wheel, I sat gulping air and trying to get my pulse to slow. I stared at my eyes in the rearview mirror, thinking I would see the reflection of a 16-year-old, a boy who didn't know a damn thing about death, having not even lost a pet. But he knew despair, and despair is dipping your toe in death's river. The toe dip turns ankle- and then knee-deep just by the act of living. I have lived to wade up to my waist in the river of death. Is this all the 16-year-old has come to know?

When people learn I work with the deceased, they tend to ask me about ghosts. Sometimes as a joke, sometimes quite serious and earnest. I tell them I've never seen one and leave it at that. But we've all felt them. We have ghosts in our heads. Science calls them memories.

You must get yourself together right now, I told myself. Go to the hospital, sign the paperwork, take custody of the body just as you have a thousand other times. Bring it back and attend to Mr. Henshaw. The Henshaw case is your single concern. Simple enough, isn't it?

I leaned toward the windshield and craned my neck to look at the sky. Still a beautiful day in Wentz Hollow, but that's no inoculation against anything. People cry on beautiful days. People die on them too. Babies and the elderly alike. The beautiful day doesn't care that I'm heading to the hospital, perhaps to retrieve the body of a woman who either ruined my life or saved it, depending on which side of the bed of reflection I woke up on, on any given day.

Which side was it *this* beautiful day?

Laughter came from outside the hearse. In the rearview mirror, I saw four boys emerging from the trees to the left. They looked to be about 10 or 11 years old and all of them carried fishing nets and glass jars. I smiled. Since the town's founding, generations of children had spent at least one summer day trying to catch tadpoles or turtles out of Wentz Creek. The boys noticed the hearse and came to an absolute stop.

CONFESSIONS

They stood clustered together, staring in fascination. With the tinted windows, I'm not sure they realized anyone was inside.

When they gathered to peer into the back window, I became certain they thought they'd stumbled upon an abandoned vehicle. They crowded the glass like they were staring into a dark aquarium. Maybe their imaginations ran rampant with ghost stories and urban legends. A hearse can be an unsettling sight, especially when you find one parked in apparent isolation next to a wooded area.

They noticed me, and with that exceptional courage children have at a certain age, when they're old enough not to be scared and young enough not to let good manners blunt their sense of wonder, the four of them came to the passenger side and tapped on the window. I regarded them a moment, finding that delicate balancing act in all their expressions. Subtract a couple of years, and these boys would have turned tail and run as soon as they saw the hearse. Add a couple of years, and they'd have walked past me with cool disregard, maybe swearing and showing me a few middle fingers. They will have been in the woods not to catch tadpoles but to smoke. But right now, they were the age of open-hearted adventurers and this was a *hearse* they saw before them.

I rolled down the window. They almost spilled into the opening.

"Do you have a body in there?"

"No," I said.

For a moment, it felt like I'd just crushed all their dreams.

"We remember you," another boy said. "You came to our school last year."

A memory surfaced. I had answered an invitation to show up at the elementary school for their career fair. I'd seen it as a chance to normalize and demystify my profession and, in some ways, death itself. What happens after someone dies? Who gets called? Where does a body go? As I recall, I had completely won the hearts and minds of the children. One boy even lay down in the middle of the bay, crossed his hands over his heart and proclaimed himself Dracula.

Then the local fire department showed up. Even a hearse can't compete with a fire engine, and I joined the other neglected career representatives—including a baker, a banker, a tow truck operator, and a park ranger with the most wonderful collection of petrified animal scat—in the corner drinking coffee and eating donuts made by the baker just for the occasion.

"I remember now," I said.

"Did you run out of gas?"

"No, everything's fine. I just pulled over to check a text message."

I thought they'd leave, and when they didn't, I began to guess at what they wanted. "Do you all want to see inside the back again?"

You've never seen heads nod so fast.

I got out and the boys joined me at the back, jostling each other with their nets and empty jars. I opened the hatch for their inspection, almost wishing I had a coffin in there to make the scenery more interesting. Empty, the hearse looked like little more than an oddly decorated SUV except for the straps and metalwork that kept the coffin secured during transport. One boy gave a tentative touch of the white padded upholstery and pulled his hand back as if he didn't know what to expect.

"Were you all there when I came to the school?"

The boys nodded.

I pointed out a chrome piece. "Then who remembers what this is?"

They shook their heads.

"This is called the gooseneck," I said. "See, it keeps the coffin from sliding around. And this is the bar where the foot of the coffin lodges. See how it locks in place?"

They nodded.

I could have stood there explaining every part and piece. But there was only so much to point out, and after a few minutes even I could hear the desperation in my voice, the desire to keep them loitering. The boys began backing away, no doubt sensing the friendly neighborhood mortician had an ulterior motive.

"Thanks again, Mister. It's creepy. Come on, guys, let's go find Jason."

They ran off, and I laid back in the middle of the hearse for a moment and took a deep breath. I should have been over halfway to the hospital by now. Why was I trying to stall the inevitable? I closed the door and then glanced up and down the lonely road. There wasn't so much as the rustle of a squirrel in the woods. There'd be no more children stumbling upon me here, their inquisitiveness an opportunity to delay me further.

I had to get Mrs. Lawrence.

I drove to the hospital, which was not a large facility by any means. I knew most of the doctors and nurses, either from trips here in my official capacity or bringing Dad in for a checkup. A hospital of this size didn't have the sort of memory care unit he really needed, but the staff were good about making sure I always left with every possible pamphlet known to man about dementia and caregiving options.

I parked around back, as no hospital wants a hearse stationed out front. There was a designated space for me that served as the unloading zone for the ambulance and the loading zone for me. I walked around to the front and approached the admissions desk. The attendant recognized me.

"Hey," she said. "Good to see you."

"Better to be seen than viewed, as the saying goes."

I confess gallows humor like that might make us sound like calloused monsters, but the nature of our work required it. I nodded and she buzzed me through a staff door. The morgue was near the end of a long hallway. The county medical examiner, Martin Lowe, had an office across from it. I heard the clicking of his keyboard as I neared his open door and gave it a gentle tap.

Martin looked up from his computer. He was several years older than me, obese the way only trueborn Southerners seem to get, very round in the belly, corpulent but somehow not slovenly. It's part of the formal heritage around these parts, an almost genetic dignity that renders the stomach more wineskin than latex balloon, so that no matter how much it bloats there's always a sense of underlying firmness. His pudgy face had a relaxed expression. The only sense of strain or stress about the man rested in his suspenders.

"Nathan," he said, working his way up out of his chair. "Here for Mrs. Lawrence?"

I only knew Martin by the way our work lives intersected. We often used the same terminology, such as cases, so hearing him say *Mrs. Lawrence* made me think he might know her.

"I am."

He patted me on the shoulder and led me out of the office. We entered the small mortuary. There were just three cold chambers, and I doubted they'd ever been used all at the same time. The polite people in and around Wentz Hollow always died at a manageable pace. Still, I found myself looking at the three stainless steel doors, wondering which one contained Mrs. Lawrence, and which one might still be housing Steve and Meghan's baby.

Martin walked over to the middle door and gripped the handle. Before he pulled, however, he turned and said, "You're a local boy, aren't you?"

"Minus the few decades I spent elsewhere."

"But you graduated from Wentz High?"

"No," I said. "I didn't graduate from Wentz. I was already gone before then."

I could see he thought I must have moved away before high school, and I suppose that's just how I meant for him to take it. He gave the handle a slight tug and the cadaver tray came forward a few inches.

"Mrs. Lawrence was something of a local legend."

"Is that right?"

"A real shit-stirrer."

He pulled the tray out all the way. The body was already bagged and for a horrible second, I thought Martin was going to pull on the zipper for a game of show and tell.

"Is the paperwork ready?" I asked. "Sorry, it's just I've got a viewing tomorrow and I haven't finished with the body. Things are a bit busy, you know?"

"Sure," he said, nodding and moving past me. "I'll go get them. Busy day myself. Had a baby die here overnight."

I pivoted toward him. "I know."

"You handling that case too?"

"The Malones want the remains cremated. A third party will handle that. I'm only the go-between."

He left. I stared down at the cadaver bag, weighing the apparent length of the body against a teen boy's memories. So much of what I recalled about her belonged to my junior year, but just then I remembered the first time I met her, as the judge at my junior high science fair. Mrs. Lawrence was wearing a white lab coat, the same one she often wore in class, and I thought she must be very important, a professor or lab researcher. I watched her moving from booth to booth, talking to other kids and their parents. Mom was standing beside me and said, "I bet that's the judge. She looks really important." Then she told me to quit slouching. At last, Mrs. Lawrence and her white lab coat came to my table. Mom sort of receded into the background, maybe because she had no idea what my dead frog was all about and didn't want to appear stupid. I was face to face with this adult and her lab coat flashed with authority.

She seemed so tall to me. Many of the boys were already as tall as our female teachers years before we graduated, but I wasn't taller than her. Her brown hair was short and had a curliness like lamb fleece. I'd never seen a teacher who wore her hair like that, and with her height and in her lab coat, I began thinking maybe I was talking to a man. She carried herself like a man according to all the assumptions of my adolescent brain. All my teachers outside of gym class had been women up to that point, women with kind smiles. Mrs. Lawrence had a different kind of smile, thin and brief as a scalpel's slit. Smiles are like accents, and hers told me she wasn't from Kentucky even before her speech confirmed it.

I'm going to have to pull down that zipper, and that old smile is going to be waiting for me, I thought.

Martin returned with the papers and handed them to me in a file folder. I tucked it under my left arm.

"Can you tell me something?"

"Depends," Martin said.

"It's about the Malone baby. Are you doing some sort of investigation on its death?"

"We'd need a pediatric pathologist for that. Why?"

"I was just curious about the cause of death."

"Poor blood flow to the placenta. Pretty common thing, unfortunately."

"OK," I said.

"Are *you* OK?"

"Yes," I said. "It's just been a hectic day. And no one wants to think about a dead child."

"You sure as hell got that right," Martin said, clapping me on the shoulder. "Ever wonder if you got yourself into the wrong career?"

"No."

He smiled and summoned an orderly to help me transfer Mrs. Lawrence to the cadaver lift. Under normal circumstances, this would be the end of whatever conversation Martin and I might have. But he followed me all the way out to the loading zone.

"Have you ever done the funeral for someone you know?"

"Not yet," I said.

"About fifteen years ago, I get this phone call. Middle of the night, you know the type. The police give me an address and I jot it down. Then I drop the pen because, son of a bitch, I recognize it. Hell, I'd been there a week earlier. I'm thinking to myself, *this is Dave's address*, and the cop is saying there's a dead male at the scene. And I know Dave lives alone. No roommates, no kids. So it's got to be him. I'm thinking that all the way to the scene."

"Was it?"

"Sure was. Dave was a poker buddy. I've got a lot of friends I call poker buddies, or used to. You say a poker buddy died and . . . I don't know, it seems lesser, you know? Dave wasn't a poker buddy after I had to certify his death. Jesus Christ, I'd lost a friend."

Martin frowned and turned his eyes to the horizon. I gulped against the tightness in my throat and thanked him.

We never thank people enough, not poker buddies, not acquaintances, not strangers.

I got behind the wheel feeling even more philosophical than before. I took a moment to check the time on my phone.

God help me, it *still* wasn't noon.

TIM

I NEVER HAD WET DREAMS, even in high school, but I started having them in Wentz Hollow after I met Johnny. He was a lot nicer in these fantasies. Sometimes he came into my office complaining of a toothache. As soon as he got in the chair, though, he grabbed my right wrist and started singing *Long John Blues*. "Oh yeah," I'd say. "You've got a cavity that needs drilling, don't you, country boy?" I should have woken up disgusted with myself for wanting a homophobe, but at the same time it wasn't like he was a white supremacist with a swastika tattoo on his chest. He was just rough around the edges and maybe closeted. Part of me knew better, but there's a fantasy in gay men that makes them assume everyone is a self-denying queer who just needs coaxing. Still, I kept Johnny's warning very much in mind. *Coax* him at your peril.

The weeks went by, and my clothes got no looser. I'd stand before the mirror poking at my belly and then go to the living room to do jumping jacks. Exercise is pure hell for people who've never had to do it before. Where had my fast metabolism gone? It'd seen me through almost eight years of college only to take a hike the moment I set foot in this humid, deep-fried hell.

On the Monday morning I met Johnny's brother, I had reached 40 jumping jacks before my side ached too much and I had to bend over, gasping. *Baby steps*, I thought. Baby food too, if that's what it'll take to lose the fat.

I toweled off as a symbolic act and got dressed for the day. On Saturday I'd surrendered to the reality of my body's temporary girth and bought new button-ups, frowning over the size tag as I transitioned from medium to large. But I'd be back to medium in a month if I just buckled down on my diet. Again, my celibate life in Wentz Hollow wasn't helping. Since I no longer had much opportunity to meet guys and have sex, I'd developed a cheeseburger libido that was threatening to make me look pregnant.

I may have been dreaming about Johnny at night, but during the day I began thinking of Nathan quite a bit despite not knowing him. It seemed inevitable we'd get together sooner rather than later. Hell, we might be the only two eligible gay men within a fifty-mile radius of Wentz Hollow, so we were bound to get along even if we had little in common. Statistical reality and hard truths had to prevail at some point. I'd already decided I'd be attracted to him. After all, I knew how handsome Bart had been as a younger man, and Johnny was hot as hell. How far from the mean could Nathan be?

That particular Monday came just shy of a month after Bart and Johnny visited me for the first time. The bells on the door jangled while I was in my little business office, recording patient data from my last rural outreach visit on Friday. I had no scheduled appointments for that morning, so the bell surprised me a little. Then Bart just appeared in the doorway, hands on his thighs, his mouth open in a toothless smile. "Well, *there* he is," he said in that eager, earthy tone, and I got up to greet him. He shook my hand and we entered the hallway. I looked toward the reception area, hoping to see Johnny. The front door was wide open.

"Is Johnny coming in, Bart?"

He looked at me as if he didn't recognize the name. I patted his shoulder and went down the hallway to shut the door if nothing else. Just before I reached it, a man came up the steps and peered in. He was just a little taller than me and skinny like I used to be in college. He wore his graying brown hair parted to the left and swept back a bit, not a good look because it pushed back an already receding hairline. There were indentations in the skin along his temples, evidence of glasses. The right pair of glasses can do wonders for the face. Rounded frames would have worked best for him, something to smooth out the sharpness of his nose and chin. Overall, he was neither attractive nor ugly, just mundane in a small-town, church-and-football-on-Sundays sort of way. Encountering this face as a Grindr thumbnail wouldn't have enticed me to click on the profile.

I figured he was either a hired caregiver or some older cousin Johnny had roped into handling his father for the day.

Standing to my right, Bart said, "There he is. What happened, you get lost?"

"You have to stick closer to me, Dad."

I heard the word, felt confused, and gave the man a closer look.

"Are you Nathan?"

He gave an almost apologetic smile. "That's me."

I confess to feeling a bit disappointed with the confirmation. I still saw nothing of Bart or Johnny in his features. Maybe he'd been adopted.

"Well," I said, "I've heard a lot about you from Bart and Johnny."

"Johnny?"

"That's right."

Bart started talking about our night of KFC, and from the impatient way Nathan nodded, I knew he'd heard the story before. But maybe he hadn't heard all of it.

I put a hand on Bart's shoulder to get him to quit talking and said, "I'm glad you stopped back in. I've been wanting to follow-up with you on your teeth. We were talking about getting some X-rays, right?"

Bart's eyes seemed to cloud over for a moment, but they cleared just as fast.

"Me and my oldest were just getting some sunshine, and when I saw where we were I had to get him to pull over to meet the best dentist in town. Tim here fixed me up real good, took care of all my pain. And Johnny goes to him all the time."

Nathan's eyebrows raised. I gave the slightest shake of the head and he mouthed, "Ah."

"Step into my parlor," I said, holding out my hand. We shook. His palm had a pleasant, dry warmth.

"Nathan, Tim here has a diploma and everything," he said, moving down the hallway. "You should see it."

"Oh, I'm sure Nathan's seen a diploma before. It's just paper."

Bart ignored me and went down the hallway, leaving Nathan and me looking at each other.

"I'm really sorry about this. These days it's about impossible to stop Dad from doing something once he gets a notion."

I laughed. "It's fine. I like him. He's . . . cantankerous."

"That's one word for it."

The grim seriousness in his voice made me feel like an asshole, like I was trying to be lighthearted about his father's dementia.

"Hey," I began, "I didn't mean to—"

"Dad!"

I turned in the direction of Nathan's despairing stare. Bart

CONFESSIONS

had returned carrying my framed diploma with him, holding it out for his son to see. Honestly, I thought this was pretty funny, but Nathan acted like the old guy had walked into my kitchen and broken every plate I owned.

"My boys have done good in their life, and I'm proud of them, but they don't have a diploma."

"Johnny doesn't," Nathan said, easing the frame away from his dad's hands. "I definitely do."

"Nice," I said. "What do you do for work?"

"I'm a mortician."

Bart went back down the hallway and Nathan started to apologize.

"It's really fine," I said. "There's nothing to worry about unless he tries to bring my chair down the hallway. But I'm pretty sure it's bolted to the floor."

"I really appreciate your understanding. Dad can be tough to manage."

"Like I said, no worries."

"You really came over to dinner?"

"Had a great time too. Johnny and I drank some beers on the porch afterward."

Nathan looked amazed, but I couldn't help wondering if it was an act. I mean, the way Johnny had gone on about wanting me to call him, and with how blunt he could be, I figured the next time he saw his brother, he said something like, *"Hey, the town dentist is a fag too. You should blow each other. His name's Tim."*

But maybe he hadn't said a word.

Or maybe they hadn't even seen each other between then and now.

I reached for the diploma and took it. "Hey Bart, why don't we go hang this back on the wall. Then you can get in the chair and I'll take a quick look at your mouth."

"Mouth's fine."

"Sure it is, but let me just take a look. That's my job."

Bart shook his head. "You got me all fixed up. I don't want to jinx it."

"I promise you I won't do that. Just follow me, OK?"

I took the diploma back to my examination room and rehung it. The framed quote from Kahlil Gibran was crooked. Bart may have brushed against it, or maybe he'd started to remove it as well and then reconsidered. *Your pain is the breaking of the shell that encloses your understanding.* I frowned. It was such a shame Nathan didn't look even a bit like his younger brother. What I understood at that moment was I felt zero physical attraction to him at all.

Neither Ashcraft had followed me into the room, and now I heard them arguing from the waiting room.

"I don't care about those!"

"Dad, if you need X-rays, we're going to do that. Your teeth—"

"There ain't a thing wrong with them! Why does everyone keep saying there's something the matter with me? Tim's got me fixed up good."

I listened to their back-and-forth for half a minute, thinking how delicate Nathan treated his dad. Johnny would either be yelling at Bart or making fun of him by now, but Nathan's responses seemed to get quieter. I imagine even someone with irrational anger can't keep yelling at someone who whispers at them. Nathan's voice had a tiptoe quality to it, a delicateness like someone tasked with rolling an inflated balloon across a cactus bed. Maybe it came natural to him or maybe he'd developed it as part of his job. Call it a coffinside manner.

I thrust my hands into my pockets and walked back to them.

"There he is," Bart said, slapping his thigh again. "We sure hope you'll come over to dinner again. I sure enjoyed last weekend, and I know John did too."

"I think it was a little longer ago than that, but you know me. I'm always losing track of time."

He began to insist it was last weekend, and I decided to agree. Nathan and I made eye contact again. I thought I recognized the look he was giving me, and I broke the stare, not wanting to lead him on. We could be friends, but I knew it wouldn't go further. Not if I didn't feel even a spark of attraction. The more I thought about the situation, the more I regretted all the hopes I'd been building up for us, and I just wanted them both to leave. When Bart showed no signs of going anywhere, I said, "Well, I better get back to work. I've got a patient coming in real soon."

Nathan gave a quick glance at the floor. "Come on, Dad. You heard him. We've taken up far too much of his time."

Bart seemed confused, like in his mind he'd only just arrived. I offered him the warmest smile and clapped him on the back. Nathan took him by the shoulders, and we fell into an unspoken team bent on maneuvering Bart out of the office.

"That sure was a good dinner we had, wasn't it, Tim?"

"It definitely was," I said. "We're going to have plenty more too. I can't wait to sit down with you all and have more of that chicken."

"You can come over tonight if you want."

"Dad, I'm sure Tim's busy."

"Can't make tonight, but we'll get together real soon," I said.

Bart slapped his thigh and gave me his open-mouthed smile. Then he broke free of us and announced he was going to the truck.

Nathan and I watched him go. Standing alone with him felt very awkward, like when you're at the end of a date that hasn't gone the way either of you wanted. You want to say goodbye and cut your losses, but you don't want to be rude either.

"Your brother, when we were having those beers, he mentioned you."

Nathan's stare followed Bart's progress. "Did he? I can imagine what he said."

"It was all good things," I said, speaking too fast. I blushed.

"Oh, OK," he said. He started after Bart, who had veered away from the truck and seemed determined to walk up the street. He didn't say a word of goodbye, but he didn't need to. I went inside and closed the door. The quiet of the lobby after losing all of Bart's energy made the little space feel deserted rather than empty. I put my hands in my pockets and just stood there, not certain how to feel and even less certain about what Nathan and I had communicated between us. I touched my stomach and wondered whether my white lab coat had hidden the pudginess.

Why the hell did I assume he was attracted to me at all? Who was I to be acting like I needed to keep him from getting his hopes up by nipping his *obvious* desire in the bud with a few subtle cues?

I went into my examination room, stretched out in the chair, and threw my thoughts at the wall like darts. I had to accept the fact my own hopes were dashed by his appearance, and that was *fine*. It's not reasonable to pursue a guy when you feel no physical attraction. It wasn't like he was a 7 and I only dated 10s. It's just that Nathan was closer to a 4.

A guy likes what he likes, and Nathan didn't check any boxes. Yet I wondered if I checked any of his. What was his type? Didn't he find me at least a little desirable? After all, I could gain another twenty pounds and still be considered skinny in this neck of the woods. What the hell kind of guy does a gay mortician go for, anyway? What would the small talk be like, since that's all we'd be doing if we did get together? Would he have a good sense of humor if I made a joke about him really liking a stiff one?

CONFESSIONS

The bell on the door jangled, almost making me jump out of the chair. I smoothed out my jacket and went to the reception area where I found Meghan Malone standing there.

"Hi," she said.

I nodded, remembering the last thing I said to her at her last appointment. *See you in six months.*

"Hello, Meghan."

She closed the door and stepped toward me. "Are you busy? I know I don't have an appointment."

"Do you need one? Is anything wrong?"

"Nothing's wrong when I get to see you."

"What?"

"This isn't about my teeth, Hermey. Do you like that as a nickname?"

"I admit I had to Google it the first time. But sure."

She smiled. I saw it, and if she'd been a guy, I would have understood its meaning right away. But I was deaf and dumb to heterosexual flirting, and despite her saying she wasn't here for a dental exam, I leapt straight into my usual consultation questions. Did she have pain in her gums or—

She touched my forearm.

"Actually, I was wondering . . . Christ, this is so forward. I can't believe I'm doing this."

"Sorry?"

"Nothing. Nothing. I've got a tooth that hurts after all, Hermey. This one."

She took my right index finger and guided it to her top left incisor. Then she gave the fingertip a little kiss.

Needless to say, gay little old me got a clue. I'd never had a woman come on to me before. Or if one had, I'd been oblivious. My queer desires were as absolute and ironclad as a childhood inoculation against polio when it came to women. Or so I thought. But as Meghan's eyes closed and she took my finger from her mouth and placed the entire palm against the right side of her face, I got hard. I looked down in disbelief. It's not like there was the slightest thing masculine about Meghan I might be responding to. She was all woman, soft and shapely, big breasts and flowing blond hair. Her face was as smooth as a candle against my skin, not at all like the bit of stubble I preferred on a guy. In every conceivable way, my penis should have been hanging due south, bored out of its balls. But Meghan had its attention.

My God, I thought. Can a gay man get so lonely and desperate his DNA straightens out? Or did I truly have a streak of bisexuality in me, never before detected, a tiger lurking in the tall tangles of my sexual hunger?

Without even thinking about locking the front door and putting the Closedsign in the window, I walked backward down the hallway and she followed me, hands flat to my chest, fingers massaging. She unbuttoned my shirt down to my belly button and squeezed my pecs the way a man would grope a woman's boobs, which only reminded me that my weight gain was showing in other places besides my stomach. I'd never had a toned chest but it was always flat. Now I looked like a budding 13-year-old girl. Meghan squeezed again and said, "You like that?"

"What are you doing?"

"I'm glad you're hairless. I like that better."

"I've got *some* hair."

"I can't wait to discover where it's hiding, Hermey."

I don't want to get too pornographic, but that's just how it went down. Meghan Malone was kerosene and I'd have struck the match then and there if it wasn't for the sudden jangle of bells followed by the immediate complaint of a little girl.

"There's no one here!"

Meghan seemed just as startled and pulled back from me like someone stumbling through a haze. I took a moment to catch my breath and shouted, "Be right with you!" Then I rushed about the room, buttoning my shirt and looking for a mirror. The only one available was my little circular inspection tool and I tried to angle it along my face to see if my hair was mussed, my cheeks sweaty. Meghan laughed and I put a warning finger to my lips. She nodded.

"What the hell is wrong with you?" I said in a low, almost seething voice. "We can't do—*this*."

"When are you free again?"

"Never."

"Oh, come on. It's obvious you feel like I do."

"I don't know how I—"

Now another girl complained, and I remembered Kelly DeSoto had booked an appointment for her twin 9-year-old girls. I shook my head. Meghan smiled. Oh, how she smiled, like I wasn't just in her pocket but had climbed in of my own accord. She turned the doorknob. Before opening it, though, she said, "Better get that thing calmed down, Tim. Though I can't wait to see it later."

Then she opened the door and made a grand announcement about how her teeth had never looked white and how I was the best dentist in the state of Kentucky. She left me standing there, listening as she and Kelly began a conversation in the lobby. It seemed they'd gone to school together.

I smoothed out my lab coat and walked down the hall. Meghan said, "You girls be good for Dr. Tim, you hear? Promise me no biting." Her exaggerated Appalachian accent did nothing to detract from the silkiness of her voice. She sounded like a sweet, sexy Sunday school teacher.

The girls promised.

"See you in six months," I said as Meghan went out the door.

She showed up at my office first thing the next morning.

MRS. LAWRENCE

NATHAN ASHCRAFT WAS NOT the only student to gravitate toward me for one reason or another. In 1988, I started the school Science Club, focusing on the *mad scientist* aspect to generate maximum publicity, though I had to bite my tongue when the yearbook editors called us the *Wentz High Wizards* and the name stuck. A simple chemistry experiment can look like magic, but that was the sort of ignorance I wanted to fight. There's no sorcery, no divinity beyond chemical reactions. It's no small irony that too much science spoken out loud will get your burned as a witch in the hearts of too many people in this part of the country. Sometimes I felt like a time traveler visiting the Dark Ages, risking life and limb to thwart the state's twin religions of Christianity and basketball.

Most years I had around ten students joining me in my classroom after school on the third Wednesday of the month. Though I specialized in biology, I had complete competency in other fields, and I led the club through experiments that demonstrated principles of magnetism, electricity, geology, chemistry, and physics. In March 1991, with the weather clear and warm for the season, I even had us dabbling in rocketry down on the baseball diamond. It was the best-attended meeting in the club's history, and even the vile Coach Skinner showed up to watch us launch an Estes Photon Probe 200 meters overhead from home plate. The cheering still rings in my ears, a redemptive sound after the past year's acrimony over my letter. In a way, I was capitalizing on the country's surging militancy. Scuds and intercepting Patriots had renewed everyone's interest in missiles.

I was a successful teacher in terms of what mattered. The principal might not like me, the football coach and half the faculty might loathe me, but no one doubted my commitment or the amount of time I spent with my students. I believed, and to this day believe, it was my earnestness that made me approachable. I cannot even remember all the frightened girls who sought me out because they were afraid they were pregnant and didn't know what to do. Sometimes these fears ended up being false alarms. Other times, the student withdrew from school and the administration received a letter from her parents announcing she was going to live with an uncle or aunt in another state—the same tidy mask used for decades.

The number of girls who cried to me in private revealed the inadequacies of both the school health class and access to practical contraception. Factor in an adolescent's tendency toward horrible decision-making, and it was quite astounding there weren't unwanted pregnancies happening every month.

I've already noted it was the encounter with Meghan Malone in my garden eight months ago that got me contemplating my teaching career and my life in Wentz Hollow. She is the one who stirred my memory, but in doing so I became convinced I should write it down to darken the posterity of this town by revealing the wretchedness of its ancestors.

CONFESSIONS

When I first met Meghan Malone, she was a 10th-grader named Meghan Garton. She came along five or six years after Nathan and made no impression on me whatsoever. A C-student through and through, the annoying sort of girl who's talkative at inappropriate moments and then goes mute the moment you call on her. She was popular with the boys and seemed to have the uncanny ability to weaponize her pheromones, releasing them in controlled bursts whenever she wanted something. Meghan Garton passed through my biology class like the wind blowing over a pile of fallen leaves, too inconsequential and slight to be a disruptive gust. I did not even talk to her in the hallways over the next two years.

But in the middle of her senior year, she came to me after school. It was the Wednesday of the science club's meeting, and I was laying out the experiment when she came in and I heard the words that, in hindsight, so often got me into trouble.

"Mrs. Lawrence?"

Short of Nathan himself walking through the door, she was the last person I expected to see in my classroom after hours.

"Yes, Meghan?"

"I have to talk to you."

I glanced at the clock. The students probably wouldn't start showing up for another 20 minutes.

Before I could respond, Meghan said, "Mrs. Lawrence, I'm late."

I could have played dumb and said something like, "Late for what?" But what would be the point of such cruelty? Nor was there any reason to go into theatrics or despair, as if she'd announced she had cancer.

"I see," I said, continuing to lay out the materials.

The coolness of the reply wasn't meant to agitate her, but she acted like I was either stupid or callous. "No, you don't understand, Mrs. Lawrence. I mean I'm *late*."

"I do understand, Meghan. When was your last menstruation?"

"Last—last month," she said, blushing.

"And you've had unprotected sex since then?"

"I . . ." Her voice trailed off.

"Well, have you? There are other reasons besides pregnancy for a change in your period."

"I . . . I did. I mean I have. I'm so afraid, Mrs. Lawrence."

There were eleven abortion clinics in Kentucky when Frank and I moved to Wentz Hollow in 1983. By the mid-90s, when Meghan came to me in class that day, the number was down to seven. I could already see the developing trend, and I've come to inhabit the future of my fears. Today the state has just one licensed facility, in Louisville, almost a five-hour drive from town, completely unreasonable for a woman without means, much less a teen girl, who also has to deal with the matter of parental consent. Still, I tithe from my pension and social security income to help fund it.

"Mrs. Lawrence, if I'm pregnant, I don't know what I'll do. You've got to help me."

"The best thing I can do is give you some numbers to call. You need a counselor who'll respect your confidentiality and anonymity."

Meghan stood there, quiet, and I glanced at the clock again.

"That's not how Jessica said you helped her."

Her voice was low but self-assured in a threatening way. I got chills and stared at her.

"I don't know what you're talking about."

"Jessica Behr. Don't you remember her, Mrs. Lawrence? She graduated a couple years ago."

I moved to the front of the class and the safety of my desk. Meghan came up to stand beside me.

"You should go now," I said. "Unless you want to stay for Science Club. It'll be starting soon."

"Mrs. Lawrence, don't make me tell everyone what you did for Jessica."

I snapped her a look. "I *said* I don't know what you mean."

"But you do. Jessica said—"

"I don't know what she said. People lie all the time."

"No," Meghan said, shaking her head, her smile so superior. "Jessica wasn't lying. She told me all about the speech you gave her about it being her body and her right."

"Come back tomorrow and I'll be happy to repeat it. But I can't offer you anything more than words and a few good phone numbers to call."

"You gave more than that to Jessica, the way she tells it."

We found ourselves in a staring match broken only by the first arriving club members. We both flinched when we heard voices in the hallway. Five students came in.

With privacy lost, Meghan left fast with her head down. I stood there in shock, wishing I could cancel the club meeting, as I no longer had any enthusiasm for the experiment. That's when I experienced a moment of arrhythmia. It made me gasp and touch my chest. The students asked if I was OK.

"Yes," I said, taking another very deep breath. I realized I was afraid of a student for the first time in my life, though like every teacher, I'd encountered my share of troublemakers. And, of course, the lives of all teachers would change just a few years later with the Columbine shooting, when no one felt safe anymore. If such violence could happen in a pleasant suburban school, it could also happen in a small town like Wentz Hollow, where half the boys in town were handling shotguns by the time they turned 12. But the intimidation I felt from Meghan Garton belonged to a different category of fear, the threat of blackmail, the terror of an exposed secret.

That secret was Jessica Behr.

I hope writing this memoir helps me understand the inner thirst for justice that sent me drinking out of so many unpromising wells. Perhaps that's being unfair. Were the wells themselves unpromising or did I do something to poison them? How could I call Nathan, with all his wonderful potential, *unpromising?* Maybe I shouldn't even give my desire a biological grounding. Hunger and thirst are somatic responses. This thing I called a thirst surpassed bodily need.

My first understanding of its nature came that March afternoon on the baseball diamond, when the Science Club launched the rocket with about a hundred students, faculty and parents encircling us. How I reveled in their enthusiasm and rapt attention as I explained the physics of it all. As I said, even Coach Skinner, the man who a few months earlier called me *dyke* and *fucking bitch* with impunity in the staff room, looked on in begrudging wonder.

The rocket launched, was successful, and everyone clapped. How strange it was to be the center of attention, but the stranger aspect was how temporary the success felt, meaningless after mere minutes. I went home feeling like the launch had been a stunt whose memory wouldn't survive past dinner time for most of the crowd.

What would make an impact on these people? What would *change* Wentz Hollow for the better and for good?

Nathan was present at the rocket launch even though he never joined the Science Club. As I gave my talk, my attention couldn't help finding him near the back of the gathering. He was looking across to Steven Malone, who stood near Coach Skinner and a group of other athletes. Maybe because he stood in the back, he thought himself safe, but anyone would recognize the longing he directed at Steven. Some might have misinterpreted it as a desire to fit in with a clique of popular boys, but I knew about the note from before Christmas break, just as I knew there'd been many more notes in the following weeks. Nathan now told me everything and came to my free period every day.

I'd spoken to him at length about the strength and the happiness that comes from embracing oneself, but I found it difficult to get him to take the step we both needed him to make. I kept telling him there were other students in the school looking for leadership, looking for community, but I started to realize it was asking him to risk too much. He hadn't yet found that extra bit of imagination and courage that transforms someone into a visionary.

After we launched the rocket, after all heads turned skyward, after all the applause and the crowd's gradual dissipation, I noticed Steve and Nathan drawing nearer, magnet and iron filing. Grins were exchanged. Steve punched Nathan's shoulder, which gave me pause until I saw Nathan's smile broaden. Steven was so much taller, so much stronger than Nathan, a leader in every visible sense.

Then and there, my true idea crystalized for me. I saw myself leading a new school club, the Wentz Hollow High Gay-Straight Alliance, with Nathan and Steve seated together to my right, and down the line were all the homosexual boys and girls who thought they'd been doomed to secrecy. *Here* was meaning; *here* was the significance that marked a permanent social change.

Here was the rocket that could achieve escape velocity and orbit above us like a star worth wishing upon.

Despite what happened in the end, I never lost the memory of that moment's heady vision, and I carried its import with me as new students with new problems entered my life. My *thirst* remained, and even if I had to surrender the notion of organizing the adolescents into a force for change, I could deal with them as individuals and try direct action when possible.

That was my mind-set when Jessica Behr approached me for advice regarding her pregnancy. It was about two years after I'd last seen Nathan, so Jessica must have been in 9th grade when the rocket of my hopes made a spectacular crash. Now she was a junior, pretty and bright, with plans to be a journalist. In fact, I knew she was already doing an internship with Geraldine over at the *Herald*.

"Mrs. Lawrence, I really need your help. I'm so embarrassed."

She told me she'd gotten pregnant and asked for advice. But advice is a cheap thing, dispensed like liquid hand soap and washed away with the same thoughtless abandon. If only it could be lotion, something to be absorbed. I started to do the same thing I'd done with other girls in her position, providing her with a few telephone numbers. But how many times had I seen those same girls shove the piece of paper into their purse and storm away with a *thanks for nothing* attitude? I thought of the school counselor, wondering what she did all day since the students came to me rather than to her. Well, why wouldn't they? I doubt they trusted the counselor to keep a secret. She was older and a local who probably knew all their parents from church. Talk of abortion no doubt crossed too many political taboos, threatened too many ethical boundaries, and the students intuited as much. So, the counselor sat in her office assuming everything was fine because her door was open and no students ever entered. No one ever conceived a more perfect bubble.

"How far along are you, Jessica?"

"Maybe five weeks."

"Well," I said. "In that case, there's something I may be able to do. I've never done it before. I need to do some research first."

Jessica leapt at this vague promise and all but threw herself at my feet in gratitude. I told her to check back with me in a week.

I've never been much of a person to read for pleasure, but

the scientist in me always gravitated toward *Frankenstein*. I was assigned the novel no less than four times between 9th grade and my final year in college, and it wasn't until the last reading that I noticed a repetition in Mary Shelley's story.

—No one can conceive the variety of feelings which bore me onwards, like a hurricane, in the first enthusiasm of success.

—Who shall conceive the horrors of my secret toil as I dabbled among the unhallowed damps of the grave or tortured the living animal to animate the lifeless clay?

—No one can conceive the anguish I suffered during the remainder of the night.

The novel is permeated with assurances about deeds and emotions being impossible for anyone to imagine. *Conceive* intrigued me too, in a sexless novel obsessed with the creation of life. I hadn't thought of that observation, or any part of the novel, until I came home that day, pondering my offer to Jessica and the step I was preparing to take. Perhaps my own sudden ethical quandary made me locate the book in our little library and start browsing pages all evening.

No one can conceive the anguish I suffered during the remainder of the night.

No sentence from a novel was ever more applicable to my life just then. Frank and I tended to go to bed together around 11:00, but I told him I was staying up. He'd already asked me if I was OK twice. He asked a third time when he came downstairs around 1:00 in the morning and found me still at my desk, with Mary Shelley back on the shelf and a lot of old botanical textbooks stacked in front of me.

"Sarah? What's going on?"

"Nothing at all."

"You can tell me."

"There's nothing to tell. I'm just researching something. It's a possible Science Club project."

He grunted his acceptance and made a turn toward the

right, in the direction of the coffee pot. Horror and annoyance spiked at the thought of him sitting up beside me. Perhaps Frank felt my mood, because he turned back and said, "Guess I'll go back to bed then. Hope you'll join me soon."

I smiled and told him I would. *Soon,* however, is a subjective measurement of time and two hours passed before my vision blurred and I felt almost drunk from fatigue. I folded my notes into the one particularly helpful book, placed that book in the middle of the stack, and pushed away from the table. Who can conceive of the changes that came over me between the moment I sat down and the moment I rose? In the space of hours, the teacher and the activist knew she had crossed a professional and personal Rubicon. But it was a necessary crossing. Someone had to stand up for young girls like Jessica. Someone had to give them more than a cold phone number.

I fell asleep within minutes and dreamed I lived a very long time ago, perhaps in the 16th or 17th century. I dwelled in cottage solitude, a crone tending to herb gardens, and people sought my help for a litany of ailments. I was a member of the so-called *cunning folk*, a wise woman or folk healer. Some might even call me a witch. I'd never had a dream like this, though it had occurred to me that I'd have gravitated to such a role had I been born in olden times. I'd have stood at a wooden table with a series of bowls, crushing roots and leaves into a paste and then extracting their juice to make a tea or a tincture to help the village women who had the same despair Jessica experienced now.

Abortifacients. To me, at least, it was a pretty word, rounded and delicate like *aperitif.* Such a shame it served an ugly need, though please don't mistake me when I say this. I of all people am pro-choice. Frank and I never wanted children, but early in our marriage we had a scare. In my case, biology's cold amorality worked in my favor. A high percentage of human pregnancies end in miscarriage, often without the woman even knowing she was pregnant. A person who gets too sentimental about blastocysts and embryos must see every sexually active woman as a walking graveyard. I could have told Jessica and the other girls who came to me not to worry too much and just let nature take its unforgiving course. But there seems to be a law passed by some cosmic Republican Congress that guarantees women with an unwanted pregnancy will always carry it to term unless external forces intervene.

In my dream, Jessica came to me, the wise herbalist, and I took her hands in mine and sat her down. Then I began to make the potion, using pennyroyal, cotton root bark, blue cohosh and mugwort. Jessica's expression screwed up with every sip, her left palm placed flat to her stomach as if expecting immediate results.

I woke feeling a little queasy but with a clear agenda and understanding of my duty. I knew the ingredients I needed, all of which could be obtained with relative ease as long as you didn't mind driving as far as Lexington. I knew I'd have to acquire the herbs myself and do the preparation. Just handing the list and the instructions off to a teen girl was tantamount to giving out a phone number. Did she even have a car? Did she have the money to make the purchases? What would she say to her parents if they discovered the list and questioned her? And even if she managed to obtain everything, would she have the understanding or the equipment needed to make the concoction correctly?

The day came, a week later, when this frightened girl arrived in my classroom after school and stood by my side watching me make the drink that might cancel her mistake. I measured and weighed the ingredients, cut and crushed the leaves and stems, and added them to a beaker positioned over an active Bunsen burner.

"I'm scared, Mrs. Lawrence."

"It'll be fine."

"Thanks to you."

She paced the room, hugging herself as I cut the flame and transferred the liquid from the beaker to a clean glass. The end result had an amber color and a faint but unpleasant odor.

"Can I drink it now?"

"Give it another few minutes to cool," I said.

She bit at her right thumbnail and rocked back and forth on her feet.

Then Jessica asked me if it would taste bad.

I smiled. "Most medicine does."

"How . . . how long will it take?"

"It's not going to be that simple," I said. I'd already told her there was little chance this single drink would cause the miscarriage, but it was clear she hadn't accepted that. I repeated the admonition, adding, "You need to have the herbs in your body as much as possible for the next five or six days at least."

Panic reignited in her voice. "But how do I do that? I don't have all this equipment. I couldn't begin—"

"You'll come to my classroom every day after school. Bring a thermos. I'll make one drink for you to have right away, and another to have first thing in the morning."

"Yes, Mrs. Lawrence. I will. I'll do everything you say."

I felt the glass. The temperature was good.

"Time for your first dose. I suggest holding your nose and downing it all at once. If you feel nauseated, do everything you can to fight the urge to vomit."

Jessica nodded and pinched her nose. The face she made as she drank told me everything I needed to know about the taste. Then she bent over. A bit of liquid dribbled from her lips and she put both hands to her mouth. I was sure she'd puke. Her body trembled and kept its tense pose for half a minute before I asked how she was.

She brought her hands to her sides, nodded, and straightened. Her eyes were teary.

"That was the grossest thing ever. But I deserve to have it taste bad."

"Don't say such a thing."

"But it's true," she said.

"No, it isn't. You had unprotected sex. That wasn't a smart decision at this point in your life, but it's not shameful. It doesn't merit punishment in any sense."

Her eyes widened. I imagine she'd expected a scolding, a moral chastisement—even now, even from me. I had no doubt every other teacher in Wentz High would have delivered on her assumption.

"Thank you, Mrs. Lawrence. I can't thank you enough."

"All we can do is try. Remember, there are no guarantees. If the natural remedy doesn't work, I'll do my best to help you with other options."

Jessica hugged me. No student had ever done that before. Even Nathan never hugged me when his trust in me was at its peak. But Jessica did and I patted her shoulder and said I'd see her tomorrow.

She came every day, but after a week of disappointing results she began losing hope and even claimed she was starting to show, as if the concoction was speeding her pregnancy along. Of course, she was not showing at all, and I worked hard to calm her nerves. She kept taking the drink despite her collapsing faith. Then, on the tenth day, she came to me while I was cutting the herbs, and I saw the bright happiness in her eyes.

"It happened, Mrs. Lawrence. It . . . it worked."

"I'm so glad, Jessica."

We never saw each other again.

NATHAN

I CAME CLOSE TO SPRINTING out of the garage and went upstairs to change into the blue jeans and T-shirt I'd started to put on before the phone call. I was allowing routine to guide my thoughts and actions. First wear the right clothes, then work on Mr. Henshaw. No, move Mrs. Lawrence from the hearse and into storage, *then* finish the Henshaw case.

I hurried to the prep room where Mr. Henshaw lay half-naked on a table. Somehow I'd forgotten I hadn't even finished dressing him and indulged in a moment of self-disgust. I felt like I'd left a confused old man alone to fend for himself and, for just a second, I thought of my father walking naked in his house, going room to room in search of my mom, with no one to help him. I squeezed my eyes shut on this horrible fantasy and reminded myself that dad had never forgotten to dress himself.

If only that was the point.

Mrs. Lawrence be damned, I thought, and shifted all my attention to Mr. Henshaw. His family had selected very smart burial clothes and provided a favorite photo of him. He still had a thick head of hair and it would be easy to match the simple way he wore it in the photo. This case really wouldn't take too long, ninety minutes tops, but I could spend the next six hours perfecting him if necessary. Get him dressed, get the hair and makeup done, get him transferred to the coffin in the viewing room.

Then I could think about that drink with Tim tonight.

I brought out the cosmetics and began working. I listened to no music and made no sound, not even a hum. Years ago, a college student interested in the profession came to watch me do last stage prep work, and afterward she made a nervous-sounding remark about how dispassionate I seemed. Maybe she worried the comment would be taken as criticism. Perhaps she even meant it as such. We had a talk about the realities of controlling one's emotions. Could I do my job if I was always crying over the dead? I felt she went away unconvinced, maybe even believing I didn't care about my clients or their families. That of course was not true, but a sort of callus does grow over your feelings when you work with corpses every day, when the process of death is demystified and routinized.

I remember a single time when I became emotional during a body prep. Early in my career, I handled the case of Vinnie Pence, a 5-year-old kidnap victim who was found dead in the woods two days later. He'd been mutilated, and working on him felt like trying to piece a shattered vase back together. I had to bring in three associates with greater expertise in makeup, and over the course of several hours we recovered the image of a beautiful child. Then we broke down and cried very hard.

The way I now suddenly found myself crying over Mr. Henshaw.

His old face blurred under the flow of the tears. I backed away, counting each retreating step as a personal failure. I went back to the garage and slumped against the hood of the hearse and wiped my eyes. I looked down the length of the hearse to the bay where Mrs. Lawrence rested.

"If . . . if it's really you . . . I don't know what to say."

It's a funny thing, the memories that stay with you like a brand on the flesh of the brain. I remember sitting in the school library—in late October, I think—reading in a study carrel. I don't recall the book, probably something by Stephen King. I shivered from loneliness. I closed the book and put my forehead down on top of it and felt damned, lost, and alone. The school library had seemed quiet until I put my head down. Now I seemed able to hear every conversation going on around me. How could there be so many? So much laughter, so much happiness. I raised my head like a submarine's periscope and looked over the edge of the study carrel. There were students everywhere. I could have gone up to any of them. They were friends, weren't they? Why did I feel so alienated, so unliked? I'd never been bullied by anyone in the room.

I saw Steve Malone at a table. He was with a girl whose name I no longer remembered. They were playing footsie. Her shoes were off and her toes were going up and down his right calf. He had his varsity jacket on and I admired how it stretched across his back. *Admired.* That's not the right word at all. Admiration doesn't cause a tingle. That tingle became a burst of anger and despair. I knew exactly what I felt and what it meant. I'd realized those feelings many times before, but for some reason my brain chose today to dwell on the lonely life in store for me.

It wasn't just Steve. There were any number of guys I had crushes on. You could have put their faces on a dart board, and I would have been happy with any person chosen by chance. I just wanted to be sitting with one of them out in the open, at a table with my shoes off. I looked at the three walls of the study carrel and almost screamed. I shoved the book in my backpack and ran out.

Did I know I was running to her? Did I ever have that intention? She'd always seemed like an outsider. When you're the kind of kid who finds himself alone a lot, you start noticing the adults who also seem to have no friends. You notice which teacher the other teachers ignore, and you catch unguarded moments of gossip and ridicule. Part of you identifies with the unpopular teacher and begins studying them like a window into your future self. I'd see Mrs. Lawrence sometimes taking a walk alone or sitting by herself with a book. It was like in elementary school when all the kids decide one of their classmates has cooties.

Shunning is the more technical term.

There was no question she represented science to me. My folks were Southern Baptists, though only my mother was a true Bible thumper. Someone might think I embraced science as a way of escaping from her beliefs, but the truth was very different. I remember us watching the evening news in the living room, with me on my stomach on the floor. For some reason they started showing footage of a gay pride parade—from Miami, I think—and my mom, who was two months shy of giving birth to Johnny, said, "Those people are just sick."

I didn't say anything. Somewhere along the way—on the elementary school playground, probably—I'd learned the word *gay*. But at the time my sexuality was more like a vague itch. I'd liken it to being 20 years old and told you've got a tumor but it's nothing you'll need to deal with until you're 60. It's real and not real. The difference is your mom doesn't make casual condemnations about a shadowy cancer diagnosis. I knew I was like the men in the news clip, even though the scene was strange and frightening. My mom had just told me how she felt about me—or would feel, if she ever discovered the secret. Far from studying science to escape Mom's religion, my impulse was to use science to get me in tune with it. I had to change myself. There must be some way. Electricity. A potion. A pill. I began to imagine myself as a scientist trying to cure myself of a deadly disease. But science fiction fantasies soon ran up against school textbook realities, the study of covalent bonds, equations, and Latin names. By 11th grade, I knew I was more of an English major at heart. I think many morticians are like me in this sense. Death straddles the worlds of science and poetry. Perhaps it bridges too.

Maybe I happened upon Mrs. Lawrence by simple chance. I heard water running from her classroom, peaked in and saw she was alone. At that moment I thought I just needed to hear a voice, any voice, talking to me. How could it be, 15 minutes later, I'd be confessing both my loneliness and the reason for it?

The memory made my face burn. It'd be many years and in a state far removed from Kentucky before I voluntarily told someone I was gay, and afterward I told that person he was the first I'd come out to. I believed it in the moment, and only later did I realize it wasn't true. I'd blocked out the experience with Mrs. Lawrence. How I wished I could go back in time and seize my younger self's thin arm and drag him away from her classroom door. I'd tell him what he can look forward to.

You will find love. You'll have many wonderful adventures. You'll live your best life.

Of course, if I actually did go back in time to say such things, the words would be lies. You can imagine a hypothetical future-self talking to you in the present, making warm assurances. But you're responsible for the person you become, so your future self has that dependency. If I could somehow stop my teenage self from talking to Mrs. Lawrence, I'd have to say, "I don't know if we'll find love. We haven't yet. There won't even be that much sex. Is it a lonely life? Sometimes. You soldier through it. Don't go killing yourself, OK? Thanks in advance."

It's a good thing I became a mortician rather than a coach,

considering the quality of my pep talks.

What comfort would my younger self find in a confession like that? He'd plunge a knife into his chest to obliterate me and the horror I represented. Or he'd go back to Mrs. Lawrence because he understood, deep down, that she was a hard woman, hard because she dealt in facts rather than emotion and facts were what he needed. He wanted to hear himself described in terms of genetics rather than feelings, to be plucked from chaos and inserted somewhere into the chain of evolution. I understood that now, and to an extent Mrs. Lawrence did that. If only she'd stopped at that point, like a normal person. But I'd come to her with needs, and she had needs of her own. I didn't understand them at the time.

Leaning against the hearse that supposedly contained her corpse, I'm still not sure I understood them.

"Future me, tell me I get through this."

You get through it just fine. It's not like you have a choice.

"Tell me I find someone."

Of course you do.

"I don't trust you."

If you can't trust me, who can you trust?

I laughed at that. Nothing like pretending to be schizophrenic to stall for time.

I returned to the prep room and looked at Mr. Henshaw. I really needed to finish his case, but . . .

I had a bell in the prep room that sounded if anyone came through the front door. It rang now, startling me. I looked down at my old clothes, wishing I had a moment to change into something more professional. This visitor would have to take me as I was.

I found an older man in the lobby, in his 70s and shorter than average, maybe 5'6". Right away I recognized the reddened, sleepless eyes of a recent widower. He had a large manilla folder tucked under his left arm. As he saw me, he extended his right hand in greeting. This surprised me just a little. Many grieving people coming into a funeral home are so shaken and off their game they forget otherwise automatic social graces.

"Are you Nathan Ashcraft?"

"Yes," I said.

He looked down at his shoes a moment, then back into my eyes. "I understand you picked up the body of Sarah Lawrence a short time ago."

"Yes."

"I have something from her she intended you to have," he said, holding out a manuscript envelope that seemed very full. "My name is Frank. I'm Sarah's husband."

TIM

I'M NOT BISEXUAL. It's just not possible. A dentist doesn't get cavities, a gay guy doesn't go for women. I kept telling myself this as I looked down at Meghan Malone's eyes. She stared up at me like some sultry porn princess. We didn't exchange words because just then she was occupied and I was the occupier.

This was our fourth get-together in two weeks. Business be damned, loan forgiveness commitments be damned, I'd started marking off big blocks of time in my appointment book and putting the Closed sign in my window so I could host her in my office.

She was threatening to make my knees buckle and I placed my hand against the wall and leaned into the Kahlil Gibran quote until I almost went cross-eyed. *Your pain is the breaking of the shell that encloses your understanding.* I wasn't exactly in pain right then, but my shell was breaking all over the place. As for my understanding—well, Jesus. I looked back down at Meghan and shook my head at her power. No wonder cavemen had spent their free time carving mammoth tusks into idols of big-breasted women. No wonder there were fertility cults. Tell a woman like Meghan Malone that you're gay and she'd just rip your wig off and say, "I'll decide what you are and aren't, got that?"

My orgasm built like it had every time with her; to add insult to the injury I was doing every male partner I'd ever had, Meghan was getting me off faster than any of them. What *was* I? I mean, sure, anything can happen one time. Arguably everything *should* happen one time if you've lived a full life. But repetition becomes a pattern, and a pattern becomes . . . fact? Truth? I looked at my white lab coat and felt like a fraud, like someone playing dress-up—but not as a dentist. Dentistry at the moment was my identity's sole anchor. No, I felt like I'd been playing dress-up as a gay man. I'd always been straight, and Meghan was showing me how to slip out of the costume.

I told her I couldn't hold back any more. She rubbed my calves and squeezed them. By now I knew that's how she signaled, *do it*. I did and held my breath, almost afraid to look down until I heard her voice. She laughed and said, "You OK, Hermey?"

I giggled. I fucking *giggled*.

"More than OK. Wow."

She got up and went to the hallway bathroom and closed the door. Water ran in the faucet. I pulled up my pants, gave my little belly a pat and then covered it by tucking in the hem of my dress shirt and fastening my belt.

Meghan came out. She didn't look like anything had happened. Not a hair out of place.

"How was it?"

"Better every time," I said, not lying.

She put her arms around me and asked for mouth wash. I gave it to her and after she'd swished and spat, she kissed me. "You ready to take the next step?"

CONFESSIONS

"Huh?"

"Tim, I know you're a dentist and all, but there's a lot more to me than my mouth."

My God, her voice was seductive and teasing, like an Appalachian Jessica Rabbit. She made me feel like the hottest guy in Kentucky and the crazy thing was hearing it made me *want* to be straight. Not just straight but dominant, like some kind of pimp. Dirty talk with guys was never much of a thing with me, I was pretty vanilla. Meghan was changing that too.

I gripped her by the arm and said, "I may have to add a gynecology service."

She kissed me again, much harder than the first time. "I'll give you a few days to recharge. Not that you need it. Want me to change the sign in the window on my way out?"

"Hell no," I said. "I need a sandwich or something first."

"Next time I'll bring one. My Hermey's so thin!"

That was another thing about her, the way she genuinely seemed to see me as being in shape, the way she made me feel attractive. When I looked in the mirror, I saw the Pillsbury Doughboy. She saw . . . Johnny Ashcraft?

Speaking of Johnny, I still dreamed about him, so at least my unconscious mind remained pure. I imagined Meghan would soon infiltrate my dreams as well. There'd be a few fantasies where Meghan, Johnny, and I shared a bed together, taking turns in the middle of the threesome. Then there'd come a night when Johnny didn't show up at all and Meghan pleasured me in dreams the way she did in life. Is that when my gay card got cancelled? What would I tell my parents?

I couldn't imagine the look on their faces if I told them I had a girlfriend. Hell, I couldn't imagine the look on *mine*. Was Meghan even thinking along those lines? She'd said she was single, but frankly she had the sex drive of a nymphomaniac. Maybe I was just one stop on her way down Main Street. See the dentist, then hop on down to the podiatrist, flash those pretty eyes at the optometrist and polish off the day getting a very special adjustment from the chiropractor. Busy day, but good for her. Take what you want, Meghan.

Own the world, starting with me.

The next few hours after Meghan left went by in a casual way. Patients came, I cleaned teeth, fought gingivitis, and in general left people smiling the way your friendly small-town dentist always should. I usually closed up shop at 5:00, but that day I had no appointments after 3:15 and felt pretty tired, so I planned on leaving early. I was sterilizing my equipment at 4:00 when the door bells jangled. "Damnit," I said, realizing I'd neither locked the door nor turned the window sign back to Closed.

Maybe it was just as well. I needed the business.

I came out to the lobby and found Nathan standing there. We faced off in identical postures, our hands in our pockets.

"Hey," I said, looking around for Bart.

"Do you remember me?"

"Sure I do, Nathan."

"I wasn't sure."

"It was just a couple of weeks ago. How's Bart?"

"He has his good and bad days. More good days than bad, at least."

"I'm glad to hear that. Is the gum pain still manageable?"

Nathan sighed. "I don't know. Dad's like a cat when it comes to that. He won't let on no matter how bad he feels."

I nodded, not knowing anything to say. The idea of my mom and dad aging and getting sick wasn't something I'd thought about. There was an eternalness about them. Even my grandparents were doing fine.

"Well, how can I help, Nathan?"

"Are you busy?"

"Not too much, actually. Had some patients earlier but nothing now. I was just sterilizing my tools before heading home."

"Oh, then I won't keep you," he said, talking fast, already backing toward the door.

"I'd love to keep talking."

"I can . . . I can pay you."

"To talk?"

His expression barely changed, but I could tell he bit back a wince. Then it occurred to me he could think I was asking him to pay for sex, which made me cringe.

"Sorry," he said. "I'm not very good at this."

Was he trying to ask me out? Poor guy, stuck in Kentucky all his life, no real local outlet and an asshole for a brother. My heart really went out to him, to the point where I'd probably say yes if he actually took the step and asked. No harm in dinner. No harm in friendship.

"It's really fine, Nathan. We're good."

"You said you were sterilizing your equipment?"

"That's right."

"Do you use MetriCide?"

The question threw me as much by its change of subject as by the change in his voice. The strain had gone out of it. Weird that someone found confidence talking about disinfectants, but I could roll with it.

"I do, but only on a few things. There are limits on what tools dentists are allowed to use cold sterilization on. Most of the time I have to use heat."

"Oh, that's really interesting," he said, and sounded like he meant it. "Well, MetriCide is a good product."

"It is indeed."

"Did I tell you I'm a mortician?"

I laughed. "Yes, you did. I think that's interesting."

"You don't think it's morbid?"

"Why would I? Death's a fact of life, right? Someone's got to handle it."

"That's so true!"

He sat down on one of the four chairs I had in the lobby, his knees bent and splayed, his clasped hands hovering in the gap. He seemed even more relieved, like I'd checked an internal box for him. I saw a bit of a resemblance to Johnny when he was seated. The line of their nose was the same, as was the firm roundness of their chin. It just wasn't fair the similarities were so meager. But if Meghan's sexual sorcery really did have me straightening out, his attractiveness wouldn't matter one way or the other.

I began to ask him questions about his work. If I wasn't so tired I might have real interest, but honestly, I struggled not to yawn as I listened. This reaction had nothing to do with Nathan's enthusiasm. I soon discovered he could talk about the embalming process with something approaching eloquence. I wondered if I could be as informative, as precise if the tables were turned and he was asking me about dentistry. Nathan Ashcraft *was* a mortician, while I increasingly felt like a guy who just ended up becoming a dentist. For instance, he started talking about going to school, and I genuinely found myself absorbed by what he had to say.

"The best class I ever took in mortuary science was called *Death and Bereavement—an Introduction*. It was the only course in the program that addressed the profession's philosophical and cultural aspects. Everything else was functional, practical—mortuary law, embalming technique, even the art of merchandising, which at first offended me so much I thought about dropping out of the program all together. What bastard would merchandise death? Who would try upselling a coffin to a grieving widow? But I was a student then, living on scholarship funds and waiter tips. Such people have the luxury of being mortified by business realities."

"You've got that right," I said, laughing.

"That one class just went to the heart of what I thought

the job was about. I didn't care about being a coffin salesman. I saw myself becoming some sort of consoling counselor who could just take the grief away."

Try as I might, I couldn't find anything close to a matching experience in my dental school program, and if he'd asked me what my favorite class had been, I couldn't have told him. Why the hell was I a dentist anyway? There had to be a reason, but just then I couldn't say. The longer Nathan went on, the more intimidated I became. I no longer had to ask probing questions. Nathan was in the zone now, going on about differences in urn types and how important it was to help the family make the right—no, the *perfect*—choice. He was like some sommelier of death, so genuine, and my tiredness went away. I realized this was the longest I'd ever listened to another guy talk, the longest by a good ol' boy's country mile.

We stayed in the lobby until 5:30, when I made the mistake saying I had to put the Closed sign in the window and lock the door. Nathan quit talking for just half a minute, but when I sat back down it was like there were no more words, and the shy awkwardness from before settled over him again. It proved infectious. I couldn't find anything to say either.

"Well."

"Yeah," I said.

"I guess I better go."

"I'm pretty tired."

"Maybe we could get a drink or something. I talked your ear off. I want to hear all about your practice."

"Sure," I said. "That'd be good."

Nathan looked at the floor as if I'd said no. Maybe my tone hadn't been that hopeful. His shyness became painful and made me feel like I was the older man. I certainly had more experience—a lot more. Could he possibly even be a virgin?

He looked like Bart just then, refusing to acknowledge pain. There are many ways to remove a tooth. Sometimes just clamping down and pulling as hard as you can works best.

The direct approach.

"Johnny told me you're gay."

His face reddened. "I figured."

"He wanted to give me your phone number."

"*Why?*" So much hoarseness in a single word.

"Because he pegged me as a queer."

"Did Johnny call you that? A queer?"

"Yeah."

"I'm so sorry."

"He's a redneck. Hope that isn't offensive."

"No, it's accurate. Did he give you my number?"

"We didn't get around to it."

Nathan shook his head. "Was he drunk at the time?"

I laughed. "I do believe."

"Then he was playing a game. Trying to humiliate me—or you. He can be tolerable for half an hour or so when he's sober, but there's nothing nice about him once he's drinking. I try not to even go over to Dad's house if I know Johnny's going to be there."

"So that's why you weren't there for dinner."

"I wasn't even invited. I'm not trying to be a hypocrite about it, though. You're right—I probably would have said no."

"What about Bart? Does he know about you? He's got to, right?"

"He *knew*. Now it's just another thing he's forgotten. I hope he never remembers."

"I didn't realize his dementia was that bad."

"It's still manageable for now. In a way I've been lucky. A lot of people start going through awful personality changes. Some even become violent. But it softened my dad."

"Really? He's so gentle and friendly as long as he's not being pestered about a mouth X-ray. It's hard to imagine he wasn't always like that."

Nathan ran his fingers through his thinning hair. "He took his cues from Mom. When I came out as gay . . . well, that's not right. When my parents learned I was gay, Mom said I was sick, and so Dad said I was sick too. Mom said boys like me got what they deserved if they didn't change, so Dad said it too."

"*Bart* said that?"

I put my hand on Nathan's shoulder and let it rest there. We were two gay men separated by about a decade, but I felt I was talking to someone who'd grown up in a much older era. I tried to imagine my parents saying—or even thinking—the things Nathan's parents had told him. My mom sent me birthday cards with hot guys on the cover and wrote messages inside like, *Since I know you won't be getting anything this good for your birthday, here's $50 to drown your sorrows.* For all I knew Nathan never received a birthday card from either of his parents after they learned he wasn't the straight son they imagined.

"Bart spent a lot of time during dinner talking about how proud he is of you. Maybe the dementia didn't change his personality so much as it brought down all the walls he'd put up over the years. Maybe you're seeing the real him now."

He nodded but still didn't say anything.

"Look," I said. "Why don't we go ahead and get that drink tonight? I'm not that tired."

But he wasn't going for it. Maybe he saw it as a pity offer. I suppose it was a pity offer and all the acting skills I thought I'd developed in Wentz Hollow weren't enough to mask that.

"I'm sort of always on the clock," he said.

"Got you."

"If I got a call to come pick up a body and I was drunk at the time . . ."

"I understand. Maybe another time? You've got to take a day off every now and then."

"Maybe when I get an assistant . . ."

"You must be the most responsible person I know," I said.

I meant it, too. I had an image of him sitting in his hearse, cell phone in his lap, waiting. Was it a lonely life? Did he ever crack under the strain? Did he ever just need to be held? These questions occurred to me after he left, when I started thinking again about what Meghan Malone wanted from me, and what I wanted from her, and what I wanted from life in general. I remembered how little talk there'd been in my past hook-ups, how little affection. Could I even be with someone who needed a long and loving embrace in the kitchen after coming home from a horrible day?

Meghan Malone didn't seem to need that. Neither did Johnny Ashcraft.

I went to bed that night realizing Nathan was superior to all three of us.

MRS. LAWRENCE

ANYONE WHO STAYS MARRIED a good number of years wonders how life would be if they'd never met their spouse. I'd still be a teacher but I wouldn't be in Kentucky. I'd have stayed on the West Coast where my interest in social progress already had appeal. We moved to Wentz Hollow because of Frank's job, though why an accounting firm had located itself out in the sticks always struck me as odd. When I joked it must be a mafia front, Frank shrugged and said, "An accountant doesn't care where the numbers come from. He just makes sure they add up." That cheerful lack of inquisitiveness so typified him.

No wife has kept fewer secrets from her husband than I have, but my plans to develop a Gay-Straight Alliance at Wentz Hollow High was something Frank need not know. I remembered his gentle late-night reproach back when I hinted that something needed to be done for students like Nathan. But that was his nature: don't push hard, don't dig deep. Keep your blinders on and walk straight. Put your fingers in your ears and pay no attention to either the surrounding screams or whispers.

But teachers are not privileged with deafness. We hear the lonely, wounded cries echoing in the hallways long after the students are gone. That's what I thought I heard on the final day of school in 1991. I stepped out of my classroom thirty minutes after the final bell, ten minutes after all other noise had dissipated. Garbage filled the hallways, wadded sheets of paper, crushed Coke cans, faded Scantron sheets, and all the other detritus from hastily cleared lockers. The locker doors, colored bright blue, were all left wide open as the students had been instructed, and as I walked past, they seemed like rows of saluting soldiers eager to pass inspection.

I seldom experienced melancholy at the end of a school year, but I dealt with a stab of it now. Nathan and I had continued to meet, and he kept on telling me about his growing friendship with Steve Malone. If I hadn't seen them together on the day of the rocket launch months earlier, I would have thought everything Nathan said no more than the romantic fantasies of a very lonely homosexual youth. The brief get-togethers he described had all the chasteness of a 12-year-old Mormon imagining what high school romance must be: the brief hugs, the supportive shoulder rubs, the secret talks that imply rather than state. These actions seemed far too tender for the high school jock whose hallway boasts I'd heard many times over the last three years.

Yet I had the visual evidence weighing against my doubts and had to assume Nathan wasn't lying.

He'd swung by during my final free period today and didn't look excited about the end of the school year. When I asked him why, he just said, "Steve."

Nathan didn't need to say much more. I think I understood. Some adolescents have their entire social life anchored in the school day, and not every relationship translates away from the classroom. The adult equivalent of work friends. Whatever he and Steve had seemed defined by the boundaries of Wentz Hollow High. The boys probably didn't live more than five miles apart, yet Nathan seemed to feel he was facing the loneliest of summers. I remembered wanting to tell him that the fall would be here before he knew it.

Now, as I left through the school's front entrance and contemplated the empty student parking lot, I felt glad I'd said nothing of the sort. How ruinous, how moronic such a response would have been! I'd forgotten Steven Malone was graduating. His next fall semester would take place at the University of Louisville, where he'd won a baseball scholarship (Geraldine gave this information pride of place on the front page of the *Herald* back in April). The hindsight of a few hours suggested Nathan hadn't been contemplating a lonely summer. He'd been contemplating a lonely *life*.

The two of us must have been the only people who wished the summer break could have been delayed a couple of weeks. For me, the summer slide meant losing all the ground I'd gained with Nathan over the last few months. I needed more time to develop my plans for the Alliance and to convince Nathan he had the courage to lead it with me at his side. Every time I'd been on the verge of bringing it up outright, I heard Frank's voice: *Just don't push too hard.* So I'd delayed, and in the process quite forgotten Steven was a senior. Realizing he was now beyond my reach proved a bitter blow. The Alliance *needed* the natural endorsement of such a popular student, someone even Coach Skinner couldn't ignore, someone too strong to be bullied.

I walked the campus perimeter to the faculty parking lot around back. Wentz Hollow High was perched atop a gently rising hill. All of the school's outdoor athletic facilities—the football field, the track, and the baseball diamond—were at the base, accessible by a winding concrete path that led straight to the home field bleachers and a brick concession stand. I could survey almost all of it from where I stood and found nothing but abandonment. I looked toward the baseball diamond and imagined how it must have looked from here, me standing on the mound giving a lecture, the impressive rocket almost waist high. Then the moment of ignition and liftoff! I should have thought to bring a camcorder. The footage would have looked amazing from this vantage point.

I went big then, I thought. That was the key lesson: go big in everything. Small was having students build terrariums to learn about ecosystems. Small was writing outraged newspaper editorials about the finer connections between language and war.

Go big, Sarah. Always, go big.

I noticed two figures standing across the way on the football field, moving toward the bleachers on the visiting team's side. From this distance it would be impossible to tell much about their features, but I recognized Nathan's red jacket. And the boy walking next to him wore a school athletic jacket, blue and yellow. He was also taller than Nathan.

I went down the walkway, hurrying as fast as I could while trying to be stealthy. Sneaking closer to them gave me the delighted feeling of being an anthropologist recording some tribal ritual. The visitor's bleachers weren't nearly as sturdy as the home team's. You could go under them, but they didn't do that. Instead, they stood at the bottom, facing each other with about two meters of space separating them. Nathan's hands were in his pockets. Steven's were on his hips. Steven said something I couldn't hear, but I did hear Nathan's delightful laugh.

They stared with such intentness into each other's eyes that I probably could have gone up to them without being noticed. Of course, I didn't do that. I just kept watching as two meters became one, and then less than one. Much less than one. Nathan kept his hands in his pockets even as Steven reached out and cupped the right side of his face. He tilted his head into Steven's palm, and he seemed like a snowman melting into a source of warmth.

They're going to kiss, I thought, almost willing it to happen. But they didn't go that far, at least as long as I stayed to watch, which wasn't many more minutes. I'd been allowed to see a beautiful moment, and I retreated with the same fast but quiet pace I'd approached. My heart felt so full. Obviously I was responsible in a small way for the joy they now shared. Nathan had gained confidence from our talks, and confidence is a self-fulfilling prophecy.

I now felt certain Nathan would lead the Wentz Hollow Gay-Straight Alliance with me when he returned for his senior year. He just needed to make the next step and come out to his parents first.

I was confident he'd accomplish this before the summer ended.

NATHAN

"I DIDN'T REALIZE the process could go so fast," Mrs. Lawrence's husband said as I led him into my office. I didn't look down at the large envelope he'd given me, but my fingers kept squeezing it. There seemed to be about an inch of paper inside. "Sarah would like that. She never had much patience. Even when it came to our marriage, she just wanted to go to the courthouse. No ceremony, no waiting."

I gestured to a chair. "Oh, thank you very much," he continued, sitting down. The man spoke in a casual but very fast tone which told me his thoughts were chaotic and lost, as they had every right to be.

"If you'll give me just a minute, I'd like to find your wife's—file." I'd started to say *paperwork*.

"Yes, of course." He crossed one leg over his knee and held it there. His dangling foot wagged back and forth like a puppy dog's tail.

I went to the cabinet and pulled out the drawer with *L*.

Robbie had been old-fashioned when it came to filing clients, cataloging couples together under the husband's name.

"What is your first name again, please? I'm sorry I've forgotten it."

"No worries at all," he said. "Frank."

"Thank you. Here it is."

I retrieved the hanging file and brought it to the desk. The paperwork inside showed the arrangements, the burial plots, the tombstones. "Everything seems to be paid for except the coffins."

"I'm sorry," he said. "That's the wrong file."

"It has both of your names listed here."

"I realize that. You'll have to excuse me, it's been such a terrible day."

"I completely—"

"No," he said. "Please don't say you understand. Maybe you will later. Maybe I will too. There should be a second file with just her name on it. If you'll please look, I would appreciate it."

Swallowing, I went back to the cabinet and sure enough he was right. The second folder looked to be far newer than the original, which might have been thirty years old. I held it up and pivoted back to him. He held out his hand and I gave him the folder. He opened it, read, and nodded.

"Exactly as she said."

"I'm not following."

"Trust me, I'm barely keeping up with her myself. Some of the answers are in there," he said, pointing to the stack of papers he'd given me.

I sat down at my desk, considered the manuscript envelope, and pushed it aside. Mr. Lawrence reached forward and pushed it back, front and center on my desk. I blinked at him.

"What is this?" I asked?

"My wife's confession, though she'd certainly never use

that term. She printed it off this morning. Two copies. One for you, one for me. I'm not sure when she began working on it. It seems she deleted the file."

"This morning?"

"Yes."

I shook my head. "But she was in the hospital. How did—"

"It seems she planned it all out. She phoned me to come home, saying it was urgent. By the time I got there, it was too late. Much too late."

He rubbed at his quivering lower lip. I sat back with the feeling of two hands pushing hard into my chest.

"She killed herself?"

"I thought you knew that already."

"No. I'm sorry, I haven't even looked at your wife's body or reviewed the hospital's notes."

Not knowing what else to do, and wanting to avoid eye contact with him, I turned to my computer and began typing. It was a pathetic attempt to make it seem like I had a course of action. Mrs. Lawrence committing suicide? There were several times when I'd wished she'd done just that, but the idea of it happening was like imagining the Great Wall of China crumbling.

"Do you have certain software?"

Mr. Lawrence's question startled me. My screen was, in fact, dark, and for a horrified second I thought he'd seen it. But he couldn't possibly from his angle.

"I'm sorry?"

"I'm always curious about industry-specific software. I know the question must sound very strange. I apologize. I just need something to ground me. Pathetic as it may seem, software and spreadsheets do that."

"No, don't apologize. There is a software platform for funeral directors. Several, actually. I like one called Osiris."

"What do you like about it?"

"It helps manage every detail."

He accepted my generic answer with a grunt and looked down at his lap.

"Nathan," he said, "I don't see any reason to avoid the subject. I know how much my wife hurt you."

"I don't know what you're talking about," I blurted.

"She was very passionate about ideas. I think she loved concepts more than people. In fact, I'm sure she did. But she did have a genuine desire to help you and many other students. She just went too far. Much too far, as you'll see."

I placed Mrs. Lawrence's file atop the manuscript envelope, opened it and surveyed her order. "Looks like she wants cremation."

Mr. Lawrence mumbled something. He was almost hugging himself. I glanced at the older file, still open to the details of the mutual burial plans of a husband and wife.

"She didn't want to rest beside me," he said. "I didn't know anything about these other plans until I sat down and read what she'd left behind. Have you ever seen a wife make separate funeral plans from her husband in secret?"

"No," I said after a moment of reflection.

"It's like she killed herself and *then* divorced me. But I'll honor her wishes. She just makes it sound like I bullied her into a traditional funeral."

"What?"

"It's in your copy of the manuscript."

"Maybe one day I'll read it."

"You *must*," he said, leaning forward. "Please."

I scanned her file again. "She didn't want a memorial service."

"You and I might be the only people to come," he said. "Maybe we're having that memorial service right now."

"It's the funeral director's job to attend the service. That doesn't make me a mourner."

My own words shocked me. Never mind the affront to professionalism, I had never said something so vicious to another person under any circumstance, much less a fresh widower.

"I'm sorry," I said.

"It's OK to be angry. It's OK to bear a grudge. I'm trying hard not to hold one against her right now, but I think I would if I were in your shoes."

We held each other's stare. I didn't remember every time I stopped by Mrs. Lawrence's classroom to talk, but a few instances remained vivid. Had she ever mentioned a husband? Had she ever mentioned anything like a private life? Did it even cross my mind to ask, repayment for all the times she listened to my problems and took my loneliness seriously? It was impossible to recapture whatever assumptions I had about her back then, though it embarrasses me now to think I could have been so self-absorbed.

"I don't know what I feel anymore. It all happened a long time ago. I moved on."

"Sarah would be glad about that. I wish this meeting between us could have taken place about thirty years earlier."

"I'm not sure I understand."

"I would have helped you," he said. "I would have kept Sarah from going to your parents. I ask you to believe that I didn't even know this happened. She was already on thin ice with the school board. Your parents could have gotten her fired easily."

"My mom didn't want anyone to know. The shame Mom felt for me kept Mrs. Lawrence safe."

"I know Sarah felt awful—"

"If she felt awful, she could have quit."

"Quitting wasn't in her nature."

"Then she could have apologized at least."

"I think she did."

"Not to me."

He gestured to the big envelope. "I think it's in there. Maybe you can accept it, or maybe you can't. But there's no harm in looking."

Mr. Lawrence rose and extended his hand. I shook it by reflex.

"I'll arrange for the cremation. I don't have facilities to do it here. She—" I looked down at the paperwork again. "She didn't select any sort of urn or mausoleum. Not even a memorial plaque. What do you want done with the ashes?"

"I don't want them."

"That's fine," I said. "But you understand they have to be disposed of according to state law. There's a designated spot in the town cemetery for scattering ashes, if you'd prefer that."

"Honestly, I . . ."

"A decision doesn't have to be made today, Mr. Lawrence. Would you like some time to consider?"

He bit down a little on his bottom lip and nodded. Then I showed him to the door. There didn't seem to be anything left to say, but he surprised me on the porch with one cryptic, out-of-the-blue remark. *"I really didn't want to be a father."* The words and the hoarseness of his voice, like he was coughing smoke from his lungs, caught me so off guard that all I could do was nod. We shook hands a final time and he went to his car.

The whole encounter lasted about 40 minutes, but it felt like hours. I pulled at my hair a moment, my shoulder blades pressed against the door like someone trying to brace it against a mob. The only onslaught was in my head. I pictured the manuscript envelope. I saw myself opening it and becoming engrossed. Alternatively, I imagined throwing the whole thing into the trash can unread. I felt like I owed the first option to my future self, the second option to my past.

But Mr. Henshaw's case was the present. That's what

CONFESSIONS

mattered. That's what had to take priority. I hurried to the prep room and resumed his case, working on him more with muscle memory than plan and purpose. I got his hair just right. I swept the blush brush across his face in short, delicate strokes that brought life to his cheeks. As much as I wanted my mind to be blank, however, Mrs. Lawrence's face began asserting itself there. I thought of her in the hearse, a suicide. Was it an act of despair? Determination? One of a hundred other possibilities? Maybe the answer was in the manuscript as well.

It was more than thirty years ago, I thought. What does any of it matter? I was over it a long time ago. I should make sure the manuscript, whatever it has to say, goes into the oven with her.

The brush slipped, making a streak on Mr. Henshaw's skin. I cursed and started wiping away the excess cosmetic. Then I put all my tools down, turned from his body and walked out to the garage. I opened the hearse and stared at her enclosed body.

My memory needed something far hotter than crematorium flames to burn her away.

TIM

NATHAN AND I never did get that drink. I didn't even see him much over the next couple of months. Our paths only crossed whenever he was taking Bart on a drive and Bart wanted to see me. Nathan and I would smile at each other and make small talk while his dad walked around. Things might seem fine, but the awkwardness of that second meeting hung over us. Still, I repeated my offer every time, and Nathan always found a reason to decline. His rejection didn't upset me too much because, after all, I wasn't attracted to him and my journey toward becoming a straight man continued unabated.

Yes, I confess my get-togethers with Meghan Malone were becoming more frequent. Sometimes it seemed I had the Closed sign on the door so much my patients must have wondered if I'd moved away. My penis seemed to be developing a genuine fondness for Meghan's vagina. At her coaxing, we'd moved away from mere oral. The dentist had forsaken the mouth and gone traditional. We'd even done it on my examination chair with her straddling me, our bodies rocking so hard I thought the chair mount would break off the floor. Her hunger was devouring. I loved every inch of her and she loved every inch of me. I really was on the verge of asking her to be my girlfriend. It'd be the most insane thing I'd ever done, but I now had little reason to doubt what I wanted. Our get-togethers still hadn't gone much longer than thirty minutes, always during the day. A few times I'd thought about inviting her over to my apartment, or out for dinner, but fear held me back. What if I was leading her on? What if this flirtation with heterosexuality didn't last?

What if she wanted me to stay forever in Wentz Hollow?

As I contemplated the possibility of being cool with such a fate, I gained a fresh appreciation for the power of pussy and the hold it could take over a man's mind. But I hadn't reached the point of no return yet. My future still very much included leaving Kentucky behind forever. It's just I now sometimes thought it'd be great if Meghan came along with me.

Around two months into exploring my new sexual identity, I heard Johnny calling to me as I stepped out and started locking the door at the end of the day. I turned and saw him waving from across the street. His truck was parked further up, next to a shoe store. He was wearing old blue jeans and a sleeveless red muscle shirt. His baseball cap was turned around backward, and his hair poked out through the adjustable strap. I watched him jog over and I knew I wasn't a full convert just yet. Damn, he looked good.

"You got a second, Doc?"

He gestured to the door. Did he want to talk to me alone? I put the key back in the door in a hot second and I locked it behind us after we were inside. Johnny must have been working all day because he had a slight funk to him. I wasn't complaining, but I couldn't get over how different men and women were now that I'd sampled both sides. Meghan's whole body always had the scent of perfume or lotion. Johnny was all sweat.

"What is it, Johnny?"

He grinned. "You make out with Nathan yet?"

"No."

"Why not? He's not good enough for you?"

"He's fine."

"Doesn't sound like you're into him."

"Maybe he's not into me," I said.

I couldn't get over how physically imposing Johnny was in the small lobby with just the two of us there. It was like he'd grown an extra inch since that night on the porch.

"I think you were lying the whole time," he said. His tone was playful but with an edge. I couldn't tell if he was teasing or accusing.

"Lying about what?"

"Being a queer."

I laughed. "Who'd lie about that in *Kentucky*? I can't think of a single good thing that would come from that, right?"

"I don't know," Johnny said. "Tell women they can't have something, and they really buckle down sometimes."

"I don't have any idea what you're talking about."

Johnny went to the window and opened a slot in the blinds. "Have you seen my truck around here the last few weeks? I've been doing some wiring work over at the shoe store. Speaker wiring this time. Why Mr. Steger wants surround sound in his shoe store is beyond me. Maybe he wants to pump in some secret messages with the music."

"Subliminal messages?"

Johnny answered with a whisper. "*'Buy shoes. Buy shoes.'*"

"That's pretty funny."

He stared at me and whispered, "*Fuck pussy. Fuck pussy.*"

I swallowed. "It'd take more than a subliminal message to get me to do that."

"You sure about that, Doc? Like I said, I've been over in this neck of the woods a lot as of late. Seen the Closed sign in the window."

"Yeah, I've been out of town for a bit."

"Did you give Meghan Malone the key? Seems she comes in and out all the time while you're away."

He was so matter of fact I didn't even dare deny it. But I thought fast and said, "She's interested in becoming a dental hygienist. I've just been—"

"You've just been fucking her, that's what you've been doing. Guess Meghan's officially your Kentucky piece?"

"Johnny, that's ridiculous."

"Pickings around here so slim for a queer that he has to get himself a bitch to drain his balls?"

"That's right," I said, trying to joke. "It's pure hell, man."

"You went from drilling cavities to drilling a cavity."

"That's a good one. You should tell it to Bart."

Johnny moved a single step closer, but all at once he was towering over me.

"Are you really choosing Meghan's pussy over my brother?"

Suddenly he looked very serious. I really couldn't tell if he was messing around or really upset. He'd spent so much time mocking Nathan that I figured Johnny hated him, but people got clannish in this part of the country. People might hate having a faggot in the family, but if that faggot got dissed by an outsider, they declared war.

"Look, I've asked Nathan out for drinks. He always says no. I swear if he ever said yes I'd be happy to—"

Johnny slapped my back. The force of it knocked me forward a step.

"Relax, Doc. I don't really care one way or the other. But since you're still kind of new in town, I wanted to let you in on a secret. Something Meghan probably didn't tell you."

"What's that?"

"She's married."

"What?"

Johnny nodded. "She never mentioned it, huh?"

"No."

"I figured. I'm sure she puts her wedding ring in her purse before she heads out the door."

"Jesus Christ," I said, sitting down with a sudden, searing pain between my shoulder blades. Johnny kept standing and we looked at each other, social butterfly and asocial lepidopterist.

"I've fucked her a few times myself. Wasn't nothing serious. I knew I wasn't first, and I wasn't going to be the last. She got married around three years ago in Louisville. About six months into it, she comes home to visit her folks and ends up crying to me about how she's never getting it the way she wants it at home. How her husband didn't want her. So I fucked her again."

A sour taste filled my mouth. "What a surprise."

"It wasn't just for old time's sake, Doc. See, she married Steve Malone."

I shook my head. "Is that supposed to mean something to me?"

"Steve's Mr. Bigshot as far as Wentz Hollow is concerned. Got out of here with a baseball scholarship in 1991. Now he coaches the high school team. I was a little kid, but I remember him, and I know things about him no one else does. No one but Nathan. Steve gave him a black eye. Or maybe it was a bloody nose. I'll never forget. I was 5 and I saw my big brother running toward me with blood on his face. Goddamn."

"He bashed your brother for being gay?"

"He towered over Nathan. That's what I remember the most. I was scared the way a little kid is scared. Steve's still a big guy. But he's gotten fatter. I could take him in a fight pretty fast. But it was more fun to fuck his wife. I sometimes imagine back when I saw Nathan getting hit. I imagine being a little boy and looking up at Steve and saying, 'I'm going to grow up and fuck your wife stupid, bitch.' These days, Steve wouldn't say shit back to me. But he would to you."

"Why's that?"

Johnny laughed. "You may put the fear of God into someone when you're scraping their teeth, but otherwise you're just a little pocket queer."

"I'm 5'10"."

"Really? You look a lot shorter. Do yourself a favor, Doc. Call it off with Meghan. Or else be a lot more discreet."

Johnny turned for the door.

"You mean you told me all this just to warn me?"

"You sound like you're about to cry, Doc."

"I just thought you were mad at me."

"Why would I be mad at you? You don't piss off the family dentist, right?"

He left me standing in the lobby, staring at the floor as I considered what my life had become. I was a gay man having sex with a woman. With a married woman. Whose husband was some local legend. And she preferred me over him.

How was I supposed to be feeling? Sad? Cocky?

By the time I got home just fifteen minutes later, my mood had blackened, overwhelmed with a sense of betrayal. Meghan had used me. I'd been her boy toy. All those thoughts I'd had about having a relationship with her, and here she was with another guy. As I stared at myself in the bathroom mirror, I thought, *Gay men are renowned whores, but there's no whore like a cheating woman.*

This bit of breathless misogyny had me turning away from myself in disgust. Where the hell did I get off criticizing anyone? I'd never had any interest in marriage or even a relationship. And if this Steve guy wasn't even touching her, why shouldn't she be out getting what she wanted wherever she could?

Still, I thought, *she could have at least mentioned a husband.* What was I supposed to do now? Keep going on with her like I didn't know the truth? Hint that I *did* know and wait for her reaction? What would I do if she admitted it, started crying, and said she wanted to leave him for me?

I swear to God, in my mind I kept fantasizing it going down that way, and every time I told her I wanted that too.

I tried changing my thoughts to another subject, but the only other topic seemed to be this Steve guy beating the hell out of Nathan when they were kids. Call me sheltered, but I really hadn't encountered that type of person growing up. Even the most homophobic jock in my high school stuck to jokes and insults. My crush Conner, as straight and popular an athlete as they came, would have defended a gay kid from bullies. I was sure of it. Would Conner have turned into a gay basher if he'd been raised in rural Kentucky in the '80s?

Steve deserved to be cheated on. After what he did to Nathan it was poetic justice for a gay man to make him a cuck.

By now it was 7:00 and I'd been pacing back and forth in my apartment, thinking about my future, thinking about Meghan. If the straight life really was my destiny and not a bizarre fling, I needed to settle the question once and for all. I'd do it *tonight*.

I showered, changed into the clothes that still made me seem slim (with the help of a club's dim lighting) and made the three-hour drive to Lexington. I arrived at 10:30 and turned into the parking lot of a gay club called The Bar Complex. I'd only been here a couple of times since living in Kentucky. The place wouldn't have stood out much in Seattle, but its existence felt like a strange miracle in the South. I heard the dance music pulsing from within.

But there weren't any dancers when I walked in and gave

a look around. The bar had about 15,000 square feet of dance space, all of it empty. I saw maybe fifty people hanging out around the edges, their faces playing hide-and-seek with the strobing lights. They seemed to be looking out on the vacant space and seeing ghosts.

I'm not a good dancer. I didn't get that part of the gay gene. I didn't get fashion sense or interior decoration skills either. What I did have was a high threshold of humiliation, so I walked out to the middle of the floor and began moving to the beat in what I hoped didn't look pathetic. I needed a few drinks to lubricate my joints and make me look a little less like the Tin Man trying to get his groove on.

I pivoted, face tilted up at the lights, whose flashes made flares and bursts of color against my closed lids. Meanwhile I felt each and every sideline stare. I'd been among that crowd many times, looking out at the weird guy all alone on the floor like it's everyone's first dance in the middle school gym. I'd made my share of remarks and snickers. I welcomed and deserved them all now.

There was a tap on my shoulder.

I stopped and opened my eyes, which took a few moments to adjust. For a second, I thought the blurred face in front of me was somehow Nathan's. Then it resolved into a man who must have been pushing 60. He smiled and an unfortunate flash of light revealed his really bad teeth.

He began to dance. He moved better than me, low bar that it was, and I restarted my dancing to keep the situation from looking too awkward. A few men had amused expressions that I accepted as well-earned karma. Shallow bitches that we are, you'll find more judgement in a gay bar than there ever was at Nuremberg. I thought of many mean things I'd said in the heat of the moment, egged on by friends when I was younger and thinner. Once, when I was 22, I rejected a guy I thought outright ugly. He got bitchy and said, "So you're one of those fags who only sleeps with 10's?"

"Usually," I'd said. "But I'll do a threesome with two 5's. Gotta make sure the math adds up, right? Find a 9 to join us and I'll sleep with you."

He stalked away, leaving me feeling so superior. Looking back on it, I find only shame.

My dance partner let his fingers graze my right forearm.

"You're pretty good," he said.

"Not really."

"I'm Brady."

The name didn't fit him at all. It seemed too young somehow, a *bro's* name. His balding paunchiness screamed *Allen* to me for some reason, just as my own name fit my bland appearance, my safe job.

"I'm Jason," I lied.

"You live in Lex?"

"Just passing through."

"That's cool," he said.

We went on dancing. Brady grew increasingly handsy. At least a few more guys had come onto the floor, dancing in groups. No lone wolves.

"You thirsty?"

"Getting there," I said.

"How about I buy?"

"Beam and Coke?"

"Sure thing."

Brady seemed nice enough, but I wasn't about to let him get the drinks unsupervised and risk being roofied. We bellied up to the bar together. He got a Bud Light for himself.

"There's a corner over there," he said, pointing. "Want to talk?"

I wanted to tell him we could talk just fine at the bar and didn't need a remote corner, but he'd just bought me a drink so I went along with it. Considering how much he'd touched me on the floor, I understood the likelihood of an aggressive groping once he got me alone.

"Talking would be great," I said.

I followed him to a table and we sat down.

"I couldn't believe you were just dancing alone out there."

"Like I said, I was just passing through."

"And you stopped off at a gay bar?"

I smiled. "Is that what this is?"

He laughed. "Well, I'm glad you did."

I sipped at my drink. It was made stronger than I thought it would be. Maybe because bourbon was the official liquor of Kentucky, the bartender felt like he had to represent.

"Do you come here very often?" I asked.

"Once a week. Depending on how busy I am." He drank some of his beer, holding it in his right hand. His left hand grazed my kneecap. "I go for weekends when I can make it. The crowd's so much larger."

"Yeah, I know."

"I thought you said you were passing through."

I swallowed. "It's not my first time in Lexington."

"Do you travel for your job?"

"Yeah, I sell dental supplies."

"Bet you know your way around a mouth."

He gave my kneecap another squeeze. *Goddamnit,* I thought. Of course, the chances were always pretty high that he'd turn out to be a pervert, but the innuendo confirmed it. Not that I had any right to complain. I'd probably age to be just like him.

"I'm not looking for anything like that," I said.

Brady leaned back a bit, his eyes narrowing. "You were just looking for a quiet place to dance, is that it?"

"I don't know. Maybe talking is what I need."

As soon as I said it, I knew I'd stumbled on the truth. Granted, it was pathetic I had to drive three hours to find anyone to talk to, and Brady wouldn't have been the one I chose. But maybe he was the perfect candidate. An older man, maybe the oldest gay guy I'd ever spoken more than 10 words to. He was from a different generation, a different time. It occurred to me he was probably my age or younger when Stonewall happened. The realization had me cocking my head and staring at him like an oracle. *Give me your stories*, I thought. *Show me your scars. Teach me your wisdom.*

"Do you like older men?"

"I've got nothing against them," I said. "I hope to be one myself one day."

He placed a hand on my thigh. "You feel so solid. You must work out a lot."

"Never miss a chance to get in the gym."

"I can tell," he said. "You're pretty perfect."

"No one's ever called me that."

"Then I'm glad to be the first," he said.

Brady leaned toward me, clearly seeking a kiss. I put my hand up against his chest and shook my head. "Sorry, man. I just can't."

"Do you have a boyfriend?"

"I do not." I thought for a second and added, "I sort of have a girlfriend."

The old guy's eyes seemed to sparkle at this revelation. "We have so much in common."

"For real?"

"Yeah, for real. I've got a wife and two grown daughters."

"Bullshit."

Grinning, he took out his phone, pulled up an album and showed me. "My wife's name is Gina. My girls are Brandi and Sophi."

He swiped through a series of pictures. The family at home. The family on vacation. I asked to hold the phone and he let me. I inspected the screen as if I thought the images were fakes.

"So you're bi?"

"No, I'm gay. I love my wife, but it's not the same as it is with a man. You know?"

"Maybe. I'm . . . new to women."

"I didn't have sex with anyone until I was 26. By then the AIDS crisis was going on and I was scared. I felt pressure to get married."

"Does your wife know about you?"

"She does now. I came out to my family a few years ago. The truth was . . . well, you know the chest-burster scene in *Alien*, right?"

"I hear you," I said. "How did she take it?"

"We're separated."

I winced and wished I hadn't. Brady shrugged it off. "We're friends again. The nice thing is how our daughters unite us. We're a solid front when it comes to them."

"How did *they* react?"

"I think if they'd still been in their teens, it wouldn't have gone too well. But they were both out of college. Our family isn't religious or anything like that. It's encouraged a new openness in our family. We all communicate a lot better."

"You make it sound incredible," I said.

"It's been a good life."

I looked around us, and even though it made me a hypocrite, I just couldn't see what was so great. A closeted guy not indulging his sexuality until he was almost a senior citizen, and then having to do so in Kentucky? But I gulped back all the cynicism. Maybe he was bullshitting about his happiness. Maybe it was a lie he'd told himself until he believed it. I wasn't going to be the one to challenge him.

"So what's going on with you and this girl? Are you bi?"

"Honestly, hell if I know. I wasn't before I set foot in this state. What else do they put in the water around here besides fluoride? I mean, how many women do you have to sleep with before it makes you bisexual? Is one time enough? Does it have to reach a certain ratio? I've easily been with over a hundred guys—"

"Holy *shit*," Brady said.

"And now one girl. One time shouldn't be enough, right? That's like someone who's eaten meat his whole life calling himself a vegetarian because he tried a salad. What do you think?"

"I think I want to suck you off."

"Come on, man. We're actually talking here. It's nice. Don't ruin it."

"We can keep talking after I've drained you."

"Goddamnit, this is what's wrong with the whole community. It's all sex, all the time."

"Sorry I offended you."

"I just want to be taken seriously," I said. "Suddenly I've been with this girl, and I'm thinking about shit like having a family. Having kids. That's messed up."

"It's worked for me."

"Has it really?"

"I'm not lying. I cherish my girls. I wouldn't be complete without them."

I shook my head. "Maybe that's what I'm trying to do—be complete. But I could have a family with another guy. Why does it have to be with a woman? I've got to figure this out."

"Figure things out with a therapist. Sounds like you need one, Jason."

"That's cold."

Brady sat back, shaking his head. "Do you want your dick sucked or not? Because I'm getting a little sick of wasting my time."

I shoved the drink to him and said, "Don't let it go to waste."

"Where are you going?"

I stood up and said, "Home."

For a second I didn't move. *Home.* Was that Wentz Hollow? Was it anywhere?

Brady called out an apology, but I ignored it and left the bar. I went straight to my car and locked myself in. But I didn't start the engine. I found myself just staring at a fragment of my face in the rearview mirror. What was going on behind those eyes? How come the answers didn't come no matter how hard I looked? I thought if I kept on looking, my reflection would get creeped out and tell me what was going on. *This is what you're after. This is what you wanted from Meghan before you—we—knew she was married.* Instead, my mirror-self seemed even more lost, more questioning, and I broke the stare and rubbed my eyes.

Had I always been some sort of self-loathing gay man without realizing it? When had I ever suffered for any reason? My tuition loan aside, I'd never felt the sting of debt. I'd never been short a dollar. I'd never known real rejection or denial. I'd never been bullied. I'd never feared. It's like I'd developed myself into this perfect vase only to become jealous of the cracks in everyone else's pottery.

But even this felt too good for an excuse. *I've just been bored*, I thought. *That's the whole of it. I'm bored in Wentz Hollow.* I needed attention and in the end, I didn't care who gave it to me.

I was staring at my lap, wondering if I'd finally reached the plain truth about myself when a tap on the passenger side window startled me. Brady stood there, hands in his pockets.

I rolled down the window.

"Hey," he said.

"Hey."

"I really am sorry. I didn't mean what I said about wasting my time. It's just—I'm attracted to you, and you seemed to show some interest."

"I've just been having a hard time the last couple of weeks. I'm trying to deal with some stuff."

"Totally get it," he said. "I'd love to hear what's going on. I know I'm a stranger, but—"

I unlocked the passenger side door. Brady got in.

"Tell me who I am," I said.

He cocked his head. Give the guy credit for not getting out of the car right away. "You're brave. You got out on the dance floor by yourself."

"What else?"

"You're kind. You had a drink with me. Most of the men in there probably would have turned me down."

I nodded. My hands were on the steering wheel, turning it a little left and right. "Tell me something about me that's bad."

"What?"

"You're just saying nice things. Bravery can just as easily be desperation, right? Maybe I'm not kind, I just crave attention no matter who gives it to me."

"You're too hard on yourself."

"Isn't that like answering a job interview question about your greatest fault by saying you care too much?"

Brady let out a long sigh. "How about this: you're a hell of a lot more fucking trouble than you're worth?"

I laughed, nodding. "I think you just nailed it."

"Do I get a prize?"

He touched my thigh.

I glanced at my eyes in the mirror. They seemed just as lost as they were before, but I believed they belonged to a good person, a generous and understanding person. I looked at Brady and found him waiting with every hope in the world stamped on his face.

I eased the seat back and closed my eyes.

MRS. LAWRENCE

I NEVER TAUGHT GEOLOGY, but in so many ways that discipline offers a much better metaphor about life than anything found in biology. There's the surface erosion from years of steady abrasion and chafing, the endless frictions and tensions happening below the surface, and then building pressure and molten temperatures threatening an explosion. We have tectonic relationships to our society. It's easy to see many full-fledged volcanoes behind the wheels of cars even in Wentz Hollow; it's easy to feel the earthquakes as they stomp by in the grocery store, muttering under their breath. We befriend, we date, we sometimes even marry warning tremors, some violent enough to put a crack in the drywall of our living. But most of the time the roof never *quite* caves in; and when there are eruptions, the ashes never get thick enough to freeze us in place for all eternity. We grow older, we look different.

Sometimes we even change.

The second time Meghan Garton came to me, she had

transformed into Meghan Malone. I hadn't seen or thought about her in twenty-five years and presumed she left Wentz Hollow as most graduates did, returning only for holidays or funerals. I recognized her right away, as you always do with one's ghosts. Her hair was as blonde as ever, but her face had lost the fit angularity of youth. She was in no way out of shape for her age, especially by Appalachian standards, but a bit of fat rounded out her chin, and she was wider through the hips. The very slight bulge in her stomach meant something else.

"Mrs. Lawrence?" she said, standing on my porch. There was enough query in her tone as to be insulting.

"Since this is her address, I suppose I better be."

Her face lit up with a joy as bright as it was false. I'd been a teacher for far too long not to recognize practiced expressions. "Oh, I'm so glad to reconnect with you again!"

"Reconnect?"

"I heard you retired."

"Yes, four years ago."

"I thought you might have moved away after you quit."

"Quitting and retiring aren't exactly the same thing, Meghan."

Her eyes widened. "You remember me, Mrs. Lawrence?"

"Meghan Garton. Yes."

"Oh, now I'm Meghan Malone. I married Steve Malone. Do you remember him?"

"Yes," I said.

"We got married four years ago too. So while you were quitting, we were getting hitched. Isn't that funny?"

I stood there staring at her and battling the most unpleasant sense of surreality. Her smile was so wide and frozen I could see the tension in her face muscles.

"Steve and I came home last year," she continued. "Steve coaches baseball at the high school."

Processing this, I thought how much the *Herald* had

changed. Geraldine passed away 10 years ago. If she still ran the paper, Steve's return would have received a special edition. Maybe there'd been an article about it in the sports section. I never read that far.

"I assume he teaches too?"

"Math," Meghan said. "But he only does it so he can coach."

I shook my head. "That went for a quarter of the staff when I was there. I gave up complaining about it a long time ago."

"I always admired you because you complained."

"Is that so?"

"Mrs. Lawrence, you were the only teacher who ever cared. Whether you know it or not, you taught all of us to care too."

I sighed, staring at her through the screen door. "What do you want?"

"To come in and talk."

"About what?"

"Just things," she said, hands touching her stomach.

I shut the door in her face and walked over to the living room sofa and sat down to stare at the wall. The doorbell rang.

If I didn't work in my garden, I sat here staring at the wall. Day after day. Frank still worked despite being old enough to retire. We'd invested well and even without Social Security and my pension we could live without any major concerns. When we were much younger, I couldn't imagine wanting to retire, while he claimed to have pinpointed the exact date he'd never work again. I still remember the two of us lying in bed talking about it.

"May 18, 2018. A Friday. I've got it all figured out."

"I'll bake you a cake."

"No, I'll want something from the Kroger bakery."

"Fancy."

"Triple-layer chocolate."

"Fancier still."

"We have to celebrate right. The day of liberation doesn't come around very often."

"No," I said to the wall. "No, it doesn't."

The doorbell rang again.

Frank's appointed future date now belonged to the past, like everything else. I made comments about how we could start doing some traveling. I suggested the New England states and even purchased a Fodor's guide to show him my seriousness. He answered with noncommittal remarks.

"Sure, we could do that. I have plenty of vacation time."

Any other reference I made to his retirement brought further evasions, doubts about the true health of our retirement funds, the fiscal benefits of delaying taking Social Security by a few more years. And how could he leave the office when it needed his steady hand to navigate for the foreseeable future? The foreseeable future stretched on and on. My Fodor's guide grew outdated and I threw it away. Next time I'd get one from the library, in keeping with the concept of borrowed time.

Meghan knocked on the door and said, "Mrs. Lawrence? Is there something wrong?"

Only everything. It had become impossible to escape the notion that my husband wanted to avoid me as much as possible. Maybe full-time jobs are the great salvation of most marriages, keeping couples from realizing they can't stand each other's company for more than a few hours at a time.

"Mrs. Lawrence? *Mrs. Lawrence?*"

God, was she going to stand on the porch calling my name for the next hour? Very well then. Let her.

I went upstairs to my little office where I kept my computer and printer. That's where I'd been before Meghan showed up on my porch. The room, too small for anything except a single bed, was probably intended as a nursery. Except for the printer and computer, the tabletop had one other possession—the picture frame Frank gave me containing my editorial. The sticky note with Frank's loving message had long lost its adhesiveness and was taped in place, but the ink retained a remarkable brightness. *Don't ever stop being you.* I never did, and I don't think Frank ever stopped being Frank.

But somehow we stopped being each other *together.*

In the 15 or 20 minutes before Meghan Malone re-entered my life, I sat looking between the picture frame and the piece of paper, reflecting on my remarkable, even miraculous longevity at Wentz Hollow High. In conservative bureaucracies, liberal squeaky wheels only get the grease so they'll be easier to immolate. Somehow, I outlasted three principals, more school board members than I could count, scores of county commissioners, and several governors. Even Coach Skinner left before I did. Nathan's parents could have destroyed me if they wished, terminating my career in 1991. It's a rich irony the homophobia I wanted to destroy is the very thing that saved me from their wrath. They said nothing, fearing the embarrassment of a public inquiry, and I went on teaching as if my meeting with them never happened.

There was, however, one physical relic of the aftermath—a piece of paper. It was a lined sheet torn from a spiral-bound notebook, folded four times into a square. I found it pinned under my car's left windshield wiper at the end of the first day of school in the fall of 1991. Steven Malone was, I imagined, already in Louisville, and I knew from the talk in Principal Thompson's office that Nathan was being homeschooled his senior year. This was something of a scandal at the time, as homeschooling wasn't as popular an option as it became in the 2000s, and teachers wanted to know what Mrs. Ashcraft's problem was. The official reason was *religious objections to the curriculum.* No one spoke a further word on the matter.

So I had no reason to think either Steve or Nathan wrote

the note when I unfolded it. Like sinister flower petals opening, the note blossomed into a hateful message—

You're the biggest fucking cunt. I hope you die.

I stared at the words, rereading them several times before turning, thinking the author would be there waiting. But the parking lot was empty, and I knew I had little chance of discovering the culprit. We wouldn't have security cameras anywhere on campus until more than a decade later, after Columbine. Even our part-time security guard mostly snacked on turkey sandwiches in his office, which was a converted janitorial closet.

The letters were in block print rather than cursive. Maybe the writer hoped to disguise their handwriting, but they need not have gone to such trouble. Biology tests required little in the way of essay writing, so I had no familiarity with the penmanship of my students. As I held the note up to read it again, though, a kind of osmosis of understanding happened between the paper and my fingertips. Nathan could not have written the note. How could he have reached the school, since his mother no doubt kept him on lockdown? I also couldn't believe Nathan capable of writing such sentiments no matter how angry he felt.

No, Steven Malone wrote the note. I stood there nodding in my certainty and debating what to do. I considered reporting it to Principal Thompson, but that might lead to unwanted questions. *Can you think of any reason someone would leave you a note like this?* Considering my lingering notoriety after the newspaper editorial, I had plausible cover. But perhaps I shared more with Nathan's mother than I cared to admit. Investigations must be avoided.

From downstairs, Meghan rapped on the door again. She said something but her voice was too muffled to make out the words.

In addition to my desk, the room contained a file cabinet and a bookshelf. The cabinet contained everything from newspaper clippings to old articles I'd printed over the years. The largest folder contained all the photocopying I'd done at the University of Kentucky back in 1990. The pages were all yellow now, ashes of a dream denied. But at the front of that folder was the piece of paper left under my windshield. At the time, I wasn't sure why I'd saved it. Maybe my mind cataloged it as more evidence of the homophobia I wanted to destroy.

I pulled the paper out and brought it to the desk as Meghan went on knocking. I unfolded the page. Like a knife's edge immune to blunting, the words still cut. The same certainty returned. Steven Malone wrote this note, a parting shot at the happiness I'd cost him.

Cost *them*.

But Steven had married Meghan. What did that imply, if anything? A closeted adult? A confused teen who'd used Nathan for self-discovery? It was impossible to think Nathan meant nothing to him at the time, not if Steven really did write this note.

And he *did* write the note. He had to be its author.

I put the note back into the filing cabinet folder, went downstairs, and opened the front door. Meghan stood there as tense as a stretched rubber band.

"Mrs. Lawrence, are you OK? Why did you close the door on me?"

"I'm sorry. I had to see to something in the kitchen."

It was a pathetic excuse, but Meghan seemed ready to latch on to anything. "Oh, I'm always forgetting to watch the stove when I'm cooking Steve's dinner," she said, stepping in at my gesture. "I can't tell you how often I've almost burned the house down frying chicken because I get lost in something on the computer. Thank God for the smoke alarm, right?"

We went over to the sofa.

"When did you meet your husband?"

"In Louisville. He went to school there, you know."

"A baseball scholarship, wasn't it?"

"Yes," she said. "For a while it seemed like he might get drafted into the Major Leagues, but he got hurt. He played a few seasons in the minors and then he got cut."

"That's too bad. I'm sorry to hear that."

"Oh, he hadn't been playing for years even before I met him. We just happened to be in the same bar. I recognized him but he didn't know who I was. He's a few years older than me so we weren't at Wentz High at the same time."

"I remember," I said.

"Like I said, it was just chance."

"So much of life seems to be that way. What were you doing in Louisville, Meghan? Did you go there for school?"

Her eyes dipped toward the floor. "I never went to college."

"I see."

"I wanted to be a model. Mom thought I had a really good shot as long as I got to a big city. I did some photo shoots. I was even on the cover of a magazine. I still have the pictures if you'd like to see them."

I smiled. "I'm glad you found success."

"I wouldn't have if it wasn't for what you did for me."

Keeping the disappointment out of my expression proved hard. Over the years, no student had ever come back to visit me after they graduated. Maybe it's the nature of the subject matter. Adolescents are impressionable and develop crushes on their English teachers. I've listened to more than one colleague share stories about how an alumnus sought them out a decade later to say, "I just wanted you to know what your feedback meant to me. You helped me grow as a poet. I just self-published this chapbook. I want you to have a copy. See, I dedicated it to you?" The bitter part of me wanted to call my colleagues liars, but they always backed up the story with evidence. Kids came back to talk to their English teachers, they came back to talk with their coaches. But no one returns to reminisce over dissected frogs.

The idea that Meghan should be the first student to ever visit me and thank me just added injury to insult. I looked at her face and saw the same simple cunning I noticed the first time she came to me for help.

"Yes," I said. "I suppose a baby would have been a terrible burden for a model."

My remark seemed to leave her speechless. I'd not intended it to be cutting, though in hindsight the dryness of my delivery must have made it sound acerbic. Meghan left soon after, and I did not imagine I'd hear from her again. This was well enough. I doubted I'd glean any information on Steven Malone that would help me understand who he was and what he'd felt toward Nathan. I could only hope, in a strange way, that at that point in time, when I saw them on the baseball field, Nathan had meant the absolute world to him. True, such a discovery would deepen the tragedy of my error; but it also meant Nathan had been loved out of pure desire. That's much more than many people get.

But my assumptions were wrong. Meghan returned the next day. I had a flower bed on the east-facing side of the house. Nothing fancy—black-eyed Susans, purple coneflower, apricot zinnias—but it occupied my time. I liked to work on it in the morning, before the heat and humidity grew too high. It was 10:00 in the morning and I was on all fours pulling weeds when I heard the footsteps. My broad-brimmed sun hat blocked my peripheral vision, but I just presumed it to be the mailman.

"Mrs. Lawrence, I'm glad I caught you."

Caught felt like the correct word. I looked up at Meghan from my knees and she smiled down on me like any benevolent warden.

"What's that?" she said.

"Excuse me?"

"The purple one, Mrs. Lawrence."

"Russian sage."

"I think you're the real sage."

I laughed at that. "A female sage is sometimes called a witch. Do you think that suits me better?"

"Of course not! Why would you say that?"

"I'm sure just about everyone in Wentz Hollow has called me that at least once. Or thought it in their heads."

"Not me. I wasn't lying yesterday. You cared and you taught us to care."

She touched her stomach. There was almost a pinching action to her fingers, like she wanted to pluck something out. It was clear she saw me noticing. At once, she became teary-eyed. Her lower lip trembled.

"I'm in trouble again," she said. "I need your help like the last time, but—"

She looked all around.

"It's not something you want to talk about where anyone else can hear," I said.

"I knew you'd understand."

"Oh, I *understand*. But I can't help you. All I'm doing is working on this garden, and then I'm going to take a nap. Mind moving to the left? You're blocking the sunlight."

Instead, Meghan knelt beside me in an unsteady crouch, as if she were months into her pregnancy rather than a few weeks. She teetered a moment and I automatically reached out to steady her. She smiled and patted my hand.

"Do you believe you have to live with your mistakes, Mrs. Lawrence?"

"I'm not interested in a philosophical—"

"Steve's not the father."

I settled back on my heels and stared at her.

"I guess you of all people might have known that," she

continued.

"What's that supposed to mean?"

"I never told Steve I'd heard anything nasty about him in high school. I was just in 8th grade when he graduated. Steve was a jock I had a crush on from afar. Then some of the older girls I knew, who were already at Wentz High, started saying he was a faggot. There was talk about him and another boy being caught together by the biology teacher."

"Nothing like that ever happened. Whispers and rumors last a long time around here."

"Yes, they do."

"Did they say who the other boy was?"

She seemed surprised by the question and shook her head. "Just some other jock. I remember when I started at Wentz and had my first gym glass. I was looking at the trophy case that's in the hallway. You know the one?"

"I can't say I spent much time around the gym," I said, reaching into the flowerbed to snag a few overlooked weeds.

"There was a picture of Steve with one of his baseball bats and a list of all the records he set. Most home runs, most stolen bases. The records still stand. I was staring at the photo, totally in love with his face and liking how the cap sat on his head. In fact, that's how I knew it was Steve when I saw him in the bar. He was wearing a cap just like he was in the picture. How many ways are there to wear a hat? I know it sounds dumb, but he just does it differently. Anyway, I'm looking at the photo and this boy came up and says, 'You think he ever put that bat up his ass?' I'll never forget that. Hell, I remembered it when I saw him at the bar. He was with a lot of guys, and I thought, *What if?* But that night he looked all man, all *straight* man, and that fierce little 8th grade girl who'd always wanted him came forward, except now she looked like a model and had confidence. I wowed him. We had sex and it was just as good as I'd imagined. I'm thinking, *Those rumors weren't true. This guy isn't a faggot*. We really did have a whirlwind romance. He proposed to me a few months later. But after we married, I found out who he really is. He's good about clearing his browsing history on the laptop, but not so good when it comes to his iPad."

I held up my right hand to gesture my impatience and exhaustion. "I'm not a marriage counselor, Meghan. Why are you telling me this?"

"Just to explain."

"You're assuming I care one way or the other."

"I know you do. Maybe sometimes too much."

"You've got that right," I said, pulling at the adjacent grass now because there were no weeds left.

"Why are you doing this, Mrs. Lawrence?"

"Doing what?"

"Acting like you don't want to help me?"

"Maybe you're not worth it. Maybe none of you girls were. I tried to make a difference—"

"You *did*."

I had to hand it to her; she was good at putting conviction into her voice. Who knew Wentz Hollow could produce such an actress? Who knew I could still be susceptible to such a performance?

She put her hand on my left forearm.

"I've already said that if it wasn't for you, I'd be a high school drop-out, doomed by a dumb mistake. I had no other options and you knew that. You took action. You saved me. Please save me again."

"But you're an adult. You can help yourself."

"No, I really can't. In some ways I'm more helpless now than I was as a kid. Steve's the breadwinner. If I got an abortion, I couldn't conceal the cost from him."

"You want me to give you the money?"

"It's not just that. I'd have to go to Louisville. Maybe spend the night. And what happens if something goes wrong?

You know how rough women have it."

"It's rougher when they're stupid."

"I know," she said in a quiet voice, though I doubted she took the criticism to heart.

"Is there something else going on here, Meghan? Does Steve know you're pregnant?"

She nodded.

"So he knows he's not the father?"

"That's just it. He thinks he is. After I knew I was pregnant, I convinced him to have sex with me. We don't do it too often, but that night he did. It was soon enough to be convincing, and I just wanted to cover up that I cheated on him. I never thought he'd be excited about being a dad."

"God, Meghan. The situation you've gotten yourself into."

"If he knew I had an abortion, it would destroy him. It has to look natural, like last time. That's why I'm here. What you gave me worked once. It can work again."

"I'm *done* with that sort of thing. I should never have—"

"You saw teen girls in trouble and you acted. It wasn't immoral when you helped Jessica or me. Thank God we could count on you."

Jessica, Meghan. Add to that Sarah, Rachel, and Brianna. Five girls who'd counted on me. Whether or not they thanked God afterward wasn't my business.

"You still don't need my help," I said. "The instructions for making what I gave you are all online. You can look up the emmenagogues yourself."

"Emmen-*what*?"

"Abortive herbs. Queen Anne's lace seeds, mugwort. Even parsley. You may have everything you need in your kitchen right now."

"Just so you know, I *have* looked on Google. But what can I say? I'm not as smart as you. All those ingredients, it makes me feel like a chemist."

"Well, this time you're just going to have to make do for your—"

My breath became short. I felt a sudden tightness in my chest, and a dull pain in my left arm. I slumped away from Meghan, hearing the sound of my heart pounding in my ears. The sound of her calling my name made a dim impression. She might have been shouting it for all I knew. I slumped over, my left temple shearing through a clump of flowers that offered no softness at all. Meghan was on her feet now. I thought she was just going to run off and leave me. But then she turned, and I saw the cell phone in her hands. She was poking the screen and shaking it. I could read her lips.

"I can't get a damn signal!"

Just at the moment she seemed ready to whirl and scream for help, the attack passed. I could breathe again and my chest relaxed. The pain in my left arm ceased with all the suddenness of a light switch being flicked. I was even able to sit up a little.

Meghan gaped at me like I'd resurrected myself from the dead. She bent down to me, one hand supporting my right shoulder. "What happened, Mrs. Lawrence? That was so scary. Oh my God."

I had gratitude for the genuine worry in her voice. The actress was gone. Fear had shocked Meghan into compassion. It didn't just seem a matter of her trying to protect her golden goose until the necessary egg got laid. She rubbed my back and asked if I had a landline so she could call for an ambulance.

"I don't think calling 911 is necessary."

"Are you sure?"

"When you get older, these things happen," I said, hoping I could be a good actress too. I took a deep breath and felt no pain or discomfort. "I've been out too long. The day's getting hotter and I haven't been drinking water."

"Why don't we go inside? Take my hand and I'll help."

I accepted her offer. She eased me up, with all the care of a dedicated nurse, and never broke contact with me as we entered the house.

"My mamaw had a heart attack a few years ago," Meghan said as she helped me toward the sofa. I started to object, realizing my clothes must be as dirty as my hands. But Meghan parked me there anyway.

"I'm sorry to hear that. Did she pass away?"

"No, she pulled through. Thank God."

I started to say, "God had nothing to do with it," but good manners stopped me. Meghan sat down on the opposite chair and leaned toward me.

I rubbed my forehead and took another deep breath. My strength was returning. The brief spell outside, scary as it had been, felt like a figment of my imagination. I met Meghan's gaze and said, "Do you love Steven?"

"I don't want to hurt him, if that's what you mean."

"It will do."

"You're going to help me, aren't you?"

"I need you to tell me something first."

"Name it."

"Who *is* the father of your baby?"

"Just a guy, Mrs. Lawrence."

"I deduced that. What's his name? How did you meet him?"

"Online," she said. "Just someone I met online. His name is Tim."

"Does *he* know you're pregnant?"

"*No.* I'm not sure what he'd do if he found out. So that's another reason I need to get this taken care of fast."

I swallowed, my throat very dry, and accepted her answer. "I see," I said.

"How soon can you make it?"

"I need to learn the process again. It's been many years,

and I don't have access to lab equipment the way I used to. Not that glass beakers and Bunsen burners are required. A few pots will work fine."

"Tomorrow?"

"No, Meghan. It certainly won't be tomorrow. I need a few days at least, and I'll need reimbursement for any ingredients I buy. I think that's fair."

"Absolutely!"

"Very well," I said. "Come on Monday. I'm sure I'll have it ready for you by then."

"But that's four days. Are you sure it will take that long?"

"Very sure."

We stood up together and she gave me a fierce hug. As she left, I had trouble seeing her as an adult woman, insulting as that may sound. She walked away like a nervous teen girl, and I stood on the porch pondering her relationship to Steven Malone. This will no doubt seem strange for many reasons, not least of all being I may have had a minor heart attack just fifteen minutes earlier. What happened to me in the garden? Shouldn't I get myself checked out? The obvious answer was yes, and I'm certain any younger version of myself would already be calling the doctor. But there comes a point as you age where you simply don't want to know what troubles lurk in your bloodwork and in your X-rays. Not investigating isn't the same as ignoring the problem. Rather, call it enlightened neglect.

I felt fine the rest of the day. Better than fine, in reality. Researching the old formula and remembering the preparation steps proved invigorating. A surprising feeling of purpose pervaded me as I went through my old books and recovered yellowed pages of handwritten notes. I didn't even notice when Frank came home. Very much like it used to be in the old days, except my preoccupation wasn't expected now, and he stopped to ask me what I was doing.

"Just fixin' to go through some old stuff."

He laughed, causing me to look up.

"Did you say *fixin'*?"

"I guess I did."

"Well, it finally happened. You've become a Southerner."

"I could only hold out so long, Frank."

He went into the bedroom to change into sweatpants and a T-shirt. This was a newer habit he'd adopted in the last few years. It used to be he kept on whatever he wore to the office, minus the suit jacket and tie, until he got ready for bed. Now he allowed himself a measure of comfort, a conciliatory gesture to the legendary and delayed *Day of Liberation*.

I had the information I needed, so I tucked away my notes, closed the books, and put them back on the shelf. For a moment, as I heard Frank humming to himself, I considered telling him about my little health incident this morning. He'd react in the appropriate manner, with concern and disbelief that I didn't call an ambulance. He might even put on his work clothes and insist on taking me to the hospital himself. The idea of his old feelings for me being so visible proved hard to resist.

But I said nothing. When I woke the next day, Frank was already up and gone, and I set about buying the necessary ingredients for the drink. This took the better part of the day.

I never wanted children of my own. After I returned and began making a trial preparation, the thought occurred to me that maybe Frank did. He'd said he didn't many times, as I'd made my own wishes crystal clear before we married. But once you've lived long enough to discover how people in relationships lie to each other and lock away troublesome truths, all considerations become possible. It seems certain to me now that he would have liked children all along. Like almost everything else at this point, acknowledgements would be a matter of too little, too late. Frank as a father: I could see it. He would have been a father in all the best ways, patient and understanding, gentle. The perfect father for a young Steve, a young Nathan. Maybe if I'd bent just a little and given him a son or daughter, the estrangement between us wouldn't seem so acute. Maybe there'd be a grandchild by now whose presence would have lured him into early retirement. The two of us as babysitters: this too I could see. Envisioning, however, will never be the same as desiring.

As I stood at the stove bringing the water to boil, it became impossible for me not to imagine Frank and I changing places with Steve and Meghan. What if I'd gotten pregnant due to a mistake and Frank found out? Would it give him the moment he'd always wanted to walk back his statements on fatherhood and say, "Maybe we should think about going through with it?" Would I crumple upon seeing the flash of hope in his eyes? Would I agree to his face while scheming behind his back to abort the fetus and make it seem like an act of nature?

Amid these questions, Frank's face became superimposed over Steve's, or at least whatever mannequin my imagination used in place of the real thing. I had no copies of the school yearbook to refresh my memory, so I had just a vague notion of what he'd looked like in high school. I supposed he'd filled out quite a bit, gotten pudgy, maybe grown a beard. A fuzzy copy of Coach Skinner, perhaps. Nothing special. But the strange amalgamation of his face and Frank's threw me. I thought I looked at two men desperate to become fathers for their own private reasons and here I stood, thwarting both.

I looked down at my cooking. The water had started boiling. The ingredients sat on the countertop in five ceramic ramekins usually used to serve ice cream.

Minutes passed as I stared into the pot, the steam moistening my cheeks. Tears were not part of the formula but I added a few drops before I even realized I'd started crying. Then I reached for the first bowl, full of crushed mugwort, and tipped it toward the water. Half the contents went into the pot. I sat the bowl down and picked up the next, containing pennyroyal herb. Once again I added half of the ramekin's contents.

And so it went down the line. I told myself it didn't matter whether I used the correct amount of ingredients or not, since this was just a test run. This was the equivalent of throwing warm-up pitches. I can't say how often sports analogies disciplined my thinking, but such occurrences were few and far between. Of course it had to be baseball. Steve Malone, what do you want? What am I about to do to you?

I took the pot off the stove and dumped the contents down the kitchen sink and ran the garbage disposal a lot longer than necessary.

NATHAN

SO MANY GAY KIDS go through the same process of total rejection by their parents. Sometimes it happens when they're old enough to make it on their own. Sometimes the only option is the street. It's their fate to be orphaned long before their parents die. Or is *orphan* the right term for children who are dead to their parents? Orphan, ghost—the umbrella word is *haunted*.

My mom died when I was 29, twelve years after I fled Wentz Hollow. Altogether, it's been almost thirty years since I last saw her, and now I have trouble remembering the sound of her voice. The memories I do have consist of the terrible final year we lived together, my senior year when I seldom left the house and saw no one but family. Dad seemed to rush off to work as early as possible and stay late to avoid seeing me. Even Johnny seemed frightened of me. Well, why wouldn't he be, with our mother always making vague pronouncements about my *sickness?* More than anything else, that's what I remember now: her voice flavored with those awful sentiments.

CONFESSIONS

"It's not right," I said, staring down at Mrs. Lawrence's covered body. I'd gotten it onto a cadaver lift without removing it from the bag and transported it from the hearse to the prep room. I began lowering it onto a sliding tray for cold storage. "I shouldn't remember your voice better than my mother's. But God help me, I do. Your voice in kindness, your voice in certainty, your voice in its damn relentlessness. I remember it in the living room as you looked me in the eyes. You were speaking to my mom but you were looking at me, and I didn't understand why your eyes were so bright. I thought you were happy to be hurting me."

I started to slide the tray into the refrigerator but stopped before her body went all the way inside. Then I pulled the tray out. My hands went to the bag zipper.

Technically I didn't have to look at her at all since she'd chosen cremation. As with Steve and Meghan's child, a third party would handle that process. There'd be no painstaking care with cosmetics, no dressing the corpse as I'd done with Mr. Henshaw. In this way, it was like fate had intervened to keep me at arm's length from Mrs. Lawrence one final time.

But to hell with fate.

I pulled the zipper down. The bag split open, revealing the old, naked flesh. Her bloodless face had no peaceful repose to its expression. Even death hadn't dulled her air of determination and decision. As I pulled the zipper lower, I felt like an archaeologist opening the sarcophagus of an ancient queen, her authority forever stamped on her remains, obvious and immutable.

The zipper reached her hands. I saw the cut on her left wrist and began sobbing.

"I owe everything to you," I said, cupping her left hand between my palms. I couldn't say if I was thanking her or cursing her, but the words themselves were right. Whatever I was and whatever I wasn't stemmed from her and the actions she took.

My tears were brief. It took a few ragged inhales, but I got control of myself to a large degree. I allowed myself a closer inspection of the cut. It looked to be efficient, like she knew what she was doing. No doubt she'd researched the technique before employing it.

I went back to holding her hand.

"I used to think about suicide a lot," I said. "Even attempted it once. I still can't believe it happened, but that's how depressed I'd gotten. It was during my sophomore year in college. Did you know I used to wonder if you thought about me? Sometimes I thought you'd somehow track me down and send me a long letter explaining everything. For a few of those early years even my parents didn't know where I was. Alone, scared, and angry don't translate to good grades in college. I almost flunked out my freshman year.

"I don't think you'd be too proud of me if I told you some of the things I did to get by. I hate myself for caring about your opinion one way or the other. You ruin my life and part of me still wants to make you *proud*? What bullshit is that? All I can say is, there was a point in my early 20s when I thought I could feel myself decaying, and I'd think of you and Mom, and this formaldehyde of hate would rejuvenate me. I imagined forcing the two of you to fight to the death. Did you read her obituary in the paper? Did you gloat? I didn't even learn about it from my dad or my brother. I got told by an older cousin who found me through a MySpace profile I created once and forgot about immediately. Mom was in the ground three months before I even knew it. That shook me in ways I can't even begin to describe.

"I've seen so much family conflict over death. More than I ever imagined could exist. Petty arguments between brothers and sisters over funeral arrangements, who gets to speak first, whose flowers get pride of place by the coffin, whose sons get to be pallbearers. And I've stood among it all trying to be this serene presence the family could turn to with their needs and desires. How would any of them react if they knew I hadn't even gone to my own mom's funeral? If they learned I didn't even know she'd died?

"Sometimes it doesn't seem like she is dead. My Dad has dementia and he forgets all the time. The living room furniture is exactly as it was the day you came over. The chair you sat in is still there, old and worn out like everything else. Dad will sit in that chair, fidgeting, and sometimes he'll crane his neck toward the kitchen and call out Mom's name. And when she doesn't come, he gives this toothless, happy smile, shakes his head and says, 'Oh, I guess she can't hear me.' Dementia is a hell of a thing. Perhaps you had it too. I could see you getting the diagnosis and deciding to kill yourself. You were always the sort to go out on your terms."

Thinking I'd said everything there was to say, I began zipping the bag up. Just as the pull tab reached her chin, though, I knew I had one thing to say, a confession of sorts, and I had to say it straight to her face.

"I wish I could have been the person you hoped for. In so many ways, the revolution you wanted seems to be here. Every other week there seems to be an article about some popular high school athlete coming out and standing up for themselves. Gays and lesbians going to the prom and having the time of their lives. It's what you wanted. Maybe, somehow, if I'd just been strong enough, we could have made it happen together here in Wentz Hollow, decades ago. Whenever I see those feel-good stories, I have so much regret. It still didn't give you the right to do what you did."

I zipped the bag up with a final quick, forceful pull.

How I wished memory could be closed with as much ease and permanence. I found myself reliving the worst impromptu parent-teacher conference of all time. It's gone now, but at the time we had a piano bench in the living room. I never knew what happened to the piano itself, but I was sitting on the bench, my hands tucked beneath my thighs. Mom and Dad were on the couch to my right. Dad looked irritated because he was going to be late to work, but he knew the importance of such an extraordinary visit and wanted to stay. I couldn't read Mom's expression at all. I think part of her thought Mrs. Lawrence was there to spring a wonderful surprise, some magical follow-up to that science fair blue ribbon she'd bestowed on me. As for Mrs. Lawrence, she sat on the armchair directly across from me, relaxed at first, like she'd been invited for coffee. She had an enormous folder with her, stuffed with documents. Not knowing what else it could be, I thought it was some official folder the school system had been keeping on me since kindergarten.

She began by saying how special I was, how bright and important. A natural leader who just didn't realize his potential. I began to relax. My parents were all smiles, beaming at me and nodding. Mom said something like, "I've always thought so too."

Then, just as naturally as the wind changes directions, Mrs. Lawrence started talking about homosexuality and oppression and bullying. She tapped one finger on the file folder as she spoke. Now Mom and Dad just looked confused. Dad said, "Are you saying Nathan's been bullying some queer kid?"

Mom turned to me and said, "Nathan, is that true?"

I shook my head, having no other response. That's when I caught sight of Johnny. He was crouched by the entry into the hallway, hugging the wall. He was staring at me as he listened.

Mrs. Lawrence said, "No, I'm afraid you don't understand. Nathan's not bullying anyone. I'm here because I think he could be instrumental in helping me start a new club in school. One that might help students like him avoid being bullied."

Mom zeroed in on the implication like a circling hawk

spotting a field mouse. "What do you mean by that, Mrs. Lawrence?"

It was the only time in my brief acquaintance with her that Mrs. Lawrence looked a bit afraid. She looked at me like she needed help, needed me to come out and say what needed to be said. I remember sinking into myself, feeling my hands tingle from sitting on them for so long. That and Johnny, who'd now decided whatever was going on must be a game. He made faces at me. He jumped up and down and then bounded into the living room, hands over his mouth with the sweetest little giggle and happy eyes. The worst miscalculation of his young life. Dad got up, grabbed him by the arm and said, "Goddamnit, I said go to your room!" I don't know if Dad had really told him this before or not, but Johnny started crying and Dad hauled him away.

"I said what did you mean about kids like Nathan being bullied? Why would Nathan be bullied? What's he done?"

I thought I saw a cloud of old suspicions in Mom's eyes, suspicions I'd never realized she harbored.

Mrs. Lawrence was overmatched and the knowledge of it showed on her face for just a moment. Then she became very sober, sat up very straight, and I could see she'd decided what she must do. In my imagination over the years, I've seen myself standing up to interrupt her before she said anything. I stand up and say, "It's none of your business. Neither of you have the right to do or say anything to me." But such moments belong to movies alone. Kids don't give bold monologues to adults, and frightened and humiliated kids speak only with a rabbit-inflected body language.

So I did not stand up. Mrs. Lawrence outed me, and my mom's face darkened almost to a shade of purple. Anger transformed her. In her light green house dress with her graying black hair pulled back from her forehead, she looked like a figure from another time, like depictions of mothers you see in photographs from the Great Depression, doomed to endless unbearable sorrow. She didn't yell at Mrs. Lawrence straight away. That came later. Instead, Mom's first reaction was to stare at me and say, "Is it true?"

"Tell her, Nathan," Mrs. Lawrence said. "It's necessary. You can do this."

Dad came back and surprised everyone by going straight out the door. We heard his truck start up. I knew he'd heard every word and just needed the safety of the mines. Mom didn't call after him. She already knew she was in charge.

I began crying. I couldn't answer either of them, and that's when the shouting match began between them. It was them screaming and me crying and Johnny wailing. Two boys in tears, two women dry-eyed with rage. Before long, Mom demanded Mrs. Lawrence leave and threatened to call the police if she didn't go.

Then Mrs. Lawrence delivered the final blow. She held out her hand like she expected me to take it and go with her. Like she intended to adopt me on the spot. Maybe she thought I wasn't in a safe place, that Mom might murder me. But that was her own doing. What kind of biologist was she? Evolution can take millions of years, but she wanted it in the speed of a minute. I wouldn't forsake the water for land, so she dragged me out of it. I wouldn't shed my tail fast enough so she chopped it off. I looked at her hand and it was like she wanted me to grip the razor blade she'd used to mutilate me.

Mom ordered me to my room, and of course I went. That's when I really broke down and went through a series of chest-heaving convulsions that were too deep for tears. I didn't hear Mrs. Lawrence leave, but all the shouting had stopped. What I did hear was the sound of a car horn and wheels going fast up the road past my house. I darted to the window and just got a glimpse of Steve's car. I closed my eyes and tried to think a message to him explaining why I wouldn't be coming to meet up.

Steve drove a beige 1989 Plymouth Acclaim. Not a cool kid's car by any means, but he looked so good behind the wheel. When I started at Wentz High, I used to see him hanging out after school in the empty parking lot, his jock friends all gathered around that car, the music blasting. Sometimes the guys were in their sports uniforms, getting ready for practice. Some were shirtless. I admired them all, their confidence, their looks, their friendship. I just wanted one of them to notice me, to wave at me. They never did.

Besides school, a geographic coincidence brought me into Steve's orbit. There was a small lake about a mile past my house. Since we lived in the last house on the road before coming to the lake, some people think we owned it. The lake belonged to no one as far as I knew. Dad used to take me up there when I was little. I'd float milk jugs and pretend they were battleships I had to destroy with artillery shells. Dad and I would throw rocks at them until they sank. He only took me up there during the day, often in the morning. By the afternoon and sometimes at night, cars full of older kids went up the road and didn't come back for hours. Mom wouldn't allow me to walk up to the lake if she saw more than one car go past.

The lake's existence seemed to be a secret passed down from generation to generation of upperclassmen at Wentz High. I'd see Steve and his buddies in that Acclaim drive past my house while I sat alone on the porch, trying to entertain Johnny like a good big brother should. One time in my sophomore year, Steve passed and honked the horn. I grinned and waved without any evidence I'd even been seen. Johnny became still and asked me who they were.

"My friends," I said. "I was supposed to hang out with them at the lake. They keep asking me and I keep forgetting."

Johnny looked at me with even more awe than usual. My life outside of the house was a complete mystery to him, but even at the age of 4 he must have been starting to sense I had no friends. No one came over to see me. No one called. What's the minimum age for a little brother to realize his older brother is pathetic?

Then the awe went out of him, and he went back to asking me to do what he always wanted. "Will you push me in the swing?"

There's a single tree in this field on the other side of the road across from the house. We didn't own the field or the tree any more than we owned the lake, but the tree felt like ours all the same. Dad put a tire swing on the lowest branch suspended by a sturdy chain. When I was Johnny's age, Dad and I went out to that swing every day, but of course those trips had stopped years ago. Dad never wanted to push Johnny, so I took over the role. Sometimes, when I was at my loneliest, I snuck over to the tree by myself and sat down, hugging my knees to my chest. And I'd cry. You can't overlook the right setting when you need a good cry. The tree was far enough away from the house that I knew I could wring the sadness out of me the way I never could in my room. The world offers few crying places, but some people are brave enough or desperate enough to cry anywhere. Under that tree I could acknowledge my loneliness and dwell in it. My private tree. My private agony.

Johnny repeated his plea. His face was so open, his eyes as wide as a Disney character. But on this particular day, I gave his head a pat and said, "I need to go up to the lake and see the guys."

"Can I come?"

"No."

He went into a pout, and I headed off. I don't know what I had in mind or what I'd say to the guys. Part of me just hoped to see them shirtless and wet, but what I desired went far beyond horniness.

CONFESSIONS

As my thoughts churned, I began running even though I thought I was speeding myself toward a disaster. I had no reason to think Steve or any of his buddies wanted to be friends with me. Maybe they'd laugh at me. Maybe they'd throw me into the lake, a baptism of humiliation. *To hell with it*, I thought. In school I was beneath notice, feeling like I had this shell around me all the time. If I didn't break it, it was going to turn into a permanent wall. You reach a crisis point where paralysis no longer works and even a terrible decision is better than no decision at all.

So I continued up that old road, slipping here and there on gravel. But it was OK not being silent. Steve would have Led Zeppelin or AC/DC blasting so loud an elephant could charge them and they wouldn't hear.

So why didn't I hear any music?

It took me about fifteen minutes to reach the lake. I saw the Acclaim parked and quiet over to the right. The engine wasn't running. The doors were shut. I stopped and stared. Had this all been a joke? Were they trying to trick me? Wasn't that a head peeking out from behind the tree on the left? Did I hear stifled laughter?

I moved toward the car taking far more cautious steps, cringing at the slightest crunch of gravel. I reached the trunk and looked toward the lake, still about 40 yards away. Steve stood at the water's edge alone. Could that be possible? Where were all his friends? I squinted at the water, thinking maybe they were diving or practicing holding their breath. Some athletic training thing. There were no strewn clothes in the grass along the shoreline.

As I waited a few more minutes, reality set in that Steve Malone had driven up here alone, though it made no sense to me. He wore a blue T-shirt that probably had the Kentucky Wildcats logo on the front. The cotton hugged his skin, inviting the eye to move down the length of his back. But I found myself staring at the nape of his neck. He always kept his hair cut short, almost buzzed, and I liked how it tapered along the base of his skull. Lots of guys in school wore their hair that way but it looked best on Steve. I wondered how it would feel against my fingertips. Soft? Bristly?

As I summoned my bravery and moved toward him, I imagined the two of us in the middle of the baseball field, me sitting with his head in my lap, stroking his hair at leisure. I've come to realize my sexual imagination has two ratings, and I prefer PG to X. Fantasies about a crush seldom conjured scenes graphic enough to put a blush on a Mormon missionary's face. Steve Malone was not my first crush, nor my only. I have to confess that if I'd found any of his friends standing there in solitude, I would have felt much the same thing, had the same hair-stroking fantasy.

But I was glad it was him standing there and not any of his friends.

Steve made a sound. It took just a second to realize he was crying. I thought someone must have died, it seemed the only possibility, and I stepped back. My foot made a noise and Steve turned around. We both froze in place. His eyes were so red, his cheeks wet. He blinked. He probably wondered who I was since we'd never had a class together.

I can't explain why, but suddenly we both raced toward the car. He reached it first, of course, and opened the driver's side door.

"Go away," he said.

"But . . ."

He wiped his eyes. "I said get the fuck out of here!"

"This is my lake. My parents live at the last house you passed."

Steve's wet eyes shifted from left to right.

"Oh," he said, looking at the ground.

"You can stay. I was just—"

"I'm going."

He got in the Acclaim and drove off. I stared after him feeling like I'd blown an opportunity I didn't know I had. I went to the water's edge and stood in his footprints and hugged myself. *A girl must have broken up with him*, I thought. Girls never appreciated what they had.

A year would pass before I ever got that close to Steve again, when fate put us near each other in math class. He glanced up as I sat down, and I thought he recognized me but didn't remember from where. He gave no other acknowledgement, and I wasn't about to strike up a conversation. Day after day, week after week his indifference to me continued. Some days I came to school feeling fine, some days terribly lonely. Sometimes he was in my mind, sometimes it was one of fifty other boys I'd have been happy to pledge undying devotion to if they'd only show some reciprocal sign.

But none of them did, and the weariness grew and brought me to Mrs. Lawrence's room. Talking to her felt a bit like watching my mom release steam from a pressure cooker. I was less on edge, less dramatic after our meetings. Sometimes though, I carried the sadness home after school. The worst afternoon happened in late October, I think, when I didn't even go into the house after school. I went to the tree and slumped against it and cried. I began to think how great it would be to be emotionless, to feel nothing and just take each day as an exercise in observation. People who can't feel loneliness are never alone, and those who can't feel loved are never loveless. I nodded to myself, convinced I could find a way to shrug off the world. But I was still crying with my forehead against my knees and not aware of anything else until I felt the tap on my arm.

Johnny stood over me, looking scared. He wasn't supposed to be out of the house—and certainly not across the road and into the field—by himself. Mom must have been too busy cooking and maybe assuming I was outside with him. He just put his arms around my neck and wouldn't let go. When I was his age, I remember having thoughts too big for words, or at least too big for any words I knew at the time.

"I'm OK," I said as his little arms began strangling me. He wasn't buying it. Call it intuition or a little boy's wisdom, that flawless ability to see through every lie except Santa Claus and the Tooth Fairy. I hugged him back and said, "Let me up and I'll push you on the tire swing."

The offer was too good for him to pass up. He backed off me, jumping up and down. I lifted him up and he held his legs out straight and rigid to let me thread his body through the tire. I settled him against the rubber and he clutched at the treads.

I put my hands between Johnny's shoulder blades and pushed. He answered with a scream of delight and begged me to make him go faster. I grinned at his happiness. For the first time I felt glad to be an older brother, and I didn't understand why I'd never taken him out to the tree before. He must have discovered it on his own since he'd found me out here, but he'd never mentioned the swing. Maybe he didn't know what it was supposed to be and thought talking about it would get him in trouble. But now he laughed and shouted and clutched the tire with all his might. I was his hero and for once he felt like a little brother instead of a pest, and I was giving him happiness and joy. *Love*. All at once the impact of that hit me and I stopped the swing, pulled him out of the tire, got down on my knees and hugged him. Jesus Christ, how he hugged back. Even now I can feel the phantom pressure of his arms around my neck. I kissed his forehead and hoisted him up and said, "Let's go back to the house. We'll make something with your Legos."

"Can we do the swing again tomorrow?"

"You got it."

And tomorrow, when it came, felt like a reward for all my long suffering.

Because that was the day Steve passed me his first note.

TIM

MEGHAN DIDN'T SHOW UP for her next three scheduled *appointments* and I began to worry her husband had discovered the affair. Then she came into my office on Thursday morning and it was obvious she'd been crying. I locked the door and just held her as she sobbed against my shoulder.

"Whatever it is, we'll figure it out. Just take deep breaths."

I was looking at my diploma as I talked.

She just sort of leaned into me and it felt nice. I could see the psychological appeal to straight guys, making them think they were some sort of protector. No wonder chivalry had been such a thing way back when. As I went on holding and comforting her, I thought about Brady back in Lexington with his ex-wife and two grown daughters and claims of happiness and expert blowjob skills. Maybe he really did have the best of both worlds.

If he could have it, so could I. So could anyone.

I waited for her to tell me what I expected she'd come to

say: that she'd been lying to me, that she was married, that she needed to decide what to do next. My life now felt tied up with hers in ways I couldn't describe. I saw myself sitting at the poker table of her love, willing to throw down my last chip and shout, "I'm all in!"

After the embrace stretched on for another minute, Meghan stirred against me and said, "We have to talk."

"I know," I said, patting the back of her head.

"I don't know what to do."

"It's very difficult," I said sagely.

"How could this have happened?"

I chuckled. "Believe me, I can hardly understand it myself."

She pulled her head away from my chest and said, "I'm pregnant."

"Wait a minute," I said, stepping back.

"Tim—"

"So we're finished, is that what you're saying?"

Meghan just stared at me in disbelief. "You're not getting it, are you? It's your child, Tim."

Honestly, my first thought was that couldn't be, as we hadn't even had real sex. This was of course ridiculously wrong, but it did take me a full minute to acknowledge it. I must have stood there with a look of denial on my face until I remembered the choo-choo had entered the tunnel several times, dropping off passengers on each occasion. Those were heady days when I used to imagine myself getting straighter and straighter with each exposure, enjoying the improbable adventure with a spelunker's enthusiasm for every dark cranny. Jesus, had I really not worn a condom even once? Had I just assumed that a gay man couldn't impregnate a woman, that my sperm would rather commit seppuku than go near an egg?

"My child," I said. "Are you sure?"

"Who else's would it *be*?"

"Um, how about your *husband?* His name's Steve, right?

What, you think you were keeping that little secret from me?"

She began crying even harder than before, weeping out apologies and excuses about being lonely. Her tone grew more and more Southern as she moved around the room, hitting her shoulder against the wall and then ricocheting toward the counter. I intercepted her and eased her toward the examination chair, where she collapsed, face in hands.

"Look," I said. "I'm sorry. I understand how it is. I'm not trying to shame you or anything like that. This is just unexpected. I don't know what I'm supposed to do."

Meghan went on sobbing. I looked to the wall and swore I saw Brady standing there like some sort of vision, nodding and smiling, telling me to join him in a life of fatherhood and marriage. I dropped to one knee beside her and put a hand on her leg.

"Does your husband know?"

She shook her head. "I just found out the other day. I haven't been able to think straight since then. I just want to get rid of it."

"*What?*"

"I want an abortion," she said. "That's why I'm here. I need you to give me the money."

"But I can't do that. I mean this is my child you're talking about. Our child. Are you out of your mind?"

Meghan looked at me as if *I* was. "Are you shitting me, Tim? You want me to have it? What am I supposed to tell Steve?"

"Tell him you don't love him and you're leaving him."

"God, men are so stupid," she said.

"I'm being serious. I mean, do you love him?"

"I don't know anymore."

"Do you love me?"

She wiped at her eyes and that's all I got for an answer.

"I really think we could make it work," I said. "You're

special. You make me feel like a changed man. A *very* changed man. I can't even begin to explain. I can't give you money for an abortion. It'd be—wrong."

I can't begin to describe the shock of hearing myself say these words. They came out so matter-of-factly, like I meant every word, like abortion somehow offended me. Hell, back in Seattle I used to attend pro-choice rallies with lesbian friends when I was still in high school. Women had the right to choose what happened to their own bodies.

That didn't mean I had to foot the bill.

"Fuck Wentz Hollow," I said. "Fuck this town and fuck this state and fuck my life."

Meghan looked up at me, squinting as we made eye contact.

"This place," I continued, "has completely messed with my head. I don't know who I am anymore. I was never interested in a girl even once before I met you, and now you're all I can think about."

"What do you mean, you weren't interested—"

"I'm gay, Meghan."

She laughed. "You're *not* gay."

"I was. Now I'm straight or bi. Maybe it depends on the weather. Hell if I know anymore. But it's all because of you. I really do have feelings for you. I could stay here in Wentz Hollow and have a family with you if you'll let me."

"Good luck getting customers," Meghan said. "Not after everyone realizes what we did."

"Then we'll move somewhere else. Ever wanted to go to Seattle?"

"I live in Wentz Hollow."

"That doesn't mean you have to! There's so much more to life than . . . Kentucky."

"Tim," she said, her voice hoarse and halting, "I don't want more than what I've got. Just help me. *Please.*"

"I don't know. I'm not against abortion or anything, it's just . . . my child. Even if you don't want to live with me, I'd be fine just sticking around and watching it grow up from afar."

"You can't be serious."

"Really."

"So a few years down the road I bring the kid in for a check-up and you don't say nothing? Tim, you're really sweet and cute and kind, and that's why I fell for you. But you have to be the only guy I know who has his head in the clouds and up his ass at the same time."

I winced, knowing she was right. Could I really watch my child growing up a stranger to me, my only contact staring into its mouth a couple of times a year? Jesus Christ, it'd be torture. Who the hell would want that?

"You're right," I said, shoulders sagging.

"It's early. I think an abortion would be around $300. Steve's the breadwinner, I couldn't get that kind of money without having to tell him why. I promise I'll pay you back."

"It's not about that."

"Then what the hell is it about?"

"Us," I said. My voice had a crack in it.

She left the chair and came over and held me. "There isn't any us, Tim. I've learned my lesson."

"I think I've learned mine too," I said.

I told her I wouldn't give her the money.

Meghan shoved me hard in the chest and called me a fucking bastard. Then she ran from the examination room, down the hall to the lobby, and slammed the door on her way out.

Well, that's it, I thought. *She's gone from my life.*

They're gone from my life.

I perched on the stool and stared at the examination chair. In the sudden stillness I realized just how fast my heart was beating. It was strange to realize I'd taken part in a pretty major altercation just now. I'd gotten a married woman pregnant and she wanted me to pay for the abortion.

The moment still didn't feel as heavy as it should have, and I chalked it up to a state of denial. Meghan would think about what I said, realize I was right, and come back. We'd blow out of here and start a life together in Seattle. Until then, waiting was my only option.

I had a busy day to help the hours pass. I did eight teeth cleanings, and even though they all had appointments I couldn't help but get excited every time the bells on the door jangled and I went out to the lobby expecting Meghan to be standing there. What I found instead was one mom or dad after another bringing in their kids. This string of families rubbed salt in the wound for sure and just reinforced the truth about what Meghan said. There was no way I could hang on in Wentz Hollow watching my child grow up from afar. More than that, I didn't see how I could go on living anywhere in the world with the knowledge that I had a son or a daughter out there growing up without me, not knowing I existed. I didn't see how I'd ever get over that or grow past it. In that light, maybe abortion would be the better option.

I still couldn't bring myself to accept that solution. I kept smiling from patient to patient, telling jokes to little kids, offering them sugar-free gum, informing parents of potential problems down the road. All dying inside. Once again my sense of isolation grew, the idea that I was just an actor with no real connection to anyone around me. I couldn't go home after work and sit in my apartment and think about abortions and missed chances. I couldn't make the long drive to Lexington tonight and hope to meet Brady again, and it wasn't like I really wanted to anyway.

When I saw my last patient out and locked the door at the end of the day, I knew what I wanted to do. There was one person in all of Wentz Hollow who wanted to see me and who'd listen. So I drove over to the nearest KFC, ordered a family-sized bucket of chicken with biscuits and extra mashed potatoes, and went to Bart's house.

With anyone else, I'd be showing up red-faced and awkward, and the fact I felt no embarrassment at all just confirmed I'd made the right decision. The front door was open and I heard Bart shouting before I reached the porch.

"Don't tell me it's the wrong number! I just talked to him yesterday. I know my brother's telephone number! You put Brad on right now!"

Bart was shouting. I'd only ever heard a few flashes of anger from him so the effect jarred me. I heard him slam the phone down and curse.

"Why don't Brad ever answer at his number anymore? I just don't understand."

I looked at the bags of food cradled against my chest and thought I'd been a fool to show up unannounced. People just didn't do that no matter how good of friends they were. If Bart was having an episode or a bad time, it'd be better if I just left without him knowing I was here.

I heard footsteps coming toward the door and started to bound off the porch and make an exit before the old guy saw me. I was too late, though, and Bart called out to me, all anger gone from his tone.

"There's the boy! I sure am glad you were able to make it this time, Tim!"

I spun back around and found him showing me that oval, almost toothless smile of his. He stepped onto the porch and said something else about an invitation. This was news to me, but I decided to play along even if capitalizing on his memory problems made me a little queasy.

"I brought the chicken," I started to say. Then I got a look at Bart's eyes. They were red and I was sure he'd been crying. "But if this is a bad time, I can just leave."

"You hush up about anything like that," he said, clapping one hand on my shoulder as he pulled me through the open door.

"Are you OK, Bart?"

"I tell you, Tim, I've never been better. This is just a wonderful day, with all three of my boys under the same roof at the same time."

"Three?"

"You and Nathan and Johnny."

He took the food from my hands and went to the kitchen table.

"Johnny's running late like he does, and you never know when Nathan's going to turn up. All of my sons have done good for themselves but work sure does keep them busy. I'm glad you got regular hours. I always liked a job with a clock. You know when you're starting, you know when you're done."

I nodded, watching him put the bucket in the middle of the table. There were no plates, cups, or utensils laid out.

"Can I help get anything?"

"No, no, just sit yourself down. You've been working all day."

"What have *you* been up to, Bart?"

"Hell if I know," he said. "Seems I took a walk. Rebecca was here with me and we went up to the lake. Sure is nice up there, Tim, just like when you were little."

"Oh," I said, trying not to frown. "That's good."

"I was thinking about how I used to take you up there with all those milk jugs. You loved throwing rocks at those bottles."

He moved past me, looked to his left and right, and then turned around. "Rebecca left. She left. I was going to tell her about the chicken, but she's gone. You take a seat now. Your brothers will be along before too long."

He sat down and so did I.

"Rebecca took me to the lake, did I tell you?"

"Yes, you sure did. I don't mind hearing about it again, though."

"I was thinking how quiet it was. Your mom and I used to go up there before you boys came along. It was special, but any place is when you're in love."

I grinned. "I like that."

"It's different up there now. It feels different. The water's not the same. Rebecca said it was, but I didn't think so."

I glanced at the tabletop a second, then back to him. His eyes were so wet and watery.

"Everything feels different, doesn't it?"

He reached across the table, pushing the chicken bucket to the left, and seized my wrist.

"Sometimes your mom is here, and sometimes she's not. Sometimes it feels black everywhere like back in the mines, and for some reason I'm down there with no headlamp. The lake smells salty like people have been crying in it. Then you wonder if you're the one who's done it. Then I'm looking for Peggy and there's a feeling like she's changed too, you've forgotten she's gone. I have, I mean."

"I'm really sorry, Bart. I don't know what else to say."

He squeezed my wrist. "Life gets to feeling like running a stop sign because you didn't see it, and you hold your breath and pray. Before you know it, you're on the other side of the intersection and no one got hurt, but you're sick thinking about what could have happened. That's all bad enough, but then life gets to where you can remember running the stop sign, but you don't know when it was, and you don't know if you crashed or not. Some days it seems like you must have, and maybe that's what happened to the people who aren't around. Then other days you pat your arms and legs and guess you didn't because nothing's broken."

He quit talking. He stared at the KFC bucket and his

expression went away. His face was like an old wind-up clock with no hands, keeping time's secrets to himself. I wiped my eyes and looked around. Where the hell was Johnny or Nathan? Where the hell was anybody?

"Hey Bart, can I ask you something? Are you glad you had children?"

He turned his face toward me. It was like he didn't understand or recognize me, and I sought to clarify the question.

"Are you glad you had a *family*?"

Bart opened his mouth, an approximation of his smile. I saw no joy there. He was silent but as he kept his lips spread wide, I couldn't help imagining a scream. He tilted his head back, and his Adam's apple bobbed in the wattle of loose skin. His eyes narrowed like he'd just noticed a crack in the ceiling. The silence between us deepened. I got the sense he was reaching for an amazing, even a profound answer and I leaned forward, determined not to miss a word from this oracle. But the next words I heard didn't come from Bart at all.

"What the hell is this?"

Johnny stood in the doorway, dirt on his face and arms, his shirt smeared with grime. He almost seemed like an overgrown kid coming into the house after playing in some field all day. He wasn't smiling.

Bart stirred, shut his mouth, and blinked. He looked at Johnny and said, "There he is. There's the boy."

"Yeah, here's the boy all right," he said, rolling his eyes. "Here I am with an ass busted from another long day of work. What are you doing here, Doc? Did Dad call you?"

"I just wanted to drop by and see you all."

"It's nice to have both my boys here with me. Go get cleaned up, John. We'll keep it all warm for you."

"I don't need to get cleaned up," he said, sitting down.

"John, I came home from the mines looking better. Now run on now and shower up. It won't take long. Me and Nathan will wait on you."

He grinned, eyes narrowing. "It'll take even less time if *Nathan* here helps me. Want to come up and scrub my back, big brother?"

"John," Bart said, an edge of warning in his voice. "You're both grown men."

"Just thinking about old times. Nate used to give me a bath all the time when I was little and Mom had other things to do."

"I don't believe that. You don't go saying things like that when she's not around to answer."

"I wasn't saying anything about Mom. I was talking about Nathan, and he's right here. Tell Dad about how you got me squeaky clean."

I stared at the bucket of chicken. "Don't know anything about it."

"John," Bart said, pushing himself up. His arms trembled to hold his spare weight but his voice had no tremor at all. "You quit bringing up your brother's ways. We don't talk about them. That's what your mother wants. And don't you dare act like Nathan sinned with you. Quit bearing false witness or get out."

"Nothing false about it."

Bart looked like he could spit fire from the black hollow of his mouth. Instead, he picked up a small Styrofoam bowl of gravy and flung it at him. The flimsy lid broke open on impact and soaked his shirt. Johnny didn't flinch. I looked back and forth between them and for a moment Bart seemed many years younger, a man with teeth. Johnny looked like a baby with a messy bib.

He dabbed his fingertips into the wet fabric and tasted the gravy.

"You and Nathan have a good time. Gum that chicken real good, old timer."

Johnny left and neither of us called out to him. A moment later, I heard the front door slam shut. I expected to hear the sound of the truck starting up. Maybe he'd go off someplace to get drunk, or shoot a gun, or whatever the hell he did when he got pissed off. But that didn't happen.

Bart sat back down and reached out for me. I gave him my right hand and he clasped it in both of his. He bowed his head. I thought he was going to start praying.

"It isn't right," he said. "You were my pride, he was my mistake. I love you both, but you were my pride. Even after you'd gone astray and we couldn't account for why. Peggy said you were a stranger in our eyes, and I should have told her my eyes weren't hers. But I honored her. Then you left and I tried to make you dead in me, as I figured I must be dead inside of you. But you wouldn't die. No lump of coal ever became a diamond harder than you, my son and pride."

He patted my hand and opened his eyes. He seemed to be staring at a spot on the table, but the stare was distant. I sat there feeling like a thief and imposter, as if I'd come here on purpose to trick out a confession.

"Bart . . ."

He pulled his hand away and dropped it into his lap. He didn't move his head or blink or give any indication of being aware of me. I sighed and looked toward the living room and the front door. *Just go*, I thought. *What else is there to do?*

I eased out of the chair, careful not to let the legs skid on the linoleum. I touched Bart's shoulder once and he still didn't react. Was it safe to leave him like this? Could he hurt himself? I looked at the stove which was off. There was a knife on the countertop. I went and put it in a drawer. I stood there a moment longer, helpless, lost. Then I made myself tiptoe out of the house.

My breathing hitched when I got to the porch. I rubbed my eyes which were on the verge of welling up. But I didn't cry. The emotions weren't mine to feel. Nathan should have been standing in my place. What was he doing right now? Handling a funeral? Driving the dead around town?

I scanned the darkening landscape across the road and noticed a figure moving away from the house, toward the old tree I'd noticed the first time I came here. It looked just as dead and lightning-struck now as it did then.

Was that Johnny? Who else *could* it be since his truck was still parked by the house and Nathan wasn't here?

I started after him, stumbling over the uneven ground. It took a few minutes to reach the tree and when I arrived, I found Johnny sitting against the trunk, his long legs stretched out and crossed at the ankles. He was drinking a can of Bud Light and he had 2 six-packs with him, though one was half gone. The fingers of his left hand darted in and out of the empty rings like little eels moving through coral.

"You here to suck my dick?"

"I wouldn't even if you were serious."

He looked up at me. "Why's that?"

"You're ugly."

"That so?"

"On the inside. That wouldn't have mattered to me before, but it does now."

He emptied his can, tossed it aside and reached for another. It didn't seem like he was going to say another word.

"Why did you say that stuff about Nathan?"

"What stuff?"

"About him washing you."

"Because he did."

"But you made it seem like he touched you or something."

"You have to touch someone to wash them. Didn't they teach you that in dental school?"

I stepped closer to him. "You made it sound like he molested you. I don't believe that."

"You don't even know Nathan."

"Not all that well. I still don't believe you."

"Queers have to stick together," he said. "You and Nathan should start a knitting group."

I kicked the ground before I even realized it and sent a clump of dirt at his face. He brushed it aside and gave me a look like he was debating whether to kill me. Maybe he wasn't sober or drunk enough to make a decision.

"Don't get your ass kicked, Doc."

"I'll just go."

"Nah, just sit a spell. It's a beautiful night. Hell, if I get drunk enough I may even put my arm around you."

I didn't sit down, but I crouched, annoyed I couldn't keep my balance more than twenty seconds before having to support myself with my right hand on the ground. "Look, I just came out here because of Bart."

"What's he got to do with anything?"

"He said some things to me after you left. He thought I was Nathan."

"Hell, that's nothing. There's a tree stump around the other side of the house. Last week I caught him talking to it like it was Mom. At least the stump didn't start bitching and preaching."

"I get that she must have been really religious."

"Oh, she read the Bible and was always watching Pat Robertson, but I only remember us going to Sunday School. After she found out about Nathan, that's when it got bad. Church on Sundays and Wednesdays, Bible readings before bed, house calls from the pastor. Guess they all thought Bible thumping would make Nathan like pussy. Who knows. Can't blame Nathan for running off, but that just made it worse for me. I became Mom's do-over. Bible camp in the summer, church all the time, not allowed to do a damn thing, suspicious of any buddy I hung out with. Thanks for ruining my life,

Nathan, and a big fuck you, Dad, for brushing your teeth and not saying a fucking word while it all went down."

Johnny pulled another beer off its ring and handed it to me. I cracked the can and took too big a gulp. I coughed.

"Hell, it's not bourbon," he said.

"Just went down the wrong hole."

He laughed. "Sounds like a queer's notion of a good time."

"Whatever you say."

"Shit, Doc, you didn't used to seem all that serious. What happened?"

"This place," I said. "Wentz Hollow happened."

"I'll goddamn toast you on that one." He lifted his can toward me. I touched mine to it and we both drank. After a moment, Johnny craned his neck to look at the tree and said, "You want to see something?"

"Sure."

"Here," he said, getting up. I was slower and he grabbed me by the wrist and hurried me to my feet. "You got your phone on you? Turn on the flashlight."

I did and aimed where he pointed. The light showed what looked to be an old scar in the bark. Leaning nearer, I realized it was carved initials. The N was legible, the S looked more like a backwards Z.

"N plus S," Johnny said. "Any guess at what that means?"

When I didn't answer, he laughed and added, "It ain't hieroglyphics."

"Nathan plus Steve?"

"Yep."

"I'm confused. I thought Steve hit Nathan."

"He did."

"Because Nathan came onto him? Or was Nathan just in love with a bully?"

Johnny chugged his beer and tossed it into the dark. "Bully? What in the hell gave you that idea?"

"You did—I thought."

"I'm not sure how it all went down. Ask Nathan."

"Why don't you ask him?"

"What makes you think I care, Doc?"

"Because you're going out of your way to make it seem like you don't."

He chuckled at that and bent for another beer. He cracked it and took a long pull.

"I think Steve carved it. I don't know when. I was 10 or 11 when I actually noticed it, and it's a lot more visible in the daylight. I'd have seen it before then, I think. Maybe I'm wrong. But Nathan never even had a pocketknife. I can almost see it, you know? Steve Malone drives to the scene of the crime years later to fix a mistake. That has to be love."

"Scene of the crime? What are you talking about, Johnny?"

"I'm talking about a detective story, starring yours truly."

"That tells me nothing," I said.

"That's because I haven't told you anything yet. Quit being so goddamned impatient!"

I held up my hands in apology and humored him even more by sitting on the ground. He stood over me like some camp counselor about to tell a ghost story.

"There used to be a tire swing about right here," he said. "The branch rotted and fell down a long time ago. Dad put it up there for Nathan when he was little. I'd get Nathan to push me in it when I could. Best thing in the world to a 4-year-old. The whole tree was this great mystery to me. In Sunday School I learned all about the Garden of Eden and the Tree of Knowledge and I started thinking about this tree as that one. But with a tire swing.

"So my whole life as a really little kid was waiting for Nathan to come home from school so I could get him to push me in the swing. I'd be in front of the TV watching Nickelodeon. *Muppet Babies* came on from 2:00-3:00, and at 3:00

CONFESSIONS

there was *Flipper*. I hated *Flipper*, but I couldn't wait for it to start because Nathan always came through the front door before the theme song finished. Then we'd go to the tree. Or if the weather was bad, he'd play a game with me. Connect Four or Hungry Hungry Hippos. That stuff."

"Sounds like a great older brother."

"Jesus Christ, Doc, I told time by his coming and going. There's no love like a little brother's. Not even a dog's devotion can compare to it. Then came the car horn to ruin everything."

"Huh?"

"It started in the spring. April. Nathan would come home, we'd go out to this old tree, and he'd put me in the tire. Push me maybe ten or fifteen minutes. Then comes this car up the road, and as it passed the house, the driver honked. The car never stopped, but Nathan sure did. Pretty soon I knew the good times were over whenever I heard that horn. Nathan would run me back across the road, plant me on the porch, and then take off running. There's a lake up there about a mile. It's where I lost my virginity. Maybe Nathan did too."

"Steve Malone was the driver?"

"I thought I was the detective."

"So they started meeting in secret."

"I know you queers are all about openness and visibility now, but sometimes I think love works better when it's got to be hidden. Know what I mean?"

"Maybe a little," I said. "But secretive isn't the same as forbidden. You shouldn't *have* to hide what you feel because someone else disapproves."

Johnny laughed. "That's the thing I don't get about you all. You act like you're the only ones who have to do that. But everyone does that over something or other. Your boss is a Democrat so you hide that you're a Republican. That sort of thing."

"It's really not the same, but I won't argue with you."

"Yeah," Johnny said, finishing his third beer. "No point in it. Nathan and Steve might still be happy little bees if it'd all been kept secret. They might be together to this day and you could enjoy Meghan guilt-free."

Did he know about Meghan's pregnancy? I fretted over that a moment and decided not to question him.

"Why did Steve hit him? Did they break up?"

"That's the detective part. See, it happened right here. Just a few days after this bitch named Mrs. Lawrence comes over. I remember being afraid of her. She didn't look nice at all."

"Who was she?"

"High school biology teacher. She's still around here. Maybe you've cleaned her teeth. Old lady who looks like a bird. Beady little eyes."

"Isn't that every old lady?" I said, and Johnny laughed and punched me in the arm. I didn't rub out the pain no matter how much I wanted to.

"She sits in the living room talking to Mom and Dad. Nathan's in there too. I was eavesdropping in the kitchen, listening. I was so scared for Nathan. I thought the woman wanted to take him away. I didn't understand anything. So my little peabrain gets the idea that if I come running into the room I can make everyone happy. Dad just yelled at me and hauled me to my room. He held me down on the bed as Mom started shouting from the living room. Dad listened. I looked up at his face, trying to see it through all my crying. Neither of us said a thing as the shouting went on. Then Dad left. Just left. And after a while the house got quiet, and I heard Nathan's bedroom door shut. Our rooms shared a wall, and I got off the bed and lay down next to the wall and wished I could see through it. Then I heard the car horn and I knew Nathan wouldn't be running up the road. And I knew that'd make him feel the way I felt when he stopped playing with me."

CONFESSIONS

"You felt vengeful."

"Fuck you, man," Johnny said. "I was a little kid who loved his big brother. Hell, maybe I was even in love with him, the way you hero worship someone."

"I'm sorry, Johnny. I shouldn't have said that."

"I'd have died for Nathan. That's what I thought I was going to do. See, the next day and the day after, Steve comes up the road, honks and goes on past. Now Nathan's grounded. Mom barely even lets him leave the room. There's no phone calls, nothing. When I try to piece it all together, I can see how it must have tortured Nathan. He just wants to see Steve, and he has no way of letting Steve know what's going on. He must have lain in bed agonizing over the motherfucker day and night. Then he gets an idea, something that will get him outside for just a bit. The afternoon rolls around and he gets me to ask Mom if he can push me in the swing. Of course, I'm all about that, and I beg and I beg, and Mom tells Nathan he can do it, but only for thirty minutes and she'll be watching.

"So we go out to the tree here, and Nathan's pushing me. My back was to him, of course, but sometimes the tire would rotate, and I'd see he was pushing me with one hand while his eyes were fixed on the road. I guess he must have been praying hard. Well, the prayer gets answered. We both hear the car coming up the road. Nathan tells me to sit tight, that he'll be right back, and gives me one massive push to tide me over while he goes running to the road. I can't make the tire stop and I'm trying to look back. I'm twisting my little body this way and that, and all it's doing is making the tire start to twist on the chain. Nathan's getting further and further away as the world goes round, and I start feeling sick.

"Next thing I know, there are hands on the tire, bringing me to a stop. Nathan pulls me out and puts me on my feet. I can't hardly stand from being dizzy, but I notice Nathan's got a bloody nose. Where'd that come from? Did he fall? Nah, of course not. I'd seen enough fights on TV to know he'd gotten punched. He's got a hand over his nose and the blood's coming through his fingers. I'm hugging his legs, and then I see the car parked down the road, a good deal away from the house, but Mom could still have seen it if she'd looked out the window. The driver's side door is open and Steve's standing there behind it, leaning forward and rubbing his forehead."

I tried to see the events as Johnny told them. By now the sky had grown dark and the tree's gloomy bark disappeared into it. He'd called this place the scene of the crime, but it seemed the road was the better location. I turned and looked toward the house, wondering whether Bart was still at the kitchen table. There were so many other things to wonder about as well. The more I thought about Johnny's story, the less I understood it.

"So," Johnny continued, "I launched myself toward Steve. I took off running, arms flailing, my whole body a missile. I'm shouting the entire time. Nothing's fiercer than a little boy out for blood. I was going to bite him. That's just what I planned. Steve stood there frozen, watching me. Watching us, because Nathan chased after me and caught me just before I reached the road. He flung me onto the ground and I began to really scream then. He was telling me to shut up and he was telling Steve to drive away. But Steve, he still didn't move until Mom came out onto the front porch and shouted. *Then* Steve hauled ass. After that the car never came up the road again. No car, no car horn. No Steve."

I shook my head. "I understand some of what you've said. But in other parts you've lost me."

"Stay lost," he said. "You're better off."

He stared off into the dark and in an instant, he was more attractive to me than he'd ever been before. He seemed almost noble, like a soldier bravely facing a firing squad. I started to touch his arm and thought better of it. There was no point in having him mistake my intentions. Just then I didn't even know what those intentions were.

"I'm going to head off. You want to come back to the house with me?"

"No," Johnny said. "I'll stay put. Finish off the rest of the beer."

"I'll check in on Bart and say goodbye."

"That'd be great, Doc. Thanks."

As I turned, I convinced myself Johnny would call out to say something like, "Maybe it'd be good if you got to know Nathan better. Maybe the two of you could be something." But all I heard was the sound of another beer tab cracking, and I walked away feeling like those words had been my better angel trying to talk to me in Johnny's voice.

MRS. LAWRENCE

THE FIRST TIME I sat down to read the town paper, I told Frank it should have been called the *Wentz Hollow Holler*, because how often do you come across a paper that uses even one exclamation mark, much less several per issue? Typical sentences were: *Milo Nelson has opened up an ice cream stand on the corner of 4th and Pearl!* or *The Wentz Hollow boys pulled out an upset for the ages last week!* Frank and I used to have a friendly wager over how many we'd find in each new issue. In the early days, when I'd report the issue total was twenty-five, Frank would say, "Really? That's incredible. I can't believe what passes for journalism among these yokels," and I'd take great pleasure in his animated tone. Now those days are gone, and if I report on anything in the paper at all, he grunts without looking up from *The New York Times* app on his iPad.

I miss Geraldine the most when I look at the paper since her passing. The *Herald* is as staid and professional as they come now, devoid of the character I spent so much time ridiculing.

There are far more photographs now, and long gone are the days of exclamation marks and breathless accounts of church picnics. Sometimes I read an article and try to imagine how Geraldine would have written it in the days when she was the paper's sole reporter and editor. That was certainly the case when I saw the brief article from around two years ago noting the sale of the town's funeral home and the name of the buyer. As Geraldine would have put it—

It appears our new funeral director is no stranger to Wentz Hollow!

The article hardly had the length of a blurb, so there was no accompanying picture. I nevertheless had several images in mind as I experienced a rush of blood to the head. A rush of blood, a rush of memories. His name was written out as *Nathaniel Ashcraft*, which puzzled me a moment. Did he go by his full name now? Perhaps a professional decision? Who would you entrust a dead relative to more, the jocular Nathan or the biblical Nathaniel? Certainly *Nate* would never do. Thinking about that brought a very old and very minute recollection to the forefront of my memory. Nathan was in my classroom once again, right before the Christmas break, telling me about some conversation he'd had with Steven Malone. I can't remember most of it, but one moment still stands out.

"He said calling me Nate just felt right. After he said it once, it's all I ever want him to say. Isn't that cool? No one ever called me Nate, and I don't want anyone else to but him."

He was moving about my classroom, almost pirouetting as he darted about the tables. I'd been cleaning up the mess from the previous class, but I found myself grinning at him. Nathan was too lost in his happiness to notice me, and I couldn't help comparing this vibrant, gregarious boy with the sad student who'd come to me just a few months earlier. Of all the times I'd seen adolescents fall in love, with all the joys and sorrows the process entails, I never saw an exuberance like his. You felt like you'd need a butterfly net to bring him back to reality.

CONFESSIONS

"Nate. I love it. But only when he says it. No one else. Is that weird?"

I remember telling him it wasn't weird at all. If anything, his pleasure made me wish Frank and I had pet names for each other. Then I felt strange for comparing our marriage to the enthusiastic first love of two gay boys and finding it wanting.

"I mean he actually talked to me. We've never done that before."

"What? I'm not sure I understand. He passes you notes but you don't talk?"

"Well . . . you know."

"I guess I don't. If you're friends—"

"We are friends! Way more than that! But it's different in school. It has to be."

Does it? I thought, troubled by how fast anxiety could reclaim him. Trying to build a future on quicksand had been the fate of all men and women like him and would continue to be unless bold people kept risking everything for a concrete foundation. Nathan would understand that in time, but by then it would be too late. Activists are seldom made in middle age. They need the imagination, the hope, and yes, the naivete of the youthful heart.

I *had* to push him to see his own potential. What other choice was there?

"Nathan, do you think you and Steve might be able to meet with me sometime soon? It could be here in the classroom, or it could even be at my house."

"I . . . I don't know."

"The two of you are leaders in this school."

"Mrs. Lawrence, I'm not a leader!"

"Yes, you really are, Nathan. You just don't see it, but I do. When you were in class, it was obvious the other students thought you were very smart. They looked to you for answers. I could see it from where I stood."

"But nobody really likes me."

"I'm sure that's not true."

"Not the same way they like Steve."

"He is a popular athlete, which is a kind of celebrity. That's useful."

"What do you mean?"

"I'll explain it all more when you both meet with me. How about at least asking him? He may surprise you."

To my knowledge, Nathan never asked. In hindsight, how could I blame him? It would mean he'd told a teacher about the two of them, a devastating betrayal. Nathan had a relationship to protect, and in my own way I sought to help him. Being exposed is the best way to eliminate the threat of exposure, like taking all your medicine in one gulp.

When I read the article in the *Herald,* only one question came to mind, the universal query every teacher makes when remembering students: what sort of person had they become, and how did I influence that becoming?

Nathan—a funeral home director? Nathan—a mortician? As a biology teacher, death was neither mysterious nor morbid to me, but I could not square the profession with the boy I remembered. Of all the things he could have gone on to do . . . was this his passion, or had he chanced into it? Would he still be a mortician if our paths never crossed?

The article mentioned nothing else, not even his age. No details of a family life, no details of any past besides an inaccurate sentence—*Ashcraft is a graduate of Wentz Hollow High.* An easy mistake to make, perhaps something Nathan even told the reporter since the true details were messy. I reread the article several times in the space of a few minutes and then put the paper aside.

We were in the same town again.

It was possible we might encounter each other.

A younger version of myself would have gone to the

funeral home and submitted myself to a reckoning. Nathan might slam the door in my face. He might even spit in my face. If I was very lucky, he wouldn't recognize me at all, evidence of a lived life, proof he gave no thought to me at all, which is what I merited. Perhaps some small part of me yearned for a happy reunion, forgiveness, understanding, but was not going to seek out approbation or condemnation. I considered myself retired from the direct approach just as much as I was retired from teaching. Wentz Hollow was just large enough, population-wise, that our paths might never cross at all in the day-to-day minutia of living. But I suspected there'd be a rendezvous one day. Nature is composed of orbits and intertwinings. Chance is never *quite* chance.

But even chance could use help. By that time, I wasn't going out much anymore. Little interested me in Wentz Hollow, and I didn't feel like driving to Lexington for some cultural pursuit. After Nathan's article, however, something very curious happened. I found myself getting in my car and driving down to Main Street. I began to walk the street and surrounding blocks, going into all the inconsequential little shops I'd ignored over the years, the gas station convenience store or the corner market where I could pay $4 for a can of Hormel's beanless chili instead of $2.50 if I made the twenty-minute trip to Kroger's. I'd go into these places at various times and sometimes stroll the aisles like a homeless person seeking air conditioning.

But these efforts proved fruitless. A year passed, and then eighteen months, and then twenty-four, and I never saw Nathan. I almost forgot he even lived in Wentz Hollow. My supposition about chance remained true, though, because after Meghan reentered my life, I began encountering Steve every time I went to the grocery store or ran errands. The first time was at the corner market about a week after I made Meghan her first drink. He'd just bought a six-pack of Bud Light and walked out as I entered. He was dressed like a man trying to perpetuate his glory days, wearing a Wentz Hollow Warriors baseball hat that looked so old and faded I figured it must be his original. In the immediate moment of realization, I almost froze in place. We made the briefest eye contact, and he made the slightest grunt. Of recognition? Or something else? In that moment, I didn't even think about the assistance I was giving his wife. All that came to mind was the note placed on my windshield decades earlier.

You're the biggest fucking cunt. I hope you die.

In my panic, I imagined him stopping to tell me this, right there in the doorway. I heard his voice saying the words. Of course, it didn't happen. I had no idea what his voice even sounded like, and the only thing that seemed to be on his mind was drinking the beer as soon as possible. He registered me as nothing more than a little old lady, a Wentz Hollow specialty.

Is it strange to say that I wish he did recognize me and say those terrible words, because not doing so felt like an affront to the possibilities my good intentions stole from him and Nathan? Did he think about Nathan? Had *their* paths intersected? I began indulging in a wild, hopeful flight of fancy. They'd both come back within a relatively short time of each other. Couldn't it be planned, a coordinated reunion? What if they were in fact together after all, living and loving right under our noses?

I began thinking of Meghan and why she maintained Steve wanted to be a father. Each time she came over to drink the next concoction, she'd sit at the kitchen table, talking in her aimless way about abandoned dreams and disappointments. It was obvious she knew her husband was not interested in her sexually but could not admit it outright. It was also obvious that she cared enough about him to go through this torturous deception. Was she misinterpreting his desires for fatherhood? Was he trying to play a role, wear a mask? I was never in a position to know. But my flights of fancy grew stronger. I became convinced that not only were Nathan and Steven covertly living together, but that Steven planned to raise the child with him. *Somehow.* Meghan didn't want kids. She'd use it as an excuse to leave the marriage, leaving him with sole custody—and an open door.

I had to ensure that future.

Meghan never commented that the drink tasted any different after I started cutting down on the ingredients. As she went from first to second trimester, she began to camp out in my kitchen during the day, one hand on her stomach, the other on her forehead as she bemoaned her fate. "It's going to work this time," she'd say, then close her eyes tight, like a little girl making a wish, before quaffing the next dose. When her eyes opened, they were always red and teary but never distrustful.

If anything, her trust in me grew as the pregnancy continued. Some of this was fear, of course. She had latched onto me as her sole savior and seemed to want to be in my company all the time. My presence offered her reassurance. The morning sessions soon became afternoon sessions too, with Meghan sitting at the table, going on and on like we were two old girlfriends perpetually catching up. She repeated town gossip, referencing the names of strangers I did not care about. Then she'd note Walmart was having a sale on maternity clothes and she felt conflicted. "My clothes are getting tight," she said, "but I know the medicine is going to work pretty soon. I'd hate to spend the money."

One day she started picking at her teeth, which disgusted me, but I made no criticism. She'd pick and then look at her fingernails. "All those times I went to the dentist, I should have bothered to get my teeth cleaned at least once," she said, laughing. The remark baffled me into asking what she meant, and she blushed.

"Cat's out of the bag now, isn't it? I'm so stupid."

"Nothing's out of the bag, because I don't know what you're talking about," I said.

"I'm talking about Tim."

"The man you met online?"

"I didn't meet him online, Mrs. Lawrence. I just said that because I wanted to protect him."

"Have your feelings about that changed?"

"Yeah," she said. "Now that I think about it, they sure have. To hell with him. Tim the dentist is the father. Do you know him?"

"I don't believe so."

"Don't you go and get your teeth cleaned?"

"I do. We go to Dr. Palmer over in Everts. It's twenty miles, but Frank and I have been going there since 1988. Call us loyal patients."

"I guess so," Meghan said with a little laugh. "Tim's a real young guy, cute and sort of pudgy. I just sort of had the hots for him the first time I saw him, and it was obvious the way he flirted with me."

"You didn't tell him you were married?"

Meghan looked away and shook her head. I sighed.

"Oh, don't do that, Mrs. Lawrence. I know it was wrong. I just needed someone else in my life and I didn't want to ruin it. Plus, later on Tim told me he already knew about Steve, so I figure it's all right."

Meghan began describing their ongoing fling. She wasn't as graphic as she could have been, but more graphic than she needed to be. I shuddered, unable to imagine the idea of sitting down in an examination chair knowing someone had sex on it an hour earlier. Was everyone's sense of ethics just dead these days?

"Does he know about the baby?"

"Yeah, he knows I'm pregnant."

"But does he know *he's* the father?"

CONFESSIONS

She blinked as if I'd just made the dumbest query imaginable. "Why who else would be? It's not like I'm sleeping around."

I raised my eyebrows, but Meghan seemed not to notice.

"As soon as I told him, the idiot wanted me to start a family with him."

"I see."

"Why the hell do I always have guys falling in love with me, Mrs. Lawrence? It's such a curse."

"I'm afraid I don't know, dear."

She went on about the misery and burden of her beauty, but my thoughts turned to this town dentist. I didn't care to meet him, but I knew the state had a Board of Dentistry that handled licensing and legal matters. Having sex with clients in your office had to violate any number of regulations. In my mind, I was already composing the complaint letter that would strip him of his license and hopefully guarantee he never practiced dentistry again.

Meghan pushing away from the table interrupted my thoughts. She was just over seven months pregnant at this point, too far along for any herbal abortifacient I could make to be effective anyway. Still, she'd gone on drinking what I prepared, oblivious to the reality that she *was* going to have this baby.

"See you tomorrow, Mrs. Lawrence?"

"Of course, Meghan. Have a good day."

"I will just as soon as I'm out of the woods. You keep on making the drink and I'll keep on drinking it and praying."

After she left, I went upstairs to my computer to look up the state's board of dentistry. I got an unpleasant shock when I found the complaint letter had to be issued in writing and signed. Some time ago, bureaucrats learned ending anonymity was the surest way to cow the public. But I had to admit I had only Meghan's story, and she'd lied about the father at least once. Lacking any direct evidence of the dentist's ethical breach, should I proceed based on hearsay? Meghan would have to be drawn into the process sooner or later, wouldn't she? The stress of it alone might cause her to lose the baby.

I backed away from the computer. I couldn't stand retreating, but I did it.

There must come a point in everyone's reckoning where you look back and think how many times you've attached your signature to something and wonder how different your life might be if you could strike your name from some of those documents—the letter to the editor, the marriage license application, the innumerable contracts you signed without even skimming all the details. Your signature on checks and tax returns, your signature on a will, your signature on funeral arrangements if you care to plan your life all the way to its terminal point.

Frank and I had done that, of course, neither of us being squeamish about reality. Without children or much of anyone in the way of relatives, there were few directives to plan. It galled me a little to think I'd rest beside Frank here in Kentucky. A graveyard in Vermont might be nice. I still cannot pinpoint the year Frank came to consider Wentz Hollow as *home*. For all the sarcasm we used to share about this damn town, that particular duet ended a long time ago, and I now sang the mocking song alone. So I acquiesced to his demand for cemetery plots and marble headstones. They are, in fact, already in place and engraved with everything but the death date. We could lay flowers on our own graves if we wished every Memorial Day. Were I younger and in expectation of decades more to live, it might be funny to whistle past my own grave. Aging does have a way of taking the comedy out of gallows humor. I've sometimes wondered if Frank's refusal to retire is his way of denying the reality of death. It's a nicer sentiment than accepting work as a respite from a woman he's quit loving.

CONFESSIONS

At some point, I should accept that I'm not so much writing a memoir as writing a letter to Nathan. The need to address him directly has been there since the start, pushing at my fingertips. So, Nathan, allow me to surrender to it as I discuss a topic you must know far better than I. The concept of burial repulses me. The idea of being embalmed and put in the ground terrifies me even though I know there'll be no consciousness to concern me. If I'd only delayed my decision, our paths might have crossed in the course of legitimate business. About four years ago, I went to the funeral home, spoke with your predecessor, and made my own private arrangements without Frank's knowledge. I don't suppose anyone is legally bound to follow through with my desire for cremation. I didn't specify what's to be done with the ashes. Since I do have a graveyard plot, it's logical they should go there. But I'd rather they didn't.

No need to curse Frank with proximity.

NATHAN

IT WAS ALMOST 7:00 in the evening when I moved Mr. Henshaw from the prep room to his casket and got him situated. I stepped back to review the work, as I did with every case, and had nothing on my mind except going upstairs to take a shower and going to bed. As I left the viewing room, though, I felt I was forgetting something important, some vital appointment. The sensation froze me in place. It was like I'd been called to pick up a body hours earlier and somehow the task slipped my mind. But of course I'd handled that call. Maybe it's the only call I ever wished I could have forgotten to answer.

Well, I thought, *it will come to me. And if it doesn't, it couldn't be all that important in the end.*

I left the viewing room. As I entered the lobby, intending to head up the steps, the door opened.

And the funeral director saw his first ghost in the flesh.

"Nate?"

The background was wrong somehow. I noticed it almost before I truly saw his face. There should have been a raging blizzard outside, the furious flakes and blast of cold air chasing him into my warmth. I caught a glimpse of the sunset through the open door. Like a magically tuned piano, the day had held its one note of beauty for all these long hours.

Though the door was wide open, Steve came in sort of sideways, as if he'd been trying to slip his body through a narrow crevice. He closed the door behind him and leaned against it, hands spading into his front pockets. He'd always worn blue jeans so well, and he still did. Goddamn.

"I, uh," he began, his tone becoming thick and hoarse. He stood very straight and tilted his head so the back of his skull tapped against the door, leaving his broad throat exposed to me. I saw his Adam's apple bob as he swallowed.

"Been a long time," he said at last. Then he did look right at me. "You going to say anything?"

"I'm sorry."

Apologies make the best bridges over chasms of time. I took a tentative step toward him, almost unsure of the soundness of the wooden floor. He made no reciprocal move.

"I should be saying that to you. I never did."

"Never had to. Besides, it was a long time ago."

He looked at me. His eyes seemed so washed out, like he'd cried the color out of his irises. "Doesn't feel like it to me."

"No," I said. "To me, either."

Now he did take a step toward me, but only one.

"I was here this morning."

"I know that."

"Was it bad that I didn't come in?"

"Steve—"

"I just couldn't do it, Nate."

"Hey, I understand."

He reacted like I'd slapped him in the face. The muscles in his jaws tensed from the force of his teeth clenching.

"Want to sit down?"

CONFESSIONS

"Is it even OK for me to be here?"

"It couldn't be more OK. I want to talk but I don't know what to say."

He let out a long breath and nodded. Then he smiled, sheepish in a way he'd never been back in high school. "Where should we go?"

I looked back toward the viewing room. Mr. Henshaw's casket was just visible.

"My office," I said. "It's just through that door."

I led him there. At first, I didn't think he was going to follow me at all. Part of me couldn't accept he was really here. I saw him, I heard him, but these could be hallucinations. My madness wouldn't extend to extraneous details like his car being in the parking lot. I saw it from my office window before closing the blinds. Then I turned and saw the stuffed manuscript Mr. Lawrence had left for me. I shoved it in a desk drawer. Mrs. Lawrence had no business here.

"You've got yourself a big old desk," Steve said.

"It came with the place."

He laughed. "Sit down first. I want to see how you look behind it."

I grinned and did as he asked. I clasped my hands together on the table-top and made my posture as rigid as possible. Then I cleared my throat and said in my most officious tone, "Can I help you, sir?"

"You look like a businessman. I knew you'd be a success."

"I suppose I am a businessman in a way. When I was in high school, I kind of figured I'd become a teacher. Things worked out a little differently."

"Yeah," he said, a bit wistful. "For both of us."

Steve looked around the office, rubbing his right cheek as he took in everything. His mannerisms, so shy and hopeless, weren't like anything I remembered about his younger self. He'd been so strong and strapping then, the all-American jock, the confident optimist, the natural leader. Now he just looked like a small-town high school baseball coach, beefy and sturdy, with just a hint of beer belly. I'd maintained my exact waist size since high school, but by any objective measure of appearance he'd aged far better than I. He looked invulnerable to balding, and there was only a trace of gray in his hair around the temples. He could pass for late 30s, I could be mistaken for late 50s.

Steve laughed and I blushed, thinking I'd stared at him too long, too openly.

"What?" I said.

"A funeral home director," he said, shaking his head. "How does that work? How did that happen?"

"It happens like everything else. You end up getting a degree in something. I have a diploma in death. I minored in mutilations."

His voice faltered. "I just never would have thought . . ."

I'd misinterpreted his attitude entirely. For some reason I thought I was still talking to the chipper, sarcastic, confident 17-year-old who'd lived in my head all these years. But Jesus Christ, I was talking to a man who'd just lost a *baby*.

"Steve," I said, getting up and rounding the desk. I touched his shoulder and we sat down in the two guest chairs. "You can't know how sorry I am. How much I'd do anything to make it better for you. I was wanting to go outside and shout it to you this morning."

"When I didn't come in."

"It's fine that you didn't. I understand."

"What do you understand, Nate?"

I looked down and realized how close we sat to one another, our knees almost touching. Memory transported me to our first true meeting, in the baseball field dugout. It was a snowy day in early January 1991, not long after the return from winter break. Our friendship to that point had been on paper, a few passed notes that were life-changing at the time. I still had a few of those notes in a box somewhere, something you keep in the heat of the moment and just know you'll look at every day. And you do for a while, whether to torture or console yourself. Then comes the day when you forget, or you just don't have the time. Days build upon each other, and you let go of things even if you don't realize it, until these poignant totems yellow and whither. But when those notes were fresh, they meant more to me than anything in the world. And after things got bad between me and my folks, I hid those notes and brought them out to remember a ruined happiness.

What I remember now—it didn't strike me as strange at the time—is that we never spoke to each other until the day before Christmas break. In my head we have a lifetime of conversations, but so many of those must be imaginary, examples of me talking to myself in loneliness and pretending it was a conversation. But I know for sure the first words he spoke to me were, "Hey, Nate." It happened after math class as I was getting up to leave. I turned and he was standing there with this halo around him and stars dotting his eyes and dimples. "Maybe we'll have a class together next year. But if we don't, it'd be cool to hang out sometime."

I wasn't even thinking about the fact we might not share a class next year. The realization would have stunned and depressed me, but how could I feel any sadness with Steve calling me *Nate*? I felt like I was hearing my actual name for the first time. The sound of it was so casual, so simple and confident. I wanted to be *Nate* the way Steve said it, I wanted to discover and live as that guy.

Did I say anything to him? I must have stood there smiling like an idiot, nodding my head. I know he grinned and hit me in the shoulder as he walked by. It was how the jocks always greeted each other, though from the sound, they hit each other a lot harder than Steve had hit me. It still hurt, but I didn't dare try to rub the spot. The lingering throb meant more than I could say.

I wouldn't talk to him again until almost two weeks after the winter break. We *didn't* have a class together that semester, and while I saw him in the halls, he never seemed to see me. How could he, with so many people always hanging around him? I began to feel a peculiar confusion I wouldn't really experience again until many years later, when dating apps came along and the concept of *ghosting* became common. There were times when my sex life seemed confined to the same cycle of a few exchanged messages and photos, followed by a suggestion to meet. Then I'd think: *This could be the one. No more being alone.* Then the messages stopped, and sometimes the other profile disappeared, leaving me to wonder what happened.

Ghosted.

Yes, in hindsight, that's how it felt when I saw Steve in the halls after the winter break. Were we not passing notes just a few weeks ago? Did he not call me Nate and say we should hang out? Did he not slug my shoulder goodbye? I started sinking into a depression and couldn't bring myself to talk it out with Mrs. Lawrence. I'd been such a fool, boasting about a friendship that didn't exist. I couldn't let her know my stupidity.

Then came a day—it was in the morning, before the first bell—when I was moping along in the hallway and I got a shove in my backpack. I spun around and there he was with the halo and the stars in his dimples and eyes. "Hey, Nate. Want to talk after school?"

"I, uh . . ."

"How about the baseball field?"

"When?"

"After school, like I said."

"Today?"

He gave my shoulder another punch, but this one was even lighter than the first. I didn't need to rub it.

"Later, Nate."

I just stood there staring after him. The encounter hadn't happened in the school's busiest hallway, but other people saw it. An open acknowledgement of knowing me. I went to class and didn't hear a word the teacher said. The clock is never your friend when you're anticipating something. Every hourglass suddenly seems clogged. But that day zipped to its conclusion as if my pulse dictated time's pace. I loitered a bit after the last bell, afraid to be seen rushing to the baseball field. After most of the crowd had petered out, I went around the back of the building and walked down the hill. There was old snow on the ground and fresh snow falling. The damp penetrated my nylon sneakers and soaked my socks before I reached the perimeter fence. I put my fingers through the chain link and scanned the field. With the snow and the frigid air, the scene looked desolate, and I began to wonder if I was being tricked. Then I cursed myself, thinking I'd waited too long to come down and Steve had given up on me. I followed the fence line, running my fingers along the icy chain link, heading toward home base and the path back up to the school.

"Nate!"

The voice called from the other side of the fence, but I still didn't see anyone.

"Over here!"

I squinted. Steve was standing in the dugout across the way, waving to me. I waved back, the most natural-feeling act of my life, and suddenly the fence seemed a hundred feet high. Where the hell was the gate? How did I get in? Steve must have read my confusion because he started pointing. I ran in that direction, slipping here and there but not falling. I found the opening in the fence and stopped there to look back up the hill. The snow came down like a protective curtain.

I went to the dugout.

Steve sat bundled up in his coat. I guess I expected the dugout to be heated, but the temperature was only a few degrees warmer. At least we were out of the wind.

And of course we were alone.

"Took you long enough," he said, without any actual criticism in his voice.

"Sorry, Steve. I—"

"Got lost?"

I grinned. Doing so, at that moment, was the *second* most natural-feeling act of my life.

"Want to sit down, Nate?"

By now he'd said *Nate* enough that part of me assumed it was his pet name for me, the first pet name anyone ever gave me. Even my parents and grandparents referred to me as Nathan. A few other men have called me *Nate* over the last twenty-five years of my life, but none of them made it seem special the way Steve did. He just had that perfect voice, perfect to my ears at least, and as I sat beside him, we started talking about that damn math class and that damn teacher. Our knees were almost touching then, and I kept stealing glances down, wanting them to connect. But even if they didn't, that was OK. Closeness was good enough.

I guess we talked for about an hour, and then he gave me a ride home. I didn't have to give him directions and he never asked. I understood then that he remembered me from the lake and that he'd always recognized me.

When we arrived at my driveway, he parked and nodded toward the road. "Maybe we can go fishing up there together when it's a little warmer."

"I'd really love that."

We found ourselves staring at each other. Have you ever been in love and looked at the person full in the face, full in the eyes at the most unexpected moment? You see openness, you see possibilities. You see all your despair and doubts sizzling to nothing like a few stray drops of water in a hot pan. It didn't occur to me at the time, but I wonder now if he was wanting to say something about the time I caught him crying. Maybe he wanted to thank me for never bringing it up or broadcasting it around school. I never knew what he was upset about. It always seemed like something we were destined to discuss. Destiny had so many other ideas.

"Me too, man," he said. "See you tomorrow. Take it easy."

He hit me in the left shoulder, but the impact felt like nothing through my heavy coat. I went inside and Johnny was there hugging my legs and telling me how cold I felt, and in the next moment he was pulling me outside to see the snowman he'd built in the backyard. I went and we even made his snowman a buddy. In my mind, its creation took on an almost spiritual tangent. There I was, a lonely snowman and now a companion named Steve was being fashioned. We made the snowman taller and Johnny declared it the best snowman ever made. Then we had a snowball fight and I let him destroy me until all he could do was roll around the snow laughing, his cheeks red from cold and glee. It's so easy to be generous with others when you're very happy. I carried him inside and convinced Mom to make us hot chocolate.

What do you understand, Nate?

"It wasn't mine," he said. "I know that."

I risked a look at his face. He was staring at the carpet and so I stared there as well.

"I guess it won't surprise you that me and Meghan don't have sex much," he continued. "I try to do right by her, but . . ."

"I understand."

"*Quit* saying that."

"I'm sorry."

"Quit saying that, too!"

He got up and walked over to the window. He looked

shorter than he was, as if the old plush carpet had swallowed up his feet.

"When she told me she was about seven weeks along, I thought back and remembered a night she'd practically tied me down to have sex."

"Did you?"

"Yeah, we fucked," he said into the blinds.

"Then the baby could have been yours."

"No, Nate. It wasn't. I can put two and two together. She already knew she was pregnant the night we screwed. That's the reason she was so hell-bent. I'd already disappointed her enough times in the past, there was no reason for her to be so gung-ho about it, except she was looking for cover."

I took a measured breath and thought about repeating Meghan's elliptical confession to me from this morning. Would confirming his suspicions be a balm or salt in a gaping wound?

"Did you want to be a father?"

He shook his head, his voice barely managing above a whisper. "I think I'd be terrible."

"Then—maybe—in a way—"

Steve shot me a look that shut me up on the spot.

"I'd like to kill whoever did it," he said, and my first thought was he meant whoever killed the baby. Then I comprehended his real meaning.

"Do you have any ideas?"

"Yeah," he said. "I do. Your brother."

Johnny?

"Meghan told me they'd fucked a few times before she met me. It wouldn't surprise me if they're fucking now."

"I don't know what to say."

"Nothing to say. It could be Johnny, it could be any number of guys. Never mind what I just said about killing whoever did it. It's not their fault. I can't even blame Meghan for cheating on me. I suck as a husband."

"I just don't believe that, Steve."

"I've had sex with a lot of girls, especially in college. I could get it up, but I never felt much from it. Not in my heart. I thought because I could fuck Meghan, that was good enough. It isn't. I used to think Meghan deserved so much better. Then she got pregnant and was acting like it was the most important thing in the world. She'd go on and on about *our* child, and asking me baby name ideas, and talking with my Mom about being a grandparent. I actually bought it. But then, after it was dead . . . it was like she wanted to wipe dirt off her hands. She acted like it should be buried in the backyard like a dead pet dog. Goddamn. Someone has to give a shit."

He stifled a sob.

"I know you do. You always have. You're the best man I know."

"Whatever, Nate."

"It's true. You wouldn't be here if your heart wasn't good."

He rubbed his eyes. "I don't know anything about my heart. But that baby never even got a chance. It was . . . doomed. I didn't want it to be forgotten just like that."

We fell into silence. I looked at his back, studying him from head to foot. An idea came to mind.

"I want to show you something," I said, getting up. I risked putting a hand on his left shoulder. Steve didn't flinch away. I felt the tension humming through his body like a horrible motor. He reached his right hand across his body and covered mine without turning. Then he leaned toward the window and flattened the blinds between his forehead and the glass.

"What?"

"It's the urn for the baby's ashes."

His body shook from a stifled sob. "I can't," he said. "Please don't make me."

"I'd never make you do anything," I said. "But I think

seeing it may help. I'd like the honor of showing it to you."

He drifted away from the window and turned, almost easing into my arms. I held him. I could have gone on holding him a hundred years, vibrantly alive with the feeling of his body against me. We began a shuffling, convalescent walk out of the office. Once we were in the lobby, though, I noticed the front door was open and seeing it shocked me out of this cherished embrace. Hadn't Steve closed it? Maybe he hadn't shut it all the way. I went to the porch and looked around. There were no other cars in the lot except ours. The sky had dimmed too much to see down to the road, but no one seemed to be around. I shut the door and turned to Steve, who stood red-eyed and dumbfounded. I put a finger to my lips and entered the viewing room, thinking a member of Mr. Henshaw's family might be here. But the room was also empty.

"What is it?" Steve said.

I slipped my right arm around his shoulders. "Nothing," I said in a hushed voice. "Let me show you the urn."

We went into the showcase room and I pointed out the model. "Meghan liked this one best."

He picked it up. "Feels fragile."

"It's ceramic," I said. "That's what she ordered. I want you to know that I got the baby a bronze version instead. Much more expensive, but I'm eating the cost."

"Why?"

"Because I thought it would hold the ashes of your child, and that's important to me."

"Christ, Nate," he said, clapping me on the back. "Now I know why you became a funeral director. All you do is care, isn't it? *Thank you*."

"It's a chance to make a difference. Maybe too little too late, but still."

"It's never too little too late. You just proved it."

He patted my shoulder, swallowed, and straightened his

CONFESSIONS

back. Suddenly there seemed nothing else to say, and a sort of panic set in. I wasn't about to be cursed with muteness when I had a million words I wanted to speak to this man.

"It's good to talk again. I've been wishing it would happen."

"Maybe I could swing by your place sometime and talk some more."

"This is my place."

"I mean your house or whatever."

"This is it."

He shook his head. "You live *in* the funeral home?"

"It's true. And no, I don't sleep in a coffin."

The stars returned to his eyes and his dimples. "Doesn't that freak you out?"

"Haven't seen a ghost yet."

He laughed but there wasn't much humor in it. He sounded a bit haunted himself, haunted and lonely, and I could only think of how I'd found him by the lake that one day. Steve stood there in front of me and I saw the young man I should have spent years getting to know. Whether we would have maintained a relationship or even a friendship, who can know? Our lives are full of voices and their echoes, and if you're lucky you experience the pleasure of the actual voice far longer than the echo of their leaving. But high school love is like how our voices change at that age, full of cracking. You get a brief opportunity to talk like that, and if you're luckier still, you're not having a conversation with yourself.

Steve bent down and kissed me. I felt the stubble on his upper lip. The gesture was too long to be a peck, too close-mouthed to qualify as intimate. He pulled back and touched his right hand to my cheek.

"Goddamn," I said.

"I'm sorry if I shouldn't have done that, Nate."

"Are you kidding? All those years wishing we could have

kissed, imagining what it would have been like."

"It should have happened at the lake. In my head, that's where I was going to do it. We'd be fishing. We'd be alone. A lot of people used to come up there, so maybe the plan wouldn't have worked. I used to drive up the road to the lake whenever I came home from college. Sometimes I even honked the horn and then went up and sat on the hood of my car, waiting. But I guess you were gone."

"I escaped Wentz Hollow as soon as I could," I said. "I spent a year being home-schooled, then I all but ran away to the northeast and had almost nothing to do with my family for years."

"All because of that bitch."

"Yes," I said. "That bitch."

"Is everything better now? With your family?"

"Well, my mom is dead," I said. "I missed her funeral."

"Jesus. I'm sorry it ended up getting so bad," he said.

I shrugged. What else was there to do?

"Why did *you* come back, Steve?"

"Maybe I was looking for you."

"Come on."

"It's true," he said. "Meghan and I were doing OK in Louisville. I'd have a couple of hookups with guys every now and then. There'd be that flash of excitement at first, but it never lasted longer than a few minutes. And I'd start thinking of you and wondering if life could have been different. I Googled your name before, but I never found anyone I thought would be you. Then one time I found a listing for you owning this place. I figured it *had* to be you."

I nodded. "Came back a couple of years ago."

"Why?"

"It just felt right."

Steve grunted at this. Then he grinned and gave my arm a light punch. "Did you ever Google me?"

CONFESSIONS

"More than once. Found a few pictures of you from 1995 in your Cardinals uniform. I may or may not have jerked off to every one of them over the years."

Steve's eyes widened and he laughed the wonderful laugh of his high school self, boisterous and just a little high-pitched and hiccupy.

"Man, I've missed your sense of humor, Nate. Some of those notes we passed back and forth, what you wrote cracked me up half the time. I'm glad you're still like that."

"Sometimes it's hard."

I didn't mean for a quaver to enter my voice. I didn't know I was feeling anything other than joy to be standing here talking to this man. It wasn't even the day's weariness overwhelming me. If anything, I felt the crush of years, the wasted opportunities, the sense of time ill-spent. I felt them and I heard them, voices and echoes all their own. All the days of just wanting to be held by someone at the end of the day after laboring over the needs of the dead. It was supposed to be Steve and I together. Few people meet the love of their life right on the first try, but goddamnit, I'd been gifted a bullseye only to have the dart pulled out by other hands.

"Nate?"

I started crying. Steve had me in his arms in a moment, but I didn't surrender to the embrace the way I thought I might. Instead, I pulled away and walked into the viewing room and down to Mr. Henshaw's coffin. Steve followed and we stood beside each other, looking at the inevitable.

"Does this feel right?" I said.

"Huh?"

"This old man. Death in Wentz Hollow. Death itself."

"You're making me worry about you, Nate."

"You asked me why I came back, and I said it just felt right. But it hasn't. It doesn't. It didn't. My Dad's got Alzheimer's."

"Man," Steve said. "I'm sorry."

"I only found out my mom was dead because a cousin called me. No one else bothered. I guess I'd given them plenty of reason to think I wouldn't care. The same cousin called to tell me about Dad's condition, and I still couldn't bring myself to think of visiting. I was nursing such a grudge. But then Dad started calling me himself."

"Your cousin gave him the number?"

I nodded. "At first I was shocked to hear his voice. I recognized it, but he sounded so different. He sounded like the way I remembered him before Johnny came along, when he used to make me feel like I was the only thing in the world he cared about. I almost had a breakdown over it. That and the way he talked like he didn't remember that I'd run away, or why. It was like he thought I'd moved out last week. I started trying to process all these feelings, and they made me understand something about myself."

"What?"

I turned from Mr. Henshaw's coffin and sat down on the first pew. Nate joined me. We sat with our legs touching. He put his right arm across my shoulder.

"After I ran away from home, I developed an attraction to older men. I didn't really get it because it wasn't there before. For a while in my 20s and 30s, I was what you'd call a daddy chaser."

I thought Steve would snicker at this, but he didn't. His lips were pressed tight.

"That's definitely a thing," he said. "I've got a few online hookup profiles. I download the apps on my phone, check them, and then delete them. I get a ton of messages from guys in their 20s."

"Anyone would go for you," I said. "You look great."

His hand left my shoulder and stroked my thinning hair. "You actually look damn good. You're super lean. And you've got more muscle than you did as a kid. If I was 17, I'd still want you."

"I doubt that."

He squeezed my arm and grinned. "So what are you saying, you only go for old guys now? No one under 60 need apply?"

"I want someone my age. But hearing my dad talking to me so gently, like he used to . . . I knew in an instant what I'd been looking for way back when, and I just thought how much of my life I'd wasted."

"You never found someone? I can't believe that, Nate. You lived out in the open, right?"

"More or less. I don't advertise it. I don't hide it."

"Meanwhile I've been living like I'm in the 1950s," Steve said.

He let his arm go back to hanging across my shoulder. The subtle weight of it pulled me toward him and I let it happen, sliding down just a little in the pew until my head rested against his chest. I stared at the casket. Mr. Henshaw here, Mrs. Lawrence in cold storage, Meghan's baby waiting for the incinerator. Variations on the same tune. What was my role in the song? Conductor? Musician? Chorus member?

It was then I understood something I'd only sensed before, the awareness that my life felt like a video put on pause. Except that's not quite accurate. The movie is still playing, the sound is still blaring, but there's a pause button symbol in the middle of the frame that all other images are subordinate to. You mash every button on the remote control of my life and still couldn't make it go away. Then you realize the pause symbol looks like an equal sign turned end over end, the ultimate indication that equality in your life is askew, and the only way to get rid of the image is to reach your hand out and turn it clockwise, somehow, through whatever artifice you manage. Then the image will go away at last.

I swallowed against a hardness in my throat. "I came back

because of my dad, Steve. Now that I . . . now that I love him again, I couldn't imagine anyone else handling his funeral, handling his . . . his body. Whenever it happens, Dad's funeral will be my last. I'll retire after I've seen him through. I don't know what I'll do. Maybe I'll live for once. I won't care. I hate myself for wishing Dad could have had dementia sooner so I could have spent more years enjoying his sweetness."

Steve held me even tighter. I cried a burst of good tears. Crying in the arms of someone you care about always produces good tears. I got control of myself after a couple of minutes. I sat back from his embrace and smiled at him.

"Thanks for that," I said, laughing a bit. "Where have you been the last twenty-five years of my life?"

"Wasting mine," he said, and kissed me on the forehead. "Whereabouts in this place do you live, Nate?"

"Upstairs," I said.

He held out his hand.

"Then come on. Let's make up for lost time."

TIM

"You don't ever stop, do you?"

"Stop what?" I asked.

"Being cheerful."

It took all the acting skills I'd developed during my time in Wentz Hollow to keep the grin on my face. I'd deserve an Oscar if it looked at all natural. Nathan couldn't know how much of a freakout I was dealing with when he came through the door. I honestly thought it was going to be the police or something. But it was Nathan, this walking embodiment of sanity and maturity. Everything my life needed. I was prepared to throw myself at him. He needed me, I needed him. Life would make sense again. A normal life. A domestic gay life, no scandals, as tidy and in order as a bow tie.

I kept thinking this during his entire visit. *Maintain appearances. Act normal.* And the whole time, even as I got him into the examination chair for the first time, even as we talked about Bart's dental problems, I just wanted to cry and confess to him what was going on. It'd be madness, it'd just confuse him, but Nathan was too decent a human being not to respond. Not to want to help. Not that he could. His line of work was more about digging graves, not helping an idiot get out of one.

Had it been possible, I would have closed up the office and hauled him off to the nearest bar, just to be near a guy who had his shit together—a guy the exact opposite of me. But with my whole career threatening to crumble around me, it'd have to wait a few more hours.

"Man," I said, trying to maintain my cheerful mask. "I'm betting I'll really need a drink tonight. How about joining me?"

Oh yeah, I thought. *I'll definitely need a drink.*

"I'd like that."

"Then that's a yes?"

"It's a yes. In fact, why don't you come over tonight after 8:00?"

I nodded.

Eight o'clock. 8:00PM Eastern Standard Time. 2000 hours military time. Something something Greenwich Mean Time.

Whatever. It was the hour I was going to get my life back together once and for all. And it was going to happen in a funeral home.

So fitting. So very, very fitting.

After Nathan left, I went to the hallway bathroom and splashed my face before entering my little office. There was an open envelope and a handwritten note on the desk. I picked up the page for the umpteenth time and began to shake as I reread the opening sentences. The cursive handwriting was small and neat, each letter tilting right at about a 30-degree angle. There was so much precision I had trouble believing it wasn't a computer font. I could register little details like this now that the shock of the message had settled over me.

I'm writing to inform you I'm aware of your terrible breach of professional ethics and the consequences that derive from it. Perhaps you'll be happy to know the baby is dead. You may not care one way or the other. Perhaps you'll find yourself caring only after the fact. If so, you and I are in the same terrible boat, even though we do not and never will know each other.

I'd found the envelope taped to my door when I arrived ninety minutes earlier, with only my name written in the middle. My first thought was it must be from Meghan. I hadn't seen her in months, not since she came asking for help about the abortion. I kept thinking she'd come around to my way of thinking and walk in the door to tell me she'd changed her mind. Some nights I laid awake wondering if she'd gone through with it. Maybe that's why she didn't want to come see me. There were plenty of reasons why that might be, and I'd hug my pillow to my chest and try to think out all the possibilities. Inevitably, my thoughts came to the same conclusion: she was going to have the baby, and she was going to leave her husband and be with me.

Perhaps you'll be happy to know the baby is dead.

I sat down, starting to hyperventilate again, nearing the same state of panic I was in the first time I read the note. Who the hell would write something like this? My first two assumptions were Johnny or Meghan herself, but there was no way either of them had handwriting like this. They could have gotten someone else to do the writing, but that didn't make sense either. Meghan wouldn't be sharing any secrets, and I doubted Johnny's friends wrote any better than he did. Besides, who in Wentz Hollow even talked like this?

We do not and never will know each other.

I'd never met Steve.

Jesus, what if *he* wrote it?

Could Meghan have broken down and told him? I just couldn't see it, but who else would she have told?

I rubbed my forehead. A blackmail letter. This was a goddamn blackmail letter, wasn't it? Whoever wrote it had enough information to get me hauled up before the state review board and flogged out of town. I'd never practice again. I'd probably have to be a Lyft driver for the rest of my life.

My career. Meghan's baby.

My baby.

Both dead.

How? When?

I tried to review my life as it'd been in the madness of the last six or seven months. Much of it had been pathetic. Without Meghan spicing up my days, weeks had gone by in a tedium of work followed by going home to sit at the computer and eat the empty calories of my feelings. I had gone up a pants size. I remembered driving to Lexington and meeting an old gay guy who had a wife and children, but I couldn't remember his name now. Johnny had brought Bart in five or six times, but I never once looked in his mouth or even tried. Bart seemed about the same each time, but he never confused me with Nathan the way he did in the kitchen. Did he ever tell Nathan directly? By God, I'd tell him tonight what Bart said, as best as I could remember it. He deserved to know.

All at once I entertained a new thought. What if Nathan knew the baby was dead? What if that's why he was acting so exhausted? He could be handling the funeral. It couldn't possibly be easy to handle. It'd have to take a lot out of you, especially when it's a baby.

What if Nathan wrote the note? He *was* the kind of man who'd have beautiful handwriting. He probably had to send out personal messages all the time, condolence cards and things like that. Could he have been showing up to see if I'd read it yet? The writer said we didn't know each other, but that could be a lie. No, no, it couldn't be Nathan. He'd never write a letter like this. He wouldn't be having me over for a drink if he had.

The bells jangled on the door again. The sound frightened

me into a whimper. I got up, smoothed out my white lab coat, and stepped into the hallway. The Reeves family stood in the lobby. Molly and the two children. Yes, that's right, they had an appointment. They weren't even early or late. Just right on time.

I shut the door to my office and waved them back to the examination room, falling into my *Tim the Dentist* routine and trusting my tongue to muscle memory when it came to saying all the right things despite what I was thinking and feeling. I cleaned the teeth of the two children, and then Sam Warbeck came in, and then Billy Demmings came rushing in with his 10-year-old son, Jason, who fell off his bicycle on his way to meet friends at the creek and had an avulsion of his central incisors. Billy held the teeth in a bag of ice and got his son to me only fifteen minutes after the accident. I was able to reinsert and save both incisors, even whistling "All I Want for Christmas is My Two Front Teeth" as I worked, which made Billy laugh as all his lingering worry evaporated.

By the time I wrapped up with the Demmings, Gladys Stein, likewise without an appointment, brought in her father, who was also about Bart's age. There wasn't much wrong with his teeth and certainly nothing wrong with his mind. I scraped away a bit of plaque and polished the enamel while we talked about whether the Cats were going to win it all this year. The smartest piece of business advice I ever got in Wentz Hollow was from the barber two blocks down, who told me to saturate my place with Kentucky Wildcat memorabilia—wall calendars, posters with the football and basketball schedules, free refrigerator magnets, whatever I could find. The barber then confessed to me he was a Louisville Cardinals fan but would never let his customers know. *"Tim, I'd get run out of Wentz Hollow in a month if anyone found out."* I remember at the time thinking he was joking.

It was 2:00 in the afternoon by the time I finished with

the Steins, and I didn't have another scheduled appointment for the next hour. I dropped my hand tools into a plastic bin filled with MetriCide solution and returned to my office to pour over the letter again.

I cannot say what your feelings are toward the dead child. Maybe you have none at all. Maybe they'll come much later. As I noted, I hope that isn't the case for you. I've found that late onset grief and guilt come with a certain amount of overdue interest and makes the bill for our actions higher than anyone can pay. But pay we must. I want you to know that I have considered filing an ethics complaint against you with the state licensing board. I think it is a fair thing for you to endure, but as you may know, such complaints cannot be filed anonymously. Therefore, consider yourself safe. You will never know who I am, but I hope this letter gives you a sober realization about what could have been: the baby, the complaint, a different future. I am sure you are a good dentist, and this is a state that needs good dentists. But are you a good person? Your misstep with Meghan does not make you a bad one. I'm not sure how many mistakes a person can have before one must no longer regard them as mistakes but patterns caused by defects of character. Believe me, it is a jarring thing to realize you are in fact a horrible person. Such ugly epiphanies can happen even on beautiful mornings.

I pulled at my hair, still in a state of so much disbelief. I could read the bit about there being no ethics complaint filed against me a hundred more times and still not buy it. But the fate of Meghan's baby . . . my baby . . . I *could* buy that. I had to know the truth.

I had one number for Meghan on file in her patient record. Surrendering to my dread, I pulled up the data and dialed the number. The phone rang and rang. I had no idea what I'd say if she picked up. And what if Steve answered? Would I just hang up?

Then she picked up. I tried to talk. I had no words and no spit in my mouth. The back of my throat made a little ticking sound. Just before she hung up, I managed to breathe out a husky, hoarse, "I heard."

"Oh," she said, her tone hushed. "Just a moment, OK?"

I heard muffled sounds I interpreted as footsteps. It was easy to imagine she was going to a different room, or maybe outside. But that would mean she's home. Surely she'd be hospitalized. You don't lose your baby and then just go home, do you?

When she spoke again, half a minute later, she confirmed a stillbirth. "Guess it wasn't meant to be," she said.

"No. I guess not."

"Are you pissed off at me?"

"*What?* Meghan, no, not ever. Why would you think that?"

"I remember you seemed really into the idea of being a dad."

"I don't know what I want."

"That makes two of us," she said with the slightest laugh. "Well, it's over now. Thank God. The whole thing was just awful. I'm never getting myself into that situation again."

"How is Steve?"

"Basking in the sympathy of friends and family. He's such a fake."

The bell jangled on my door. Every muscle tensed when I heard it. Fear flashed through me. I imagined some representative of the state dental board standing in the lobby.

"I've got to go," I said.

"That's OK, Tim. Maybe I'll see you around."

"Yeah."

"Cool then—"

"Meghan?"

"Yeah?"

"How are you?"

"I'm going to be fine. The pregnancy just took so much out of me. I'll sleep a lot better knowing you're not mad."

"No."

"It wouldn't have worked with us. What happened is for the best."

I hung up. A woman's voice sounded from the lobby, asking if I was here. I called back and said, "Just a minute." Then I went across to the bathroom and splashed my eyes with water until the salt was out of them. I couldn't hide their puffiness though.

I walked into the lobby drying my eyes and saying, "Sorry, I've just got the worst allergies today. My eyes are so irritated."

I used the same excuse for the next few patients and worked with a dead feeling in my chest, as if I'd taken an injection of Novocaine right in the heart. Then, sometime around 4:00 p.m., a strange feeling of ease settled into my chest. I started accepting the note's warning at face value. There *wasn't* an ethics complaint lodged against me. I *wasn't* in trouble. Acknowledging this made me quit feeling like I was living at high altitude. My breathing became deeper. As for the baby, I needed to be more like Meghan. *What happened is for the best.* Such a Zen quality to those words, such a graceful acceptance. I took a quick break to stretch my back as I worked on my last patient and spied the Khalil Gibran quote on the wall. What had Nathan said when he read it this morning? That's deep, or something like that. Well, the quote was past its sell-by date and now I had a replacement.

What Happened is for the Best would do just fine.

As I resumed working on my patient, though, something happened. My hands developed a fresh tremor. Nerves, I think, is what's left over when you realize you've been involved in a narrow escape. You see you've gotten away with something you never should have gotten away with and didn't deserve to get away with in a moral universe. I'd fathered a baby with a married woman, a patient, and the baby was stillborn. All the alternatives that could have ruined me raced through my mind as I was scraping the tartar off the gum lines of my patient's molars.

Dentists don't need the sure grip of a surgeon, necessarily, but you don't want your fingers to shake when you're working around someone's gums with a tartar pick. The little hook slid and struck into the soft, pink meat of my patient's bottom gum. She grimaced, her fingernails digging into the ends of the armrests like a convict in an electric chair. I pulled back, apologizing as the blood began to pool along the interior of her bottom lip. She knew to lean over and spit without being told, and I began offering little cups of water.

"I'm so sorry," I said. "I was going for this one stubborn piece."

She shook her head in understanding, still in discomfort. But the bleeding had already stopped and she was good with letting me continue. I cleaned her teeth without further incident and when I finished, I told her there'd be no charge. Like all the good people of Wentz Hollow, she insisted that wasn't necessary, that it was her fault for not flossing correctly. So many people—most people—are polite to a fault, even when they've been hurt.

After she left, I locked the door and put the Closed sign in the window. Then I went back to staring at the letter. I seemed to find something new in it on every reread. This time the note seemed to be calling me to ask all the *What Ifs?* of my life. No question straddles the line between profundity and annoying like a good *What If?* Because you can ask it of yourself every minute of the day. Hypothetically, it might be life-changing that a series of sneezes on your way out the door sends you back into the house for a tissue, making you leave a minute late; and that delay is enough to change whatever algorithm it is that just never lets you through *that one red light* you hate with such a passion. But this time, because you went inside to get Kleenex, you arrive when the light is green.

CONFESSIONS

So, of course, you go through it, only to find another car has sped through the intersection and crashes right into your driver-side door. All because of a few sneezes that could have been yours, or the other driver's for that matter. In the world of *What Ifs?* we're always a hair's breadth away from meeting the love of our life or the gunman who ends our life decades too soon. You're always just escaping from or just getting caught in the natural disaster, the terrorist attack, the freak accident. No *What If?* bothers with the idea that the thousands of choices we make and random twists of fate all add up to a bunch of nothing, which is the same influence our lives exert on the people around us, never mind the world.

Yet there was a baby dead, and that baby wouldn't exist if I hadn't come to Wentz Hollow and gotten my head screwed up about who I was, and who I wanted to be. Who knew what that baby—my baby—might have done had it lived. Maybe nothing. Maybe everything.

Tonight, I told myself, I'm going to see Nathan and somehow I'm going to tell him all this. Not *tell him* tell him, but get to the point about the *What Ifs?* I'm going to say I find him attractive (he'll never be Johnny, but then neither will I) and I enjoy his company (true as far as I know). I'm going to say I'm glad to be in Wentz Hollow because if I was back in Seattle, I'd probably be screwing a frat boy and not sitting down with someone who means a hell of a lot more. I'm going to say I've been looking for a deep person, and as an undertaker he must be at least six feet deep. Yes, I'm going to use all my humor and wit to win him over. I will charm him, and if charm fails there's always the liquor.

Tonight the past gets flushed as much as it can be flushed, and I race toward a future named Nathan Ashcraft. Tonight the floundering ship of my life gets an anchor, and its name is Nathan Ashcraft. Tonight, my bologna has a first name, and it's N-A-T-H-A-N. Tonight I come alive fully and for the first time in a funeral home. I couldn't wait until 8:00 p.m.

Eight o'clock. 2000 hours military time. Something something Greenwich Mean Time.

I finished sterilizing my equipment and returned to my office one more time to stare at the letter. The words still stung me but I felt their impact less than ever. Nothing was going to happen to me. Meghan had it right. Everything was for the best. I threw the envelope in the trash can and almost put the letter in there too before thinking better of it. I needed something to remind me about consequences in case I ever went crazy again, so I folded the paper and put it in my right front pocket. Then I went outside and locked the door behind me. The streets were pretty empty. Unless it was the 4th of July, nothing much happened in downtown Wentz Hollow after dinner time. After 7:00 p.m., the ice cream shop two blocks down had a monopoly on anyone's interest and didn't close until 9:00. Maybe Nathan and I would go there as a couple. But not tonight; there were too many other things that needed to happen tonight.

I noticed Johnny's truck parked along the curb by the shoe store. It seemed like he'd been doing odd jobs in the downtown area for months, though for the most part I only saw his truck, never him. I probably hadn't seen him in three weeks—the last time he brought Bart in to wander around the lobby. There hadn't been much said between us.

Did he know about Meghan's baby?

Johnny came out of a building and started rummaging through the tools in the bed of his truck. I shouted at him and waved. He waved back and resumed searching for whatever it was he needed. I ran across the street to him, which made him squint.

"Going to run the Wentz Hollow Classic, Doc?"

"What's that?"

"Hell if I know. Just made it up."

"I had to talk to you," I said, embarrassed at how breathless I was. *Christ,* I was out of shape.

"Didn't have to rush," he said. "I'll be here another hour at least."

"What are you doing?"

"Electrical upgrade for Ms. Peters. Between you and me, she's lucky this place hasn't caught fire. If it did, it'd give the fire department something to do. Might give Nathan a bit of business too."

I nodded, trying to figure out how to come to the point. Instead, I said, "How's Bart?"

"Probably not on his last leg but definitely on his last tooth."

"I wish I could help him out."

"Not your fault, Doc. Old people are like that."

"Like what?"

"Determined to hold on to whatever's left. I can promise you he'll take that last tooth to the grave."

"Is he still having a lot of pain?"

"You know, I don't think so. Nathan stayed over at the house last night. I know that made Dad happy because he was still asleep when I got there early this morning. When Dad's agitated or hurting, he won't sleep more than fifteen minutes at a time. So he must have been doing OK."

Johnny turned back to the truck and pulled out a drill bit set.

"Wait a minute," I said. "Where were you?"

"Had myself a date and it turned into more than that. Jealous?"

He flashed that little smirk that did and always would turn me on. I started to boast there was no reason to be jealous because I had a date tonight myself, and between me and Johnny's girl, I was by far getting the better deal, the better Ashcraft. Instead, I shook my head and said, "I thought maybe

Meghan called to tell you. I remember you were friends, right?"

"Called to tell me what?"

I told him.

Johnny's face paled despite his perpetual near-sunburn. He looked at the ground and spat on the sidewalk.

"When?"

"I think last night. Maybe the night before. I don't know."

"How did *you* find out?"

"I heard it from a patient," I lied.

Johnny shook his head. "She'd have told me herself if it was true."

"I'm sorry, man."

"Fucking bullshit," he said, throwing the drill bits into the bed. He stalked past me to the driver's side door.

"Where are you going?" There was almost a squeak in my voice. Johnny looked to be in such a rage, I felt like I'd accidentally lit the fuse on a stick of dynamite.

"Just done for the day. Going home to listen to the old man ask me where Nathan is, because that's all he fucking cares about. I'm going to tell him he's too busy to visit because he's making money on dead babies. I'm going to tell Dad that until even he gets it."

"That's not fair!"

Johnny raised his middle finger at me without looking back. "You're the one who said I was ugly, remember? Guess you got that right." He got into the cabin and slammed the door. The engine started. The street had a slight incline and the rear bumper slid toward me, almost striking my hip before I jumped onto the sidewalk. Then Johnny gunned the truck forward, blew through a stop sign, and turned left. I felt like I'd never see him again.

What the hell had I done? Nothing? Something I couldn't even guess at?

CONFESSIONS

Not knowing what else to do, I went back to my office. There was still almost two hours to go before my future began with Nathan. I slumped into my examination chair and took the letter from my pocket. Once again, its tone had changed. The words no longer seemed scolding or threatening. I pictured the writer as a very old man looking back on his life. The crazed notion struck me that some future version of myself had written the letter, a confession intended to stop me from becoming him.

I've found that late onset grief and guilt come with a certain amount of overdue interest and makes the bill for our actions higher than anyone can pay. But pay we must.

I closed my eyes, repeating the words to myself until the message that had seemed profound now became gibberish. Profundity is very much a first impression experience with me. It never survives repetition. I read a poem and think, wow, that's so profound. I'm likewise quick to see profundity in a painting, or a statue, or a building. Then the novelty wears off and I think, *There really should have been a comma after that word. The color scheme seems a little off in that one spot. The statue's proportions aren't quite right. The building tilts just a bit to the left.* The same holds true with words and phrases of wisdom. I can visit any number of websites filled with famous attributions and every one of them will strike me with awe—at first. This is particularly true when I see quotes attributed to Kahlil Gibran, like the framed print on my wall. *Your pain is the breaking of the shell that encloses your understanding.* I remember thinking, *My God, that's amazing, that's so profound.* It had long turned to bullshit in its frame as far as meaning was concerned. I'd stared at the quote for too many months for there to be any impact left. But then dentists make poor philosophers. We know how to pull, we know how to patch, we know when to spit.

Above all else, we recognize decay.

Your pain is the breaking of the shell that encloses your under-

standing.

Now if Kahlil had been a dentist, he would have referenced the enamel, not the shell, and he would have understood that poor brushing and eating habits lead to the deterioration of the enamel, which in turn leads to an eventual understanding of pain. In that sense, the quote had become an unintentional inside joke—an inside-the-mouth joke, if you will—with no other intention beside that.

But pay we must.

I opened my eyes and considered the letter. That sentence, no matter how I tried, would not yield to repetition. I could not make it become nonsense.

I eased off the chair, a slight tremor in my feet as they touched the floor. I checked my watch. My rendezvous with Nathan grew closer. If I went by car, as I'd intended, I still had forty-five minutes to kill before going home to shower. I just wanted to set off to his place right now. *I should walk*, I thought. That would eat up the time. I could take it slow so I wouldn't be sweaty. Nathan had walked here this morning, after all, and it wasn't too hot or humid outside now. A walk would burn off all the nervous tension and let me collect myself, maybe lose a last minute .0001% body fat and make me look more appealing.

I tossed the letter on the chair and set off, more certain than ever I'd made the right decision. The walk gave me time to think up conversation starters. It was strange to consider how very little we actually knew each other, and how much advantage I had because of what Johnny had told me. I had to capitalize on that. Pump him for questions about the funeral business, ask about the hearse, pretend to have a fascination with coffins.

Or I could simply ask him about his day and see how the ball rolls from there.

Yes, I thought, and I felt like I'd hit upon a very profound realization. I needed simplicity, domesticity. Both appealed to me now as they never had before I came to Wentz Hollow. That's really what I'd been after from Meghan, but now I could have the best of both worlds with a guy like Nathan. *How was your day?* Nothing pretentious, just openness and truth.

My pace quickened. I didn't want to arrive in a sweat but how could I stop myself from hurrying toward my future? Nathan began to take on new dimensions in my mind. I had the sense that I wasn't walking toward him. I wasn't even on land. I was in a rickety lifeboat on the ocean, rowing in the direction of a lighthouse. So what if he didn't look like Johnny? So what if there was about a fifteen-year age difference between us? What were these concerns against the possibility of a lifelong romance, a real commitment, a real relationship? I was almost jogging now. My imagination ran much faster. We were going to embrace inside the funeral home, clinging to each other, vowing to never be parted. We'd care for each other, we'd never be lonely. I'd delete every dating app I had, erase every online profile, because that's what happens when two people find each other and their lives merge. You throw away junk you no longer care about since something better occupies the space.

The funeral home was very large and stately, almost palatial. I saw its roof in the distance. It never occurred to me until now that it must be the largest building in Wentz Hollow. As I marveled at the roof, my right foot tripped on a rock and I stumbled forward but did not fall. I grinned. This was an evening for portents and signs. I wasn't going to land on my face tonight. Goddamnit, I was going to stand tall.

Then I reached the funeral home and saw the single car parked out front. I recognized it. Meghan usually drove a little Honda Fit, but she'd shown up a few times in a white Toyota Highlander. I'd never thought to question that, but now I realized one car must be hers, and the other belonged to her husband.

Damn, I thought. They must be seeing Nathan about the funeral arrangements.

For my child.

I stood there staring, my heart rate made faster more from sudden shock than anything the walk had done. How long would they be there? I stood in place for a few minutes, telling myself I could just wait out whatever was happening and then proceed when the other car left. I was already moving forward, though, staring at the car, watching it and the funeral home get larger and larger. At last, I reached the start of the driveway which looked to be at least a hundred yards long. The main floor windows were lit. The upstairs windows were all dark.

I'm just here to hang out with a friend, I told myself. I'm innocent. I'm Tim the Town Dentist, popping in for a drink. I'm going to act like the idea of finding Nathan busy was the last thing on my mind, and I'll just say, "No worries. I'll visit again another day." I'm going to be understanding, the soul of generosity and charm. Because like Nathan said, I don't ever stop being cheerful.

And if Meghan and I see each other, how will she react? How will *I* react?

Despite every little voice I had screaming at me to come back another time, I began marching up the driveway, leaning into the walk even though the ground was flat. Sometimes you get in those weird perceptual situations where it seems like you're walking forever but never making progress. I experienced the exact opposite. It's like I conquered the entire driveway in five strides and suddenly I had my right foot planted on the first step leading up to the porch. I stopped again. Who built this house? Were they going for the slave plantation look? Had slaves ever worked here? Did Kentucky even allow slavery? Jesus, what if slaves were buried on the grounds? I should

CONFESSIONS

step aside and hide behind that tree over there while I consult my cell phone for all the answers.

Just climb the goddamn steps, I told myself.

And don't forget to keep smiling.

At the front door, I caught myself on the verge of knocking. But of course this was a business first. You didn't knock on the door here anymore than you'd knock on the door to Walmart. I tried the knob. It turned and I pushed forward a couple of inches, just enough room to spy. There wasn't a sound or any sign of life, which I guess is appropriate for a funeral home a lot of the time. Taking a deep breath, I stepped in and eased the door closed behind me. The first thing that struck me was the odor, a kind of mustiness like when you come home after being away for a few weeks. Not unpleasant, at least to me, but surprising. Maybe it was the smell of so much wood. The walls, the floor, the staircase—polished wood everywhere.

I tiptoed toward another room almost straight ahead. Its double doors were wide open, the interior lit. I caught a glimpse of pews and then I saw the coffin at the end of the room. My first thought was this was for the baby, but that couldn't be. It was far too big. Was a funeral about to start? Where were all the mourners?

I stood there by the doors, staring at the coffin and wondering who else was dead in Wentz Hollow when I heard a raised voice to my left.

"What do you understand, Nate?"

A deep voice, a broken tone. Someone was on the verge of crying. I looked toward another door over to my right. The space looked to be an office, but I wasn't about to poke my head in and find out. Instead, I walked toward it on cautious steps, listening, trying to make my breaths deep, few, and silent.

"It wasn't my son. I know it wasn't. Big surprise that we didn't have sex much. I tried, but . . ."

"I understand."

"Quit saying that."

"I'm sorry."

"Quit saying that too!"

I closed my eyes as I listened, and I put my forehead against the wall. There was a moment of silence. Then:

"When she told me she was about seven weeks along, I thought back and remembered a night she'd practically tied me down to have sex."

"Did you?"

I strained to hear the answer. But it was too low, too mumbled.

"Then the baby could have been yours."

"No, Nate. It wasn't. I can put two and two together. She already knew she was pregnant the night we screwed. That's the reason she was so hell-bent. I'd already disappointed her enough times in the past. There was no reason for her to be so gung-ho about it, except she was looking for cover."

"Did you want to be a father?"

I gripped the wall, waiting for Steve Malone's answer. The intensity of the silence produced a buzz in my hearing. Then Nathan said something, a little too low for me to make out word-for-word. But Steve's response was loud enough.

"I'd like to kill whoever did it."

I backed away, heading for the front door. I was still trying to be quiet, but I heard movement from inside the room and more speaking.

What have I done?

What have I *done?*

The question kept repeating through my thoughts, and every repetition landed like a slap to the face. I reached the door, opened it, and stepped out. I was halfway across the porch before I realized I hadn't gotten the door shut. Fuck it. I thought I heard footsteps inside and didn't dare get caught out here. I bounded down the steps and took off running. My footfalls sounded like gunshots to me, and I was sure Nathan and Steve must have been standing on the porch, watching me flee. At least it was dark. The sunset had just ended. I didn't stop until I was on the other side of the road and on the trail that led back to downtown. I looked back several times, always able to make out the warm glow of the funeral home's windows. The last time I checked, just before I reached the trailhead, it seemed like the upstairs lights had gone on. It was impossible to say. Maybe it was something else.

I heard Steve Malone's voice. I heard Nathan's. Maybe I'd never unhear them.

What have I done?

Who have I ruined?

So many things. Everything and everyone. I closed my eyes and thought something like a prayer toward the house in the distance and whoever might be inside it, both living and dead. It was no more than babbled thoughts, nothing even a real God could piece together.

Forgive me for fucking everything up. I'm leaving. I'm done.

I staggered back to my office and went to the examination room. I took the letter off the chair and tore it in half. Then I ripped all the Wildcats shit off the wall and stuffed it into the trash can. I took down my diploma, placed it on the floor, and stomped on the glass. I kept stomping until there was a big filthy shoe print across the paper. I turned my attention to the framed quote from Kahlil Gibran. I took it off the wall, undid the back clasp and threw the quote away. I went to my office, pulled up a blank Word document and typed out a more fitting replacement. I printed it, slid it into place and returned the new quote to the wall. It was good to leave behind profound words of confession and acknowledgement, words to explain my otherwise inexplicable and permanent departure from Wentz Hollow this night.

And best of all, neither I nor anyone else would ever know who authored them. Maybe that's because we all do—in time.

But pay we must.

MRS. LAWRENCE

NATHAN, if you've read this far, you'll have noticed I did not start off with the intention of writing a letter. Somewhere along the way, the impulse to do it became overwhelming, and now I accept the entire work only makes sense as a letter to you. I want to draw your attention to something I wrote a few pages back. I mentioned my ambivalence about Frank's plans for our funerals, and how I made private arrangements with your predecessor. I mentioned how our tombstones are already in place in the town cemetery. The humor of walking past my own grave had long eluded me, but this morning I did visit it. One of many things I accomplished, in fact. It's possible I haven't felt this productive since the day I drove to the University of Kentucky library to collate all that research.

At around 7:00 in the evening yesterday, Meghan called me to say she'd gone into labor two hours earlier. She was also calling to thank me. "Mrs. Lawrence, it worked. Thank God it worked. I'm so relieved." I sat in the living room holding the receiver to my right ear, at a complete loss for words. Frank was in the kitchen, and I suppose my long silence aroused his curiosity. He came into the room and stood nearby, mouthing, "What?" I shook my head at him and finally found a few poor words.

"Well, that's wonderful. I'm glad I was able to help."

"I'm doing OK. I feel pretty good really. The hospital's letting me go home in a couple of hours."

"I see."

"Anyway, I hope we can get together again soon. I really like talking to you, Mrs. Lawrence."

"Me too," I said, and smiled at Frank.

The call ended and Frank still awaited an explanation. "That was a former student," I said. "She was just calling to say she's decided to get her PhD. She said I inspired her."

"Wonderful!" Frank said, and I thought his excitement sounded too genuine to be an act. I suppose he wanted so much to believe I'd made a difference in the lives of my students. "Want a little ice cream to celebrate?"

"Chocolate?"

He went to get it and returned with one of our largest bowls. It looked like he'd scooped me half a gallon, far more than I could hope to eat. But I made no complaint. It was so nice to feel adored by my husband.

None of the ice cream's sweetness reached me. Perhaps I had too much bitterness on my tongue. I ate and pondered all the details Meghan hadn't supplied. I could only guess she had a stillbirth. No cesarean if she was already going home. Other questions, unwelcome questions about fetal development came to mind, but I tried not to give them the consideration they demanded.

Last night was almost sleepless. Frank snored beside me while I stared at the wall and thought of many implications. My fantasy of you and Steve Malone somehow raising the baby together was now broken like all my other hopes. At some point around midnight, I started crying. You won't be surprised when I say tears don't come easy to me. Frustration and depression may afflict me, but I never cry. Funerals for friends and relatives haven't wrung them from me. But I cried for a nameless baby whose death was hailed as the greatest blessing in its mother's life. I cried for a faceless baby whose life I may have helped to end despite my efforts to sabotage the drink that would kill it.

To my extreme surprise, Meghan called me again in the very early morning, just before sunrise. Frank was in the bathroom, showering for another day at work. Meghan apologized for calling but said she needed talk.

Steve was now insisting on a service for the baby.

"No, not a burial, Mrs. Lawrence. He wants to cremate it and keep the remains, like you do for cats and Great Aunts. I can't talk him out of it. We're going to the funeral home in about half an hour. We're just going to sit there until they open, I guess. Can you believe this?"

"He's grieving, Meghan."

Her voice changed all at once. *"Hey, don't you think I know that? But Jesus Christ, I'm the one who miscarried! I guess I better go if you're going to take his side. I just had to let you know what was going on."*

I wasn't bothered that she hung up on me. All I could think about was how you'd be coming face-to-face with Steve in just a few hours. While my greatest hope had been that the two of you were engaged in a clandestine relationship all along, it occurred to me now that this meeting could be the first time you've seen each other since high school. You can't imagine how fast my pulse was going at the possibility, and I so much wanted to see this reunion no matter how horrible the circumstances. I thought to myself, *if nothing else, I could just drive by the funeral home a few times and play it by ear from there.*

CONFESSIONS

What harm could there be in that?

How long should I wait before leaving? Meghan said she and Steve would just be waiting in the funeral home parking lot until you opened. (Is *open* the right term? I suppose it must be, in the business sense, but I find the phrasing odd in association with a funeral home. As if Death keeps official hours). You'll understand that my rational mind had taken a back seat to my emotions just then. Perhaps it was not even the back seat, but the trunk. My scheming thoughts astounded me. I could show up in the parking lot to tell Meghan I'd come to offer emotional support. Anything to let me be on hand at the moment you arrived.

Frank left the bathroom fully dressed and ready to go, like always. He was never a man for a full breakfast, and his morning appetite remained meager. This worked in my favor. He ate a banana, drank a cup of coffee, kissed me goodbye (the barest peck) and headed out. I waited until his car was gone, and then I hurried to get dressed. Showering would have to be foregone, but I don't believe I had a bad odor. My presentation was serviceable.

I stepped outside and was struck by this morning's promise of a beautiful day. Noticing the glory of sunrises, etc., was among the list of duties I'd vowed to fulfill upon my retirement. I suppose I had some notion of sitting on my porch sipping coffee as I watched the sun come up every day. But my porch faces west, and *glory* has religious overtones that sicken me. There's no God, no Apollo. It's just a constant nuclear reaction that keeps us all alive, and could also kill us all, and will soon, relatively speaking, extinguish.

But this morning I felt a notion of *glory*. The sky was three different shades of blue from east to west, like a paint color swatch from Home Depot, and the air held an invigorating crispness. I never drive my car with the window rolled down, but I did this morning. Have I ever breathed as deeply as I did during that drive?

There's a concept in biology called homeostasis, when the body is stable and optimal. Though not at all a philosophical or theological concept, I nevertheless entertained it as such during that drive. I was never more aware of my body: of my fingers gripping the steering wheel and the whiteness of the knuckles; of my stomach's emptiness; of a slight need to urinate, brought on by extreme anticipation; of the tickle of the wind along the finer, almost invisible hairs of my body. I understood the sights and sounds around me as something more than the product of my senses. It may be as close as I've ever come to having a true *religious experience.* I suppose driving to a funeral home is a good excuse for one.

As you can imagine, I'd never make for a good mystic. I understood my psychosomatic responses, and while I didn't quite hyperventilate, I knew I was having a little trouble drawing a full breath and decided to pull into the parking lot of the convenience store to settle myself. I let the car idle while I closed my eyes and inhaled deeply. A disorientation threatened to steal over me, similar to the time in the garden when Meghan was pestering me for help. I should confess there have been a few other times this happened as well, which I have not bothered to record. Who knows what a doctor might tell me or a lab report might reveal. I know the body ages, but there's something to be said about not becoming old until the day you *feel* old. I didn't feel old yesterday or the day before, and I sure wasn't going to let myself feel old as I sat in the car on the way to the funeral home.

Then I saw you. More specifically, I saw your hearse, and my chest got so tight I thought maybe I was having a heart attack. There was a momentary pounding in my ears. *That's him*, I thought. *That's Nathan. It has to be.* If we were in a city like Los Angeles, some place large enough to host quirky subcultures, it might not be unusual to find people driving

CONFESSIONS

hearses just to garner attention. But in Wentz Hollow? It could only be the undertaker.

It could only be you.

The hearse was parked near the front door. You must not have been there too long. Maybe you pulled in to take a call or send a text message. The parking lights were on. Then they went off and you got out. I hunched forward, almost hugging myself against the steering wheel. I didn't get the clearest look at your face, but my thoughts were confirmed. You'd grown an inch, but you had the same slight build, the same color hair, though quite a bit less of it than the young man I remembered. You weren't inside more than a few minutes and came out with a cup of coffee. The hearse backed out and for a second or two, I saw you in perfect profile. I thought you might have noticed me in your peripheral vision, but you didn't turn your head my way, and then the hearse lurched forward. The business of death never stops, does it?

I almost went inside to get coffee too, just to stand where you'd stood, just to be having the same experience with the drink. I asked myself: has he been happy? Is he happy *now?* Has he found someone, if not Steven Malone then someone even better? They were questions of the heart, and just then mine felt so full of wonder and agony. You may be the only person in the world for whom I can feel any sentiment at all now. When the hearse was gone, I began to question if I'd seen it at all. I cursed myself for not getting out of the car and throwing myself in front of the hearse.

If you'd forgiven me, you wouldn't run me over.

My questions about you intensified, narrowing into specifics as surely as a magnifying glass focuses the sunlight to a searing point. What were your days and nights like? Why in the world did you become a funeral director? Where did you live? What pleased you most about your life even if few things seemed to? Or were your blessings so profound it'd be impossible to limit yourself to one choice?

I didn't realize I was crying until I noticed my reflection in the rearview mirror. I saw the tears but didn't feel them. I touched my face, and my cheeks didn't detect the pressure of my fingertips.

I lifted my arms, checked my vision, examined my face for slackness. I'm sure I wasn't having a stroke. The numbness meant something else, maybe an allergic reaction to tears. I kept telling myself this as I waited and waited. Ten minutes passed. Then twenty. At last, I thought I'd recovered my composure and I drove out of the parking lot and continued toward the funeral home. I saw Meghan's car there but I didn't see the hearse. Maybe you parked somewhere else. Maybe you had other duties before attending to the Malones at such an early hour. They're the ones who'd chosen to arrive at a time when no one would be open. Why should you arrange your schedule around their needs?

But I knew you had done just that. I intuited it. I drove past the funeral home about fifty meters before turning around to make another pass. There was no traffic on the road. It was just you and me and Steve and Meghan on this sunny day. I passed the driveway again and once again turned around. The funeral home loomed over me, this old manor house shadowed with pretensions of a plantation lifestyle. Up on the high porch, the front door appeared to be wide open. I was too far away to know what activity might be occurring in the windows.

I had to get closer.

After yet another pass, I turned the car and this time I let it roll into the driveway. I didn't even apply the gas but the car kept moving forward, drawn as if by a magnetic force. I heard nothing except an insistent pulse that drowned out any telltale sign of my approach, the skitter of gravel under the tires or whatever other various sounds a car makes. I came closer and closer to Meghan's SUV and fought to turn the wheel so that I wouldn't pull up right next to it. I was close enough now to see Steve Malone in the car, hands on the steering wheel. He seemed to be shouting. Screaming. But he was alone. Meghan must have gone inside. I saw the cords standing out in Steve's neck. I imagined the most fantastic shriek.

I put the car in park but let the engine idle. Was I really going to carry out the plan bubbling in my thoughts? I undid my seat belt. I opened the car door. I got out of the car and approached the SUV. So much healing needed to occur for everyone. I had to talk to him, to you. Meghan I could care less about. I got closer to the SUV. The wonderful sunlight made its white surface very glossy and reflective enough to let me see my own approach. I saw the sort of deformity you expect from a fun house mirror, and I paused. If Steven turned his head even a fraction, I would surely explode into his vision and awareness. His head did not turn. He went on screaming, and now I could catch the faint sound of them through all those layers of metal, plastic, and glass. Maybe he was shouting, "No! No!" I couldn't tell. Then he stopped, and in that moment the world felt reduced to the two of us. Steven's head dipped until his chin met his chest, and his body shook. I watched this grown man cry and could not comprehend the complexity of his feelings. There are several famous videos showing the decomposition of a dead animal over the period of weeks, sped up to a time frame of mere minutes. That's how Steven's reactions seemed to me, the total disintegration of a human being on the spot.

I did this. I am responsible for this. I made Meghan the drinks and I made them incorrectly, but in the end not incorrectly enough.

If he'd just turned his head, I might have gone forward. Instead, he tilted his head back, almost skyward. One could believe he was considering higher matters.

I understood his thoughts, you see, because I retreated, got into my car, and drove home. Then I went to the bathroom and gave my reflection a hard stare in the vanity. I must have stood there a full ten minutes, blank, afraid to allow myself a thought. The thinking came a bit later, when I sat down to add this postscript. After all the years of pondering what might have been between you and Steven; after all the years of wondering how you'd grown up; after all the years of wishing I could go back and not do what I did to you, but realizing I'd have probably done it again without change; after hearing the cries of Meghan's thwarted child in my imagination—that's when realization set in, that's when I truly felt old and worn out, that's when a surge of hatred came for myself and for Frank and for Wentz Hollow and for Steven and for you. God damn everything.

But God damn me most of all.

We almost met earlier this morning. We *will* meet before the night is over, I imagine. Or maybe tomorrow? I'm not sure how fast these things go. Not as fast as escaping blood.

I have a few things to do before I go. It is still quite early in the morning, and I have another quick letter to compose and deliver, so Meghan's dentist knows what happened to his child. I will tell him what I think of his ethics in hopes that he changes his ways and does not become like me. Then I will return home and print this long overdue confession for you and for Frank. If you both read it or if neither of you do, I will have nonetheless set it down. Know that I come to you not as a person but as an entire cemetery.

My mind is a graveyard of dead babies and ruined chances.

ACKNOWLEDGMENTS

I'd like to thank several people for their friendship and support in writing this novel. Thanks to Darren Buford for reading and commenting on an early draft of the story. Thanks to Bret and Jeanni Smith for their edits and attention to detail. I must also thank the members of my writer's group and their willingness to review the manuscript as a work in progress. So, my appreciation to Carter, Abe, Dirk, Sam, and Linda. Above all, I must express my profound thanks to my friend, frequent collaborator, and publisher, Josh Viola, for taking on this project for me. You're the best.

CONFESSIONS

ABOUT THE AUTHOR

Sean Eads is a librarian and writer living in Denver, Colorado. He has been a finalist for the Lambda Literary Award, the Shirley Jackson Award, and the Colorado Book Award. *Confessions* is his fifth novel. You can find him online at *www.seaneads.net*.

CONFESSIONS

Other Hex Publishers Titles by Sean Eads

NOVELS

Lord Byron's Prophecy
Lost Story
Seventeen Stitches
The Survivors
Trigger Point

ANTHOLOGIES (SHORT STORIES)

Blood Business: Crime Stories from this World and Beyond
Blood and Gasoline: High Octane, High Velocity Action
Georgetown Haunts and Mysteries
It Came from the Multiplex: '80s Midnight Chillers
Nightmares Unhinged: Twenty Tales of Terror
Psi-Wars: Classified Cases of Psychic Phenomenon
Shadow Atlas: Dark Landscapes of the Americas
StokerCon 2021 Souvenir Anthology

I'd like to thank several people for their friendship and support in writing this novel. Thanks to Darren Buford for reading and commenting on an early draft of the story. Thanks to Bret and Jeanni Smith for their edits and attention to detail. I must also thank the members of my writer's group and their willingness to review the manuscript as a work in progress. So, my appreciation to Carter, Abe, Dirk, Sam, and Linda. Above all, I must express my profound thanks to my friend, frequent collaborator, and publisher, Josh Viola, for taking on this project for me. You're the best.

CPSIA information can be obtained
at www.ICGtesting.com
Printed in the USA
BVHW070015090223
658191BV00023B/654